ARMED
MEMORY

Books by Jim Young

The Face of the Deep
Welcome to Reality: The Nightmares of Philip K. Dick
by Uwe Anton (English translator)

ARMED
MEMORY

JIM YOUNG

TOR®

A TOM DOHERTY ASSOCIATES BOOK
NEW YORK

ARMED MEMORY

Copyright © 1993, 1995 by James M. Young

All rights reserved, including the right to reproduce this book, or portions thereof, in any form.

Parts of this novel appeared in a slightly different version under the title "Microde City" in *Asimov's Science Fiction,* June 1993, copyrighted 1993 in that version by Bantam Doubleday Dell Magazines.

This book is printed on acid-free paper.

A Tor Book
Published by Tom Doherty Associates, Inc.
175 Fifth Avenue
New York, N.Y. 10010

Tor® is a registered trademark of Tom Doherty Associates, Inc.

Library of Congress Cataloging-in-Publication Data

Young, James Maxwell.
    Armed memory / Jim Young.
        p.   cm.
    "A Tom Doherty Associates book."
    ISBN 0-312-85766-7
    I. Title.
PS3575.07945A76   1995
813'.54—dc20   95-6321
                                      CIP

First edition: June 1995

Printed in the United States of America

0 9 8 7 6 5 4 3 2 1

To the memory of my mother

PART
ONE

CHAPTER 1

I

Johnny always wanted scales. At least that's what he told me the time we saw an exhibit of life-sized dinosaur models in St. Paul when we were about nine or ten. Maybe that wasn't the only thing that was strange about him, but it shows he was going in a kind of distorted direction even then.

Johnny Stevens was my cousin. Probably my best friend at one time, when we were both in our early teens. I guess he was a lot smarter than me—but he was also a lot less stable. Unlike me, he went through an accelerated high-school program and finished a couple of years at Princeton before he dropped out. That was when he was nineteen. He called me once sometime after that when I was out somewhere and left a message with my mother, and that was the last any of us heard from him. I always figured he went to live in California. Surf, cheap drugs, endless summer—everything a wild-assed Minnesota boy would ever want.

Several years later (in fact the summer after I finished my master's degree), I went out to New York to stay with friends for a few weeks with the idea of maybe writing about the music scene. I had quit playing in bands by then, and I had been working part-time as a proofreader and getting occasional free-lance jobs at a Minneapolis entertainment cable channel.

A couple of my friends from the station had gone out to New York and found jobs, so I figured it was my turn to try.

That's how I wound up going to hear a scope band called the Skopsies play in a bombed-out theater on Avenue A. It was about eight o'clock at night, and I was riding the R train into Manhattan from where my friends Moustapha and Alice lived in Brooklyn, when I ran into Johnny. He was standing on the platform, letting the joneses pass him by, watching the creatures carefully.

I wouldn't have recognized him because he'd had himself microded into a wolfman, except that he was wearing a Minnesota Vikings muscle shirt. That made me look at him carefully; and beneath all the hair, and even with the snout and the canine teeth, I could see it was him.

"Johnny!" I yelled as the doors of the car opened.

He looked around, stared right into my eyes without recognizing me, and the hair on his neck and shoulders raised up. Then he bared his fangs.

"Johnny, it's me, Tim!" I yelled as I dashed through the crowd onto the platform, where the smell of piss and vomit and the heat assaulted me. "Tim Wandel. Your cousin."

"Son of a bitch," he mumbled, scratching his crotch. "Tim." He looked at me for a moment, then leaned forward very casually and said softly near my ear, "Get the fuck outta here. Something's about to go down, and I don't want you around. Here," he told me, as he leaned away, reached into a back pocket of his shorts, and pulled out a strip of paper about the size of the fortune you get in a fortune cookie. "You take this, get back on that train, and call me tomorrow."

I looked down at the paper, saw there was a phone number printed on it, and stumbled backward.

"Get going. Quick."

The warning chime rang, and I stepped back into the subway car. At least the air conditioning was working in there. As the train pulled out of the station, I saw Johnny walking casually toward an approaching group of people, but then the train accelerated into the tunnel and I couldn't see any more.

I had a couple more stops to go before I got off the train, so I stared at the people in the car for something to do. It occurred to me I was one of maybe three people there who hadn't been microded in some way, at least for muscles and height. And the subway car was filled with ads for microde shops, ranging from very chic morphing studios to the "Ears too big?" variety.

Although the car was filled with Elvis and Madonna look-alikes, oddly enough, there were only a couple of creatures in that car—two wolfmen seated near the door, holding hands.

II

As scope goes, the Skopsies were pretty lame. But my friend Monica Sammler was there, so I hung with the program to the end. Monica had worked at the station with me until she moved to New York last year and got a job with *Scope* magazine. After the last set, Monica and I went outside and sat on top of a parked car that belonged to the group, waiting for the band members to show up. It had cooled off, though it was so humid you could see your breath in the glare of the streetlights. The air reeked of the sickly sweet aroma of gasohol, as New York always does.

"So," Monica said, "was that def or what?"

"It didn't do it for me."

"Well, they're def in this town."

"They're okay," I told her.

That was when the band finally showed up. Monica introduced us as we crowded into the car and drove off toward midtown for food.

The lead singer, a woman with a snakeskin microde job, was squeezed beside me.

"So you like us?" she asked me.

"Yeah," I said as convincingly as I could.

"My name is Eva. Monica said you were from Minneapolis?" The woman had the damnedest accent I'd ever heard. Sort of generic Eastern European.

"Yeah, that's right. I'm Tim."

"It's quite a town. We have played it."

"Yeah, well, it's okay."

"I know someone from there. He's my microde synthesist."

"What's his name?"

"Johnny."

I glanced into her eyes. Her microde job was so good even her pupils were snakelike; as I looked at her, she blinked using her nictitating membrane.

"It's not Johnny Stevens, is it?"

"I do not know his last name. He never uses it."

This was too weird for me; I hadn't even heard from the guy in eight years, and then I not only run into him, but meet one of his clients.

"What are you thinking?" the snake-woman asked me.

"If it's the Johnny I know, then that's really strange."

"Johnny is the very best microde artist there is, you know," she said, smiling oddly, as though she were amused by something only she could sense. Then she looked at the keyboard player. He was driving manually, even though we were in one of the computerized high-security zones of Manhattan. "Vlad," she told him, "take me somewhere where I can have steak tartare."

"But that's raw meat, Eva," Monica said, disgusted.

"I know," the snake-woman replied, smiling again.

III

My friends Alice and Moustapha lived in a tiny apartment near Prospect Park, and they both worked day jobs. In the early-morning twilight, I heard them setting up the water-recycling equipment and taking showers and fixing breakfast in the kitchen and getting ready to go, so I forced myself awake and staggered in from the sofa in the living room.

"Good morning, sunshine," Alice said. "You don't look too much the worse for wear."

"Good morning to you, too."

"You didn't have any—security trouble last night, did you?" she asked.

That was the year when "security trouble" had become the polite term of art for a gang attack by the hammerheads, so I told her, "No."

She smiled; she seemed relieved.

Just mentioning the hammerheads, however obliquely, tended to dampen any conversation. So we both fell silent for a while. But I guess that's only natural when you consider that the *Times* had just called the 'heads the "most horrendous criminal group ever created."

At last Alice said, "I'm always scared here, Tim. The sooner we get out of here the better, as far as I'm concerned. This hammerhead stuff. . . ." Her voice trailed off.

"It scares me, too," I told her. "But it's just another underworld fad, like that Band-Aid punk thing last year in Los Angeles. It'll blow over."

"I don't know. It seems to me like they're—well—something sicker than anything I've ever heard of before. Wait till you see some of the local news coverage about them. Then you'll see what I'm talking about." She chewed on her thumbnail for a bit, then realized she was doing it and pulled her hand away from her mouth. With an effort, she smiled and asked, "So how was the band last night?" She still sounded nervous to me.

"It was okay." I could have said more, but it wasn't worth it. "The really funny thing is that I ran into my cousin. I may wind up staying over at his place. I'm going to try to get in touch with him today."

"Well, just let us know so we can program the security system."

"You're up awful early," Moustapha said as he walked into the kitchen carrying Alice's Kevlar safety cloak. He has a very strong southside Minneapolis accent, which seemed so out of place in this overpriced safe-deposit box of a Brooklyn apartment that I couldn't help but smile. "So how was the big band last night?"

"I wasn't very impressed."

"How was Monica?" he asked. He had always hated her, back when they both lived in south Minneapolis and worked at the station with me.

"She's got herself microded. She's an amazon."

Moustapha said, "Hmm," and he and Alice exchanged glances.

"Some of us are content to be joneses," Alice announced in a stagy Brooklynese accent.

"And some of us have to get to work," Moustapha told her, as he held up her silvery cloak. She allowed him to drape it over her shoulders, and then Moustapha got his own protective gear out of the hall closet and put it on.

"Leave us a note about your plans," Alice said as they were walking through the security exit. "By the way, we want to take you out to dinner Friday night."

"Fine," I told them. After the security system had cycled shut, I plodded back to the sofa and went to sleep.

It was three in the afternoon when I woke up, according to the antique dial clock on the wall. I went into the bathroom, set up the water recycler and showered, then programmed a cup of coffee on the kitchen system. For a few minutes I sat there at the rickety kitchen table, drinking my coffee and eating a bagel with cream cheese on it, wondering what Johnny was up to.

I accessed the phone and punched in my credit-card code

and then typed the number Johnny had given me the night before in the subway station.

The telephone screen phased through several colors, and then a parade of creatures marched across it. It took me a while because the screen was so small, but finally I figured out they were all Egyptian gods. Gradually the volume increased, and the images began to dance to some kind of Caribbean-sounding music as the words "Microde City" formed in the background. The camera did a spiral pull-in and focused on an ibis-headed creature; Thoth, I told myself, impressed by how real it looked for a computer-generated graphic.

"For the very best," Thoth announced in a breathy voice, "you have in you, Microde City—" And here the view cut away to a shot of Eva, the snake-woman of last night, as she began to sing, "Let me wrap you, wrap you, in my arms; let me squeeze you till your cells cry out; let me twist you, sister. . . ." I realized then this wasn't a graphic, but a video. The song accelerated for about a minute in a very fast scope tempo—and it was so emotional that I couldn't believe it hadn't gotten in trouble with the censorship board because of the National Mental Health Act—then cut away to a viewer dialog panel. I punched in the code for a private appointment.

"Your cost-free initial interview can be scheduled for the following times," a sexless synthovoice announced. A list of dates and times, starting next week, flashed on the screen. I pressed in the code for "other."

"How may I help you?" asked the synthovoice.

"I want to talk to my cousin, Johnny," I replied.

The screen went blank.

For a moment, I thought the answering system must have panicked, figuring I was the cops or something, but then a simple blue screen appeared with the words "Please hold" blinking across it.

I finished my cup of coffee while waiting, and then Johnny started speaking without a visual.

"Tim, thanks for calling." He sounded like any jones sounds on a business call.

"What the hell was going on last night?"

"You have to deal with some scary people in this business sometimes, man. It was just part of the job."

I thought about that for a while, then said, "I met one of your clients last night. She's the singer with the Skopsies, the one with the snakeskin in your phone ad."

"Oh, yeah, for Microde City. Her name's Eva. She's sweet."

"She eats raw meat, Johnny."

"Well, that's legal."

"But it's—disgusting."

"Life in the big city, guy. So when you want to get together?"

"Hey, I'm open. I'm just hanging out for a couple of weeks." I didn't want to tell him I was really looking for a job; it might seem like I was hitting on him.

"You got plans for dinner tonight?" he asked.

"No."

"You do now. Get over here around nine." He gave me an address in lower Manhattan and I wrote it down on a scrap of paper. "Square?"

"Square."

"Hey, Tim, you see my mom recently?"

"Naw. She moved to Guam to work on the new rocket base down there."

"Oh."

I couldn't think of anything to say for a moment, and then I figured I'd ring off.

"Well, I'll be seeing you," I said at last.

"Uh, listen, Tim. Don't tell your parents you're in touch with me, okay?"

"Okay."

"And listen. You may not recognize me when you get here."

"Huh? Didn't I recognize you last night?"

"That was a replicant, Tim. I've got a different thing."

"Is that why you don't have the camera on?"

"It's for security. Listen, I've gotta go. See you tonight."

He broke the connection, and the screen went dead.

IV

Johnny lived in the high-security zone around Washington Square, so I had to stop at a checkpoint on West 10th Street to get a transponder pass valid for twenty-four hours. But instead of what I expected would be a five-minute wait, I got stuck with several hundred other people trying to get to the entrance while it was being blocked by a group of demonstrators.

"End microding now!" one woman screamed into a portable public-address system. "Expand the Mental Health Act to cover microding! It's a form of violence against the individual, just like violence and horror on TV!"

A young man with a crew cut, wearing cross-shaped earrings in both ears, came past us distributing leaflets. When he tried to give one to the portly older man standing in front of me, the man started arguing back.

"You can take your leaflet and shove it," the older man growled, a mix of Brooklynese and Yiddish framing his accent. "What you're trying to do is just like Prohibition was a hundred years ago. The more you try to repress these sort of things, the more curious people get, and the whole situation just gets worse."

"Microding is just as bad as violence and horror," the kid with the crosses in his ears answered, and then he pushed on and tried to hand one of his fliers to me.

"No, thanks," I told him, and waved him away.

"Okay, break it up," a cop announced from his own P.A. system. A police car arrived and several plainclothes officers got out and started directing the crowd away from the entrance.

"Demonstrators are free to disperse, but may not enter the high-security area," the cops announced. "All others may start in-processing."

And with that the line started moving.

Once I got through the gate, I noticed the portly man waiting for me.

"You're from out of town, aren't you?" he asked.

His question startled me and I couldn't answer him right away. We stood there silently, both of us rather anxious, smelling the roasting chestnuts that the street vendors were selling.

"I don't mean to bother you," he went on, "but I couldn't help but notice how polite you were to—those people. Take it from me, you're better off just ignoring them—not saying a word to them—if you can't bring yourself to be rude to them." He smiled reassuringly, then nodded and walked off toward the New York University buildings.

I figured he must have been a professor at NYU or something. Then, looking down at the transponder pass in my hand, I tried to forget about the whole thing and concentrate instead on meeting Johnny. It was about a five-minute walk down to the address he had given me on West 8th Street, an early-twentieth-century apartment house by the look of it. It seemed to be a kind of a quaint brick-and-granite building that made me think of New England, especially when I glanced up at the towering brutalist-revival projects that thrust across the horizon there like the rotting teeth of giants.

To get into the lobby I had to present the pass card and put my palms on an identiplate; almost without delay the doors valved open. Just inside the entrance stood the largest T-man I've ever seen. Dressed in what looked like black kevlar, he was well over two meters tall and must have weighed at least 200 kilos. It was hard to make out his face because he wore a kind of Maori tattoo all over it.

"You are Mr. Stevens's guest?" the giant asked me. Another funny accent I couldn't place.

"Yeah."

"Welcome to the Adams. Mr. Stevens is expecting you."

"What floor is he on?"

"Take the elevator to the penthouse."

"Thanks."

He nodded and turned to face the door again.

Must be another example of Johnny's handiwork, I told myself as I got into the elevator. Nobody ever grows that size naturally, not even on steroids.

I pressed the button for the penthouse, the doors closed, and a synthovoice announced, "Mr. Stevens is expecting you, Mr. Wandel."

The elevator took me to a small, dimly lit lobby decorated in an Egyptian motif—hieroglyphics and paintings of animal-headed deities covered the walls, and the floor was a burnished, red stone. At the far end of the corridor, above a short flight of stairs, stood a monumental door.

When I reached the bottom step, the door opened. A jackal-headed T-man wearing only a pair of red soccer shorts stood at the threshold, staring down at me.

"You Tim?" the creature asked.

"Yeah."

"Come on in." I went up the stairs and entered a long reception area that looked something like an ancient Egyptian temple, defined by two rows of terra-cotta pillars with tangerine-colored sheer curtains behind them.

"You guys are really into Egypt, huh?" I asked.

"Yo. It's big this year. Have a seat," he told me, gesturing at a chaise longue. "The boss's almost done. Wouldya like somethin' to drink?" The more he spoke, the thicker his Bronx accent became.

"I'll take an ice-tea if you've got one."

"Sure. 'Scuse me. I'm just leavin', but I'll tell da night staff to bring you a' ice-tea. Ya want sugah in it?"

"No."

I sat down on the chaise longue and looked through the pile of magazines heaped on what looked like a genuine wood coffee table. They were all fashion magazines, most of them from the avant-garde microde monde.

"Hello," a woman said. "I'm Ray-Lee."

I looked up to see a rather good-looking blonde dressed in a blue jumpsuit. As far as I could tell, she was as jones as me.

"If you like iced tea," she added, "I recommend Earl Grey."

"Fine." She looked at me quizzically for a moment, and then I couldn't help but ask her, "How come you're not microded?"

"Leavening. Johnny likes a bit of jones around the place." She walked over to a table and typed in the order for my tea on a built-in keyboard.

"Your drink will be ready in a few minutes. Excuse me, and I'll see if Johnny is ready for us." She turned and put her hands in her jumpsuit pockets and strolled away through the columns.

As I watched her go, I thought about trying to get to know her better; then I rejected the thought. It was her use of the word "us." The way she said it, it was a highly exclusionary term.

"Tim!" Johnny's voice boomed from behind the sheer curtains at the far end of the hall of columns. "Come in, come in!"

So I got up and walked toward the curtains. For an instant I hesitated this side of the screen; I could see there was a massive desk in the room beyond, and a shadowy figure behind that. As I passed through a fissure in the curtain, the figure swiveled in its dark judge's chair, turning to touch a control panel behind it. All I could do was stare at the desk that glowed with gold leaf in the twilit office; it looked for all the world like an Egyptian sarcophagus.

"Johnny?" I said. My voice sounded hoarse.

"I'm just putting some music on," Johnny replied. I could glimpse his hand typing in instructions on a console behind the desk.

Then the chair swiveled.

A creature sat there. It was vaguely like a man, but covered with scales rather like a pangolin's.

"I said you might not recognize me," Johnny said. If he smiled, I couldn't tell; the scales covered the corners of his mouth.

"How are you?" I asked. I couldn't think of anything better to say.

"Well. Top of the world. All that shit. Sit down," he gestured toward a divan, and I stumbled over to it. Classical Indian music began to play softly from ceiling speakers.

Johnny walked from behind the sarcophadesk. He was naked, but his scales hid his genitals. Strangest of all, he had a long prehensile tail.

"So, what are you doing in New York?"

"I came out to visit some friends. Try to write a little. That kind of thing."

"You want a job?"

I swallowed and asked, "D'you have one?"

"I've got an opening in my public-relations office. You're welcome to take the test for it. But there's a catch."

"And that is?"

"You can't stay jones."

"But—uh, no offense, Johnny—I don't want to be a creature."

"I'm not saying you have to be creative." He may have smiled; I couldn't tell. "But you've got to be a T-man for the job. You get it free, along with housing and medical." Maybe he smiled again; he paused long enough to do so. "I'm a good employer."

The woman in the blue jumpsuit entered the office pushing a tea trolley. She handed me my glass of ice-tea and gave Johnny an Irish coffee, and then she sat down in a bowl chair.

"Have you been introduced?" Johnny asked.

"We've already met," she said pleasantly. I nodded back at

her; she had one of the three or four best smiles I've ever seen.
Then I forced myself to look back at Johnny.

"Listen, what is it exactly that you do?" I asked him.

He tilted his head to one side—a gesture that reminded me
of an iguana.

"Think of me as a revolutionary." He paused again and
might have grinned behind the mucus-colored scales. "Because what I've done in the last five years is a total revolt, man.
Other people started it. I admit that. They've been using
viruses to cure genetic diseases for almost thirty years.

"But I'm the one who came up with the idea of turning it
into the microding industry." He sipped at his Irish coffee,
and then he paused once more. Maybe it *was* a smile; I still
couldn't tell. "And that solved the race and the crime problem
at the same time."

I wasn't sure if he really believed that or not. At the time, I
know I didn't.

"Somebody had to be the revolutionary, Tim," he added at
last. "It just happened to be me."

"Well, you've certainly made some enemies. I just waded
through a demo against microding to get in here."

"Was it in front of the building?" he asked, his voice
sounding strained.

"No, it was down at the entrance to the high-security area."

"And who were these people?" His eyes glanced briefly at
the woman, then back at me.

"They were some kind of religious rightists I guess. They
said they wanted to put microding under the Mental Health
Act, along with violence and horror."

"Ahh. Those people." Johnny nodded and put his hands
together as though he were praying. "We're not worried about
them. And besides, I'm pretty sure the Mental Health Act
won't last out the next session of the Supreme Court. It's just
not constitutional."

After an awkward pause, Ray-Lee said, "I'm going to get
dinner."

"What are we having?" I asked.

"Garlic shrimp. It's one of my specialties."

She got up and pushed the tea trolley off through a break in the curtains, and glanced back at Johnny as though she thought she might lose him by leaving the room. It was so intense, it made me squirm to be caught in the same building with it.

"So what was going down last night with your replicant in the subway—a sideshow in the revolution?"

"In a manner of speaking. I was doing a little research on the hammerheads," he began to say, as the sitar music swelled; when the musical storm subsided, he turned to me and began to speak once more. "You know, the hammerheads are something I didn't anticipate. They've even got their own keiretsu. But I think we'll be able to handle them. Eventually."

I filed that away for future reference. Johnny was the first person I'd ever heard who acted as though the hammerheads were a normal part of life. Everybody else on Earth was convinced they were either space aliens or mutants caused by pollution or the spawn of the devil, depending on their particular religious persuasion, but Johnny matter-of-factly thought we'd be able to handle them.

Eventually.

Ray-Lee entered with the food on the tea trolley, and the raga built to a new climax.

We didn't say much during the meal, although Ray-Lee tried to make light dinner conversation. Johnny seemed to be brooding over his food, but it was hard to tell about him through the scales. Afterward he told me he had another appointment and got up to escort me outside. As he walked me back into the terra-cotta corridor, he asked very casually, "Do you want to work for me?"

"I'll have to think about it."

"I can offer you a hundred and fifty grand and housing. I know the salary isn't much, but you get full medical and microde benefits, too. You've got the number. Call me." He opened the massive door leading out to the elevator lobby. "Either way, call me. But let me know by the middle of next week, okay?"

He shook my hand for the first time then. His palm was dry and scratchy, and I had the sense he was much stronger than I would have thought.

"Okay?" he asked again.

"Okay, I'll call you."

I had to think about it.

CHAPTER 2

RECONSTRUCTION OF EVENTS SURROUNDING THE "MICRODE CITY" INCIDENT PREPARED FOR THE SENATE INTELLIGENCE COMMITTEE

I

What you are about to see is illegal."

Ullrich let the words wash over the sixteen sweating rubes in the cramped theater. The nearly-worn-out speakers gave his voice just the rasping metallic edge it needed to set them ill at ease.

"According to the Mental Health Act, each one of you faces fines of up to one hundred thousand dollars and two years' imprisonment for viewing this film."

It was late fall outside in the ruins of New York's Soho district, and Ullrich had the heat turned way up. That was just the way he liked it—the more the rubes sweated, the more they would absorb the chemicals sprayed on the arms of their chairs.

"If any of you want to back out, this is your last chance." Ullrich opened the jewel box and popped out the disc, then hesitated a moment before he put it in the video player.

He looked down at them from the air-conditioned comfort of his control booth: a Midwestern businessman and his wife dressed in '90s retro-grunge suits, looking for a cheap thrill, the wife's sister from New York (obviously along to make sure the out-of-towners didn't get in trouble), three rich Ivy League Elvises celebrating the end of their midterm exams, and a scattering of the art-world types. You could always tell the artistes, Ullrich thought to himself; they were the ones with pierced noses who usually showed up clutching one of Stephen King's outlawed books.

And there wasn't anyone in the crowd who looked remotely like a plant from the Mental Health League or any of the action committees against horror and violence.

But, most importantly, none of them looked like cops.

When he felt sure of that, Ullrich smiled to himself and thought, "Well, you people are sure as hell going to get more than a one thousand dollar video tonight.

"They're all alike," he told himself as he inserted the disc into the player; "but by the time it's over, they won't be thinking about how much they paid to get in the door anymore." He keyed the control board, and the house lights faded to darkness.

"This is a sound recording," Ullrich began to intone as the television screen started to sparkle. "But as the show begins, I'll tell you a little about how we made it." Abruptly the screen flashed to a shot of a large indoor swimming pool taken from a camera apparently placed in the ceiling some 20 meters above the water. At first the view wasn't clear, but then the camera focused on an enormous hammerhead shark swimming in the pool.

"You wanted to know about the hammerheads," Ullrich said, smiling grimly. "So here's what you asked for. We penetrated a hammerhead tank here in Manhattan with a spycam to get these pictures. Shortly after we recorded this, the hammerheads found the camera and destroyed it, and then they abandoned this particular tank. The police raided the structure only after the hammerheads left. Smart. The cops here are plenty smart."

The businessman's wife and her sister started whispering to each other. It was a good sign, Ullrich thought. He cued the subsonic generator and turned to watch the screen, now covered by a vision of a horde of human figures rushing onto the white-and-gray-tiled walkway surrounding the pool. The speakers began to boom with the oddly slurred chant of the crowd: "Farang, farang—farang, farang," and the near-subsonics pounded out a beat just beneath the audible range in time to the chant. At that point the camera zoomed in on two people being held by a group of oddly deformed men. That was where Ullrich stopped the action.

It was a full-color, freeze-frame of a crowd of nearly human monstrosities, most of them with vast lobes rearing out of the sides of their hairless heads, each one a parody of a hammerhead shark. Their bodies seemed distorted, too, as though their musculature weren't quite human any longer—though that might have been the result of the blurring caused by stopping the action. But even through the fog of frozen motion, it was clear they were hustling two naked young men toward the swimming pool.

"So . . . this is one of the rites of the hammerheads," Ullrich said at last, as he touched the contact button that made the action resume. He lowered the volume as the chanting began to rise. On the screen, the two young men were thrown to the immense shark in the pool. The camera pulled back its focus, but it caught only a rush of dark gray beneath the water and a blurred magenta spreading of blood.

Several of the hammerhead figures on the tiled walkway threw themselves into the water, then, and the great shark rushed on them as well. More blood billowed in the pool.

At that point the chanting stopped, and a single voice began a recitative in a language that might as easily have been Tagalog as Navaho: the genetically restructured mouth of the hammerhead leader distorted the speech into alternating liquid and guttural sounds.

"What you've got to understand," Ullrich told his audience, "is that the great shark in the pool is the real leader of this particular triad. It was a human being once, too. But they've put it through additional microding until there isn't much human left in it. But there is some. There"—he stopped the action as the shark neared the surface of the pool—"you can see the head is bigger than a normal shark's. It's still got a lot of brain left in it. And what you'll see now proves it." Ullrich touched the glowing key, and the action resumed.

On the screen the great shark broke the surface and sculled water for a moment, then roared, "Fa'ang, fa'ang." It rolled beneath the water again, and the crowd resumed its chant.

Ullrich turned off the video and rheoed up the lights. The rubes were drained. One of them had vomited. Considering the subsonics coming through the floor and the human-fear pheromones sprayed on the arms of the theater seats, Ullrich thought their reaction was surprisingly subdued. "Damn," he told himself, "I'll have to use more pheromones next time." He looked at the clock on his control panel; fifteen minutes had gone by.

"My associate will escort you up to the high-security area." Nobody protested as they stood up and got ready to leave. As Ullrich removed the videodisc from the player and stored it in the armed safe, he rubbed his hands together and said to himself, "What a scam!" It was wonderful what you could do with computer graphics nowadays. This was so good that no one could guess it wasn't real.

He keyed opened the theater door, and the rubes got up and began to stagger out, some of them leaning against the wall. On the monitor in front of him, he watched them gathering in the dimly lit corridor outside the auditorium to wait for Corrigan. He turned away to activate the armed memory on the safe, and after a few minutes glanced back at the monitor. Corrigan still hadn't shown up.

Ullrich charged down the spiral staircase and unlocked the door to the theater. The smell that assaulted his nostrils was a mixture of sweat and vomit and the reek of people nearly frightened to death. He held his breath and crossed the room to the exit.

Out in the bare concrete vestibule beyond the exit, the

rubes were too sick to need blindfolds. Ullrich shepherded them into the freight elevator, figuring none of them would remember the route through the basement maze that led back to the cheap hotel where Corrigan had escorted them in. He pressed the worn button on the control panel, and the doors closed. After an interminable, stuttering ride, the doors opened, and he herded them out to the side entrance, just beyond the limits of the Soho quarantine zone.

Good riddance, curiosity seekers, he thought as he watched them leave. You came here to kick the law in the butt, and you didn't learn a goddamn thing about the hammerheads. That suits me just fine.

And I'll bet the bigwigs who actually work for the 'heads don't know any more about what's really going on, either.

As Ullrich retraced his steps, he let himself grow increasingly angry at Corrigan. "When I find you, Eddy, I'm going to kill you," he said out loud.

II

Somebody's out there, Corrigan thought to himself again. He fished his pack of cigarettes from the breast pocket of his motorcycle jacket and tried to coax one out, but his hands were shaking so much that it took several tries before he got one into the corner of his mouth. He nearly dropped the pack when he tried to put it back in his pocket.

For a moment, he stopped and looked down at his boots. There was a twinge in his gut, almost as though he were going to hurl. There was definitely something wrong about to happen.

He could feel it.

And it wasn't just the news about the Midtown hammerhead frenzy he'd seen on TV that was making him feel that way—although just mentioning the hammerheads could sometimes make him feel simultaneously scared and guilty, just as his mother used to before dragging him into church on

Sunday when he was little. Corrigan tried to tell himself he was just feeling weird because of the film of the 'head attack he'd seen.

"How can you let some stupid gang attack get to you like this?" he asked himself.

But there was no arguing away the feeling. This was different, like there was actually something inside him that felt . . . wrong.

It was like the time the cops made that big bust on his neighbors for selling horror comics through the mail. He'd felt this way just before it went down. And when he heard the story, he finally understood what had caused it.

Corrigan looked up at the biohazard warning signs posted on the cyclone fence that marked the limit of the Soho quarantine zone and then ducked through the hole in the wire mesh. Once inside the fence, he got out his lighter and lit up. Corrigan smiled; it might be illegal to smoke in this town, he thought as he inhaled, but the cops sure as hell aren't going to bust me for it in the quarantine zone.

And the funny thing was, he told himself, smiling as he exhaled the smoke, there wasn't anything to it. Some developer had gotten the bright idea of claiming there was a biohazard spill on Spring Street so he could get everything condemned and buy it up cheap, but then the government had closed the whole place down. It had been that way for years.

He looked up at the shattered building tops and a shiver passed down his back. You could almost smell 'em up there, looking down and planning something. That was how he'd felt back in the hotel lobby, but the feeling was worse here. Maybe he should have just taken the chance and phoned Ullrich from the hotel, after all.

But if the cops were going to make a bust, they were sure to be monitoring the phones.

Corrigan took a long drag on his cigarette, exhaled and started running. As he rounded the corner, the rubber band that held back his long black hair broke, and the wind started whipping his hair in his face so he was running blind part of the time. That only made the feeling worse.

He turned another corner and saw Ullrich standing in front of the alley that led to the theater entrance.

"Corrigan, you piece of phlegm, where the hell were you?" Ullrich shouted at him.

He slowed down and walked the last few meters toward Ullrich.

"Don't give me any shit, Fader," he said, out of breath. "We're being watched and we gotta get out of here quick." He took a last drag on his cigarette and threw it in a puddle.

"Jesus Christ, Eddy, that's all we need is you smokin' and gettin' the cops down on us here."

"Fader, shut the fuck up and get going." He grabbed Ullrich's arm and tried to pull him away, but Ullrich snatched his arm back.

"Listen Eddy, I pay you to do certain jobs. One of them is escorting the people out of the theater when the show is over so the cops don't find out where we are. So tonight what happens? You get heavily involved in some kind of personal psychodrama and don't show up. At the very least, why didn't you call?"

"If the cops are out to make a bust tonight, they've got the phones tapped. That's why. And to make matters worse, I just saw this newscast about the biggest hammerhead frenzy there's ever been, and it's coming this way."

Ullrich stared at him and asked, "So what do you suggest we do?"

"Take my bike over to Jersey and wait and see if they try to hit the theater."

They stared at each other in silence.

"I'm goin', man," Corrigan said at last. At the same time, he thought to himself, "You can never figure this guy out; is he paying any attention to what I just told him, or is he so bored with life he doesn't give a rip?"

"All right. I'm coming with you."

Something scudded down the street just then—a piece of cardboard blown by the wind.

Ullrich jumped at the sound, and Corrigan realized that Ullrich could feel it, too.

"Can you spare a cigarette?" Ullrich asked.

III

From the rooftops the triad watched the two men rush off, out of the strike zone. All nodded as they watched the two leave. They were ready for the attack and eager to taste blood. But instead of making the gesture to initiate the breathing ceremony, the leader gave the tone that meant the directive was not yet ready to be implemented and that the target jones was to be given a reprieve of limited duration.

IV

Ullrich's kevlar cloak wasn't very warm, and to keep from freezing as he rode on the back of Corrigan's 150cc Russian motorcycle, he tried practicing a little highway zen, rotating the arguments for trusting Corrigan in his mind. Months ago, when he and Corrigan had first started the shows in the abandoned porno house in the quarantine district, he'd decided he definitely couldn't trust Corrigan's girlfriend Lisa. Now he just didn't know if he could trust Corrigan anymore, either.

You can't stake your life on people who always make decisions on the basis of some kind of goddamn metaphysical crap, Ullrich was thinking as Corrigan took the first exit past the Newark arcologies into a worn-out warehouse district of beige-brick buildings. They rode a few blocks farther until they reached the warehouse where Corrigan had his loft. Corrigan stopped the bike in front of a garage door, keyed the automatic opener, drove the bike inside when the door rolled upward, and parked it out of the way of the three cars of the other tenants as the door began to close again.

"God, I'm cold!" Ullrich dismounted and took off his helmet.

"How about something to eat? That'll get you warmed up."

They walked up a flight of unpainted wooden stairs and along a dark corridor to Corrigan's loft. Corrigan unlocked the door and Ullrich followed him inside.

"Sit down anywhere but on that one," Corrigan said, pointing at a massive puce sofa upholstered with a kind of fake leather. "I've just sold that one to the Museum of Modern Art for their new Naugahyde exhibit."

Ullrich took a seat on a massive beanbag chair while Corrigan went off toward the kitchen. He tried stretching out his legs, but he just couldn't get comfortable. There was something about Corrigan's case of nerves that was catching, and he'd been infected by it.

Corrigan came back with a couple of bottles of beer and handed one to Ullrich.

"You want another one of these, too?" Corrigan asked, holding out his pack of cigarettes.

"Thanks." Ullrich took one and Corrigan lit it for him.

"I'm going to cook up some dinner. Turn on the TV or the music system if you want." Corrigan shook out a cigarette from his pack and put it in his mouth and lit it. "Help yourself if you want another one." He tossed the pack down on the table beside Ullrich.

"So where's Lisa?" Ullrich asked.

"She's got a job interview in Philly. She won't be back until tomorrow."

"Oh." Ullrich didn't try to hide his relief, but Corrigan had already left for the kitchen.

Ullrich found the remote control for the television and turned it on. He zapped around until he found a news channel. There was some coverage of a big flap in Washington and a fire in Queens, and then some video of the hammerhead frenzy in Midtown.

"There's something beautiful about the shape of these hammerhead bodies sprawled in their own blood on 46th Street," Ullrich thought as he watched the TV. "It's like some kind of Jungian symbol made flesh and put on the eleven o'clock news." As the newscaster droned on about the property damage and the number of dead, Ullrich began going into his hammerhead mantra: they are the symbol of the rebellion against life as we know it; against law, against thought, against civilization.

That was why he loved them so, down to the last piece of glass they'd left broken in Midtown. The fact that they were able to run circles around the media and spew the most incredible black propaganda into the headlines made him admire them all the more.

When the story finished Ullrich hollered, "Jesus Christ, Eddy, more than a hundred people died in that frenzy tonight!"

"I told you it was bad," Corrigan hollered back.

"And now for a related item," the TV anchorman said, "here is our special correspondent, Judith LaValle." The screen cut to a close-in shot of a woman wearing a golden kevlar cloak, walking down a dark street.

"This is the edge of Greenwich Village, not far from the Soho quarantine zone," the woman began. "Somewhere in this maze of streets I was taken to one of the most horrifying films I have ever seen in my life. I was blindfolded and led through a series of passages in one of these buildings along with a group of some twenty other people, each of whom paid one thousand dollars to see what we were told was a film of a secret hammerhead rite."

"Corrigan, get out here!"

"What?"

"Get your ass out here! We're on TV."

". . . We were warned before the film began that it was illegal to see it under the Mental Health Act." A close shot of a biohazard sign attached to a cyclone fence flashed on the screen; then the camera panned back to the reporter. "But where did it come from? Was it obtained illegally from the police? We spoke to Lieutenant August Drummond of the New York City organized-crime investigations unit. . . . "

The screen cut away to a close-up of a thin, balding man in a poorly lit office, and Ullrich turned down the sound.

"That credit-card software of yours sucks," Ullrich said. He took a long drag from his cigarette and then crushed it out in the ashtray. "We might as well have prescreened everybody with a sieve."

Corrigan combed back his hair with both hands.

"I told you I had a hunch something was going down tonight."

"Hunches! Jesus Christ on a crutch, how can you live with all these hunches of yours?"

Ullrich glanced over at Corrigan. You just couldn't trust the guy, Ullrich thought to himself. As he reached down to pick up the remote control for the the TV, his beeper went off. He leaned back and pulled the block out of his coat pocket.

He looked down at the display and shook the thing.

"It's gotta be a mistake," Ullrich said.

"What's a mistake?"

"Look." Ullrich held the beeper toward Corrigan.

The display was blinking two messages: first, "Territory violated," and then "Safe detonated."

"That's it, then," Ullrich muttered, sounding as though no one else were there. Then he glanced up at Corrigan. "Goddamn you and your hunches." He turned away, trying to calm himself down.

"Okay," Corrigan told him, speaking as quietly as he could, "so the safe blew up. That's what it's supposed to do. The system worked."

Ullrich wanted to holler that it was all Corrigan's fault. But at the same time, he told himself that wouldn't do any good.

"Listen, Fader, you were always worried about somebody finding evidence they could use against you. Well, now there isn't any evidence. It blew up."

"Don't be too sure. This could be some kind of software glitch."

"I don't think so."

"You can live with your hunches, Eddy. But me, I've got to find out what happened." He got up and walked out the door.

V

"Fader—where the fuck do you think you're going?"

Corrigan chased down the dimly lit hall after him.

Ullrich turned his head as he walked and said, "Back into town to see what's left of the place."

"Ever think about who might be waiting to find you there?"

Ullrich stopped and turned around.

"What do you mean?"

"Just what I said. Somebody was after us tonight. I figured it was the cops, but I could be wrong. So who else would it be?" Corrigan smiled at Ullrich. "Think about it for a minute."

They stood there in the dingy hallway without speaking until Corrigan thought he could almost hear Ullrich's synapses clicking. That was a dangerous sign, Corrigan told himself; Ullrich had a talent for coming up with really horrible ideas.

"So why don't you go back to your apartment and check your computer?" Corrigan asked.

Ullrich nodded. "Yeah," he said after a moment. "I suppose that's the safest thing to do."

Considering the source, Corrigan thought that was a pretty big admission.

"But before you go, let's eat. It's probably ready by now."

As they reentered the loft, Ullrich asked rather quietly, "Would you give me a lift back into town?"

Corrigan thought about it. He was tired, but he figured he'd better go along to make sure the guy didn't do something really stupid.

"Okay," he said.

VI

The triad smelled the two men as they rode the motorcycle toward the flashpoint. But now the leader gave the signal that meant the moment for the kill had passed, followed by a new call that meant there would be a different form of attack, one that they had never tried before. The triad members exchanged the look that meant they were prepared for the challenge and then focused once more on the streets below.

Down there wafted the scent of the target, the one whose film transmissions they had monitored.

Now that the target had killed one of their own with the explosive in the safe, they were particularly ready for the hit.

VII

Ullrich had an apartment on the edge of the Soho quarantine district, only a few blocks from the abandoned theater he'd taken over for his shows. Corrigan pulled into the high-security garage around the corner from Ullrich's apartment building and parked his bike. The two of them dismounted and walked to the entrance of Ullrich's building without saying a word.

Even though he didn't like doing it, Ullrich found himself looking down the street at the police booth that marked the boundary of the Greenwich Village high-security zone. He pressed his palm against the key plate, and the building's security system let him in. Once he was inside, he told the computer he was bringing in a guest, and Corrigan, too, had to put his hand against the plate so the system would recognize him on the way out.

"You know, Fader, I'm awful tired. Any chance you could make me a cup of coffee?"

"I probably got somethin' up there that'll do."

Both of them had to palm the security plate once more before the building's system would let the door open, and then they took the elevator to Ullrich's fourth-story flat.

They had to go through the palm-identification routine yet again to get the apartment door open, and once inside, Ullrich turned the lights on, let Corrigan enter the crowded one-room efficiency, and shut the steel-reinforced door behind him.

"I think I've got some instant coffee in the cupboard," Ullrich told Corrigan. "Help yourself."

Ullrich unpiled a series of half-finished paintings from his computer equipment and logged on. He initiated the security-check routine for the theater and watched as it started to phase through the last three hours.

"You've got some weird shit in here," Corrigan said as he looked around his shoulder, "but I can't find any instant coffee."

"Jesus, Eddy, you couldn't find the floor if you weren't standing on it!" Ullrich got up and went over to the kitchen cupboard. He bent down and swung a water-recycling tank out of the road, pushed the tubes that connected the tank to the sink out of the way, then removed a bottle of pickled pigs' feet and a box of firecrackers and pulled out a nearly empty jar of instant cappuccino and handed it up to Corrigan.

"Now, that stuff is strong enough to wake up Lenin," he said as Corrigan took the jar.

"I bet it tastes bad, too," Corrigan muttered as he examined the powder through the glass.

"I wouldn't know. I never touch the stuff."

At that point the computer began beeping and Ullrich walked over to it. The screen was flashing:

SAFE DESTRUCTION: 11:41 PM

He sat down and typed in a request for a report on the intruder who detonated the safe. After a moment the computer flashed:

NO INDICATION OF INTRUDER

"What?"

"What what?" Corrigan asked.

Ullrich looked up from where he was sitting and muttered, "It says there wasn't any intruder in the theater before the safe exploded."

"Huh?"

Ullrich repeated himself.

"Maybe it just can't figure out what the intruder was," Corrigan told him. "Maybe it was somebody who was microded, so the recognition system couldn't figure out it was a person. So, no intruder."

"Let's see what we get for a visual." Ullrich typed in the commands and the computer screen split into quarters, each quadrant running the playback of the four main cameras monitoring the entrances and exits from the theater. At about ten minutes before the time the safe exploded, the four sections on the screen all wavered noticeably, but none of them ever showed anything that could be construed as the figure of an intruder.

When the screen had gone back to digital gray, Ullrich turned to Corrigan and said, "Somebody jammed the system."

"I thought you said it was so cop-proof."

"It *is* cop-proof, man." Ullrich looked over at his bookshelf and stared at the spines of his hard-copy books without really seeing them. "So it wasn't the cops."

He looked back at Corrigan, and that was when the window shattered and fog started billowing in through the opening.

For a moment he could see the hammerhead standing on the fire escape outside the window, its clothing glistening in the sick yellow glow of the streetlights. It was holding some kind of gun that exhaled the white fog into the apartment. At that point Ullrich couldn't hold his breath any longer. Even though he held his arm over his nose and tried breathing through his coat sleeve as he started typing an emergency notice on the computer, some of the gas seeped into his lungs and his head exploded.

Briefly, very briefly, he accelerated into a sharp gravity well, going down fast.

CHAPTER 3

TESTIMONY OF TIMOTHY J. WANDEL

I

When I woke up the next morning on Alice and Moustapha's sofa, they'd already left for work. I wandered out to the kitchen, hardly awake, and made a small breakfast for myself. While I was waiting for the coffee to brew, I turned on their TV to watch one of the news channels. It was the midsummer silly season, and I blipped through the spectrum until I saw coverage of a new line of microde fashion for the fall—the full-body stuff, not the nip-and-tuck morphing business advertised in the subway—mostly a line for men and women who wanted to look like ravestars of the last decade, designed by someone (or something) called Saavedra.

Then there was a break for an ad that showed a black woman talking on the phone, saying, "Hey, girlfriend, wanna look like Madonna for the party tomorrow night?" And then it cut to a time-lapse of two moderately good-looking young black women turning into blond, white sex vixens, just in time for a monster rave in Central Park.

It had to be some of Johnny's biggest competition.

While I sat there munching my toasted whole-wheat bagel and reflecting on that ad, I started thinking that New York seemed to be a separate country of its own. In Minneapolis, or other places I'd lived in the U.S., the changelings weren't the majority. Well, there were look-alikes everywhere, and Minneapolis was certainly filled with as many Elvis and Marilyn and Kennedy clones as anywhere else, I suppose. But the big difference was that microding was bound to have an enormous market in the high-crime, high-racial-tension areas like New York. Eventually it would probably spread out to the rest of the country. If you could spend a lousy five grand and become Conan or Wonder Woman, why not?

And then there was the social security crisis to consider: since Washington decided it would pay for genetically engineered rejuvenation as long as you agreed to work for another thirty years without receiving retirement benefits, that only added momentum to the whole thing.

Which brought me down to the big question: Should I accept Johnny's offer?

I just wasn't sure. If I really trusted him it would have been different.

He was a bright guy. No doubt about that. But there'd always been that twisted quality about Johnny, and it seemed as though it had gotten worse with time. Okay, so maybe his pangolin suit was state-of-the-art microding. But to me it just made it clear that he had created a permanent kind of a Halloween costume to keep everybody at a distance because he hated human beings; and worse yet, because he hated himself for being one.

Or at least that's the way it seemed to me at the time.

My mind wandered to Ray-Lee; she had to be a lot stranger than she looked if she was living with him.

For one thing, she had to like scales.

II

Alice and Moustapha took me to their favorite Chinese restaurant over in the Bay Ridge high-security zone. Over dinner, they complained about the international entertainment network they both worked at, and I told them about the offer Johnny had made me.

"I'm not sure if I should take it or not," I added.

Moustapha didn't like the idea. I could tell by the way he sort of hunkered over his moo-shu pancake. When I looked across at Alice, she sipped her tea rather demurely so that she wouldn't have to make eye contact.

"Don't get me wrong, Tim," she said finally. "I'm not a supporter of the Mental Health League or anything. But it seems to me that microding is so dishonest." And that was as near as I got to discussing with them what was on my mind. Eventually we finished our meal and walked back outside. It was a high-security zone, so they didn't put their bullet-proof cloaks on until we reached the checkpoint adjacent to the subway station.

We joined a line of people going through the checkpoint. The line stalled, and several of the people ahead of us started yelling at the cop in the kiosk to fix the turnstile.

Abruptly the siren on top of the police kiosk sounded.

"What the hell?" a fat man in front of Moustapha muttered, turning to look at us as though we knew what was going on.

There was a popping sound. At first I thought it was somebody setting off firecrackers, but by that point Moustapha was pushing me and Alice to the sidewalk. He threw his gray kevlar cloak over us.

A woman was screaming somewhere on the other side of the checkpoint. There were several more gunshots. Somebody else started screaming along with the woman, and then a couple of squad cars screeched to a stop down near the subway entrance.

"Okay, everybody up!" hollered one of the cops. "Please exit the checkpoint in an orderly fashion. Everybody up."

Moustapha pulled his cloak off me, and I looked around. Alice was rubbing her elbow, and there was a funny quiver in her eyelids. Moustapha took her hand and helped her to her feet.

"What happened?" I asked.

"Dunno," Moustapha answered. "I guess we'll see."

We went through the turnstile and saw a team of paramedics working over a woman who was sprawled in the middle of the street. There were three dead hammerheads strewn across the road down by the subway stop where the squad cars were parked.

All three of the corpses wore the same style of baggy, shiny clothing. Somehow their bodies didn't seem quite right underneath it. Their enormous eyes stared outward from vaulting lobes very much like a hammerhead shark's, and blood oozed away from them across the pavement.

"Jesus Christ!" Alice muttered, looking up at Moustapha.

"How the fuck did they get down here?" Moustapha asked.

"That's the first frenzy we've had in Bay Ridge," the heavyset man in front of us said to no one in particular.

We walked past the corpses of the hammerheads before we got to the subway entrance, and I heard one young cop telling another, "This is fucking unbelievable," as he shook his head.

When we got into the safety of the subway station, I said to Moustapha, "I've read about hammerheads, but I've never seen them before."

Alice looked away nervously.

"I thought we were getting over random violence in this country," Moustapha muttered. "But this is worse than the drug lords ever were. They're trying to soften us up for something."

"Like what?" I asked.

"I don't know." He hugged Alice briefly and then stared at the tiled floor. "You know, I used to think the hammerheads were just the start of something really crazy and new that, sooner or later, would be surpassed by something even newer and crazier. But after seeing that"—he nodded toward the station entrance and looked me in the eye—"it makes me think they're—like the killer instinct personified."

"Now you're getting metaphysical on us," I told him. "The hammerhead creation's just like a tattoo or getting your ear pierced. It's a fashion in some particular gang—that's all."

"And there are always killers in gangs, Moustapha," Alice added.

After that none of us felt like saying much anymore, and we stood there in the embracing heat and thought. I leaned against a girder and felt the sweat trickling down my sides underneath my shirt. "Be thankful the station doesn't smell too bad," I told myself. "And be thankful you weren't here five minutes earlier, Wandel," We could easily have been hit in the frenzy; but I didn't say anything about it because the expression on Alice's face was so bad. She looked as though she'd just had something ripped out of her. That was the first time, I guess, that I realized that the hammerheads were something more powerful than just a new mafia.

They had the ability to rob people of the sort of ordinary strength you need to get through the day. I could see that's what had just happened to Alice by the sunken look to her cheeks.

That was when I decided I was going to work for Johnny. At least for a while.

A guy's gotta do something to protect himself.

III

There isn't a whole lot to getting microded. They draw a little blood, separate out your genes and splice them with whatever else you need. After that, they pack it into a synthetic virus, shoot you full of it, and the virus infects every cell in your body. Within a couple of days, the first effects start showing, and within a couple of weeks you can start to tell what you're going to look like when it's all over.

My problem was that I turned out to be one of the unlucky few who come down with something like the flu after being injected with microde virus. For about a week I had a fever and stayed in bed in the tiny efficiency apartment Johnny put me in when I signed the contract with him.

So I managed to get into the office—located several floors beneath Johnny's penthouse apartment—some ten days after getting my microde shot. By that time, my face had broken out in acne and my hairline, though nowhere near as bad as my German grandfather's at my age, was starting to fill in with golden fuzz.

As it turned out, Ray-Lee was my boss. I wasn't sure if I liked that.

When I entered her office that morning, she had some kind of classical rock playing; The Doors or Echo and the Bunnymen, something like that.

"Good morning, Tim," she said as I entered the room. She turned down the music. "How are you feeling?"

"A lot better."

"Have you talked to the medics this morning?"

"Not yet. I'll see them after this."

"Let's get down to business, then," she said, leaning back in her chair. "For the first six months, we're going to have you on a physical-development program. How does that strike you?"

She was wearing a mauve herringbone jumpsuit with the zipper open to somewhere near the ground floor. It took me a moment to react to what she'd said.

"All right," I finally managed to answer.

She looked at me quizzically; then an expression of faint disdain crossed her face.

"First off, you need to read the computer file on the upscale division, the 'Johnny' line. I want you up to speed by the end of the week. We have to get the fall selections ready for in-house previewing next Monday." She smiled conspiratorially. "We're going to do chameleon," she said softly through her smile.

"But you'll read about it. And when we get done with that, we have to work on recycling the Egyptian stuff into the Microde City discount line. Any questions?"

I shook my head.

"Fine." She gazed at me and said, "Listen, Tim, there are some closely held projects going on here. Eventually you'll get in on all of them. In the meantime, if you come across a file you can't get access to, tell me. Don't talk to anyone else about it. You understand?"

"Worried about leaks?"

"Not really." She smiled once more. It was a smile that should have been in video; she was wasting it working an office job. I hardly noticed the gritty tone in her voice at all when she did that.

"Why don't you go see the medics, then, and after that, we'll get started." She glanced back down at the screen built into her desk and I turned and left her office. The door valved shut behind me.

IV

When you get into a routine divided between intense physical workouts and equally intense paper shuffling, you don't notice time. Seasons, yes; it was summer. That much I could figure out.

As the doctors told me, after you get microded your body does a rerun of late adolescence, and that only adds to the time-dilation effect. I was horny and hungry most of the time I wasn't exercising.

The other reason I didn't notice the time was Ray-Lee's practice of working you till you dropped, and screaming at you if you stopped to see what you were going to land on once you reached bottom. One of my coworkers, a Conan from marketing named Henderson, told me Ray-Lee had been an actress at one time. She was talented, all right. I just wish she could have focused that talent at somebody else.

Looking back on it, I'm sure they were working the bejesus out of me to keep me from whoring across Manhattan and winding up dead somewhere. There's nothing like adolescence the second time around.

Johnny and Ray-Lee must have known it intimately.

V

My job was to write publicity releases for the company's fall line without really saying what it was all about. There is an art to these things, and whenever I thought I'd figured out a way to do it, Ray-Lee would tell me to do it differently. Maybe it would have helped if I'd have had some idea of exactly what they were going to do with the fall line; but Ray-Lee didn't tell me much, and Johnny was spending all of his time up at the laboratory in Connecticut.

The week before we were going to host a big party to open the fall publicity campaign, we had a staff TGIF. We celebrated at a couple of different night spots, and a couple of hours later, I wound up at a rooftop bar talking to Henderson from marketing and the woman from the lab in Connecticut, Meryl Ellen Merril, who tracked what the competition was doing.

Meryl Ellen was an earth goddess, about two meters tall and weighing about 100 kilos, but she'd been drinking green russians all night and was suddenly very drunk.

"Y'know what," she said, turning to me as though she'd just realized I was there, "Johnny's up t'somethin'. It's big. Real big. We've put new security on at the lab. And nobody's seen him for days."

"He's always like that before he announces the fall line," Henderson told her.

"No, no—it's not that. You can feel it up there. I think he's working on the hammerhead stuff again."

"What hammerhead stuff?" I asked.

"The same stuff he was working on when Karnovsky defected. You can just feel it up there." She finished her drink. "Tension, I mean." For a moment, she sat there, looking past us. Then she excused herself and went to the women's room.

"So who was Karnovsky?" I asked Henderson.

"Some guy who supposedly defected to the hammerheads. Actually, the cops thought he was kidnapped. But he took a bunch of stuff from the lab, so they've been calling him a defector ever since."

We waited for Meryl Ellen to return for quite a while. After nearly twenty minutes, Henderson got up to see if she was all right. He never came back, and neither did she. I was getting sleepy, so I made my way back home.

The next week, just two days before the debut of the fall line, I came across my first secret file.

It was in a folder marked "Hammerhead," in a library Ray-Lee had given me the entrance code for that morning. There were three items in the folder: a chronology of reports on the hammerheads from the press; a file containing nothing but an address and phone number in Oakland, California; and a final one called "Retromicrode," with a blinking "access limited" beneath the title.

I couldn't get into the document with my access code, of course.

As far as I knew, no one had ever developed a reliable way to reverse a microde job completely. You might be able to eliminate a lot of the new characteristics introduced by a microde virus, but nobody had managed to get rid of all of them.

So it meant Johnny was trying to retromicrode hammerheads.

And however he was trying to do it, he didn't want anybody to know anything about it.

I didn't have any doubt he had some kind of connection with them. For a moment, I even wondered if Johnny might not have created them. I tried to argue myself into trying to break into the file.

Instead, even though I was getting fed up with her, I went in to see Ray-Lee and told her what I'd found.

"That shouldn't be there," was her response. She looked quickly at me, then typed away frantically at her keyboard. When she finished tapping away at the contact spots, she looked up at me again. "There. That's taken care of. Thanks for letting me know you found that, Tim." She gave me one of those really incredible smiles of hers—maybe the first one I'd seen in several weeks.

"You didn't tell anybody else about this, did you?"

"No."

"Good." She looked out her window at the street below and then back at me. "We had some trouble with one of the people at the lab a few years ago. He put a lot of things in public access and then disappeared. If we're lucky, that's the last one left in the system."

"What's it all about?" I didn't let on about what Henderson and Meryl Ellen Merril had told me a few days earlier.

"We're trying to figure out where the hammerheads came from."

"I thought it was Asia."

"That's not what I mean. We're trying to pin down the lab that first produced their microde. It's awfully hard to do." She smiled again.

Maybe my second adolescence was already starting to wear off. I don't know. But when she smiled, I thought she was lying.

CHAPTER 4

RECONSTRUCTION OF EVENTS SURROUNDING THE "MICRODE CITY" INCIDENT

I

After vague dreams of hearing people talk about him, Corrigan woke up in the isolation ward of the hospital. A very young doctor wearing a green hospital jumpsuit—Corrigan figured he was probably an intern—was looking in at him from behind the plastic cocoon.

"Hello," the doctor said.

"Hi," Corrigan answered. His voice sounded oddly distant when he spoke.

"I'm Dr. Katzner," the man said. "Do you feel good enough to talk a bit?"

"I guess so."

"There's a man here from the police department who wants to see you."

"About what? I didn't do anything." Despite Corrigan's grogginess, some of his natural paranoia began to well up inside of him.

"I know you didn't, and so do the cops. The police are just trying to figure out what happened to you and the other fellow."

"So—what did happen to us?"

"You were gassed. You had us worried for a few days, in fact."

"Yeah, come to think of it—" It seemed so distant in his memory, it was almost like a dream.

"After you've eaten breakfast and shaved and showered, and if you feel like it, we'll have the man from the precinct office stop by."

II

Ullrich woke up with his skin itching as though he'd been sleeping on a bed of poison ivy. He had been lying naked on the heated floor of a dimly lit cell when he awoke, and he tried rubbing his back against the pebble-grained wall.

Then his genitals began to burn—a throbbing itch deeper than any cut.

"Hey, anybody there? I need help."

His voice echoed slightly in the cell.

Ullrich rubbed himself and patches of his skin came off, as though he were a snake shedding its skin.

"Hey, can anybody hear me?"

For a few minutes the throbbing ebbed, but then his entire body began to itch so badly he gritted his teeth and tried to concentrate on rubbing only his chest and arms. That was when he noticed he had gotten a couple of injections in his left biceps. Even with the terrible inflammation of his skin he could feel two welts there.

For a few seconds, the itching abated. When it rose to a new climax, he gritted his teeth and squeezed his hands together until he drew blood. That was when he noticed for the first time that his teeth seemed to be loose in his gums.

III

The hospital office made Nemetz think of a court building and, despite himself, he soon found himself thinking about his divorce again. He couldn't stand the way it continued to intrude on his life, and he fumbled through his suit-coat pockets until he found his bottle of phokus, opened it, and popped one of the pills. Almost immediately he found his life and his problems receding.

At last he decided he could concentrate on his job once more.

So he looked at the computer readout on the survivor of the hammerhead attack: name: Edward Stassen Corrigan, age twenty-eight, unmarried, self-employed as art historian, no microding, no criminal record—though received two tickets for public smoking (both paid). A note from the hospital computer said that Corrigan's girlfriend was waiting to see him in the lobby.

Funny, Nemetz thought to himself; he seems like a pretty nice kind of guy to be hanging out with somebody like Ullrich. But then, he told himself, Ullrich was in the art racket, and the relationship might have been strictly business. Nemetz decided he'd play it straight. He shut off the notebook computer, dropped it back in his coat pocket, straightened his tie, and walked down the corridor to the doctor's office to see Corrigan.

"Hi," Nemetz said, holding out his hand as he entered the room.

Corrigan partly got out of his seat, sank back, and then shook Nemetz's hand weakly.

"A pretty narrow scrape." Nemetz shook his head.

"Yeah," Corrigan answered, a little nervously.

Nemetz thought the guy looked awfully thin, but the effect was exaggerated by the overly large hospital dressing gown Corrigan wore.

"Tenth case like it we've had. Hammerheads are behind it, of course, but we can't figure out what they're up to."

"They were definitely behind this," Corrigan said as he combed back his hair with his hands and then shook it out over his shoulders. "I saw one of them just before I passed out."

"You were at Mr. Ullrich's apartment at the time of the attack, then? Was Mr. Ullrich with you when the attack occurred?''

"Yeah."

"Can you remember if Mr. Ullrich was carried away bodily by the hammerheads?''

"Sorry. I really don't remember anything after I saw the one hammerhead at the window shooting gas into the room.''

"Well, we haven't been able to find Mr. Ullrich since the incident, so we have to suspect they kidnapped him.'' Nemetz wondered if he was pressing his luck with this kid, then decided to push on. "Did you know Mr. Ullrich well?''

Corrigan didn't answer right away; but Nemetz thought he seemed more thoughtful than guilty.

"Well, we worked together on a few film projects. He did a lot of computer graphics for some of the more avant-garde companies. Maybe you've seen his phone ad for Microde City— the one with the Egyptian god motif?''

"Who hasn't?''

"I did the script for it. Fader did the graphics. Fader— that's Ullrich's nickname. His real name is Nils. We worked on a couple of other things, too.''

"So you knew him pretty well.''

Corrigan managed to smile. "You know, I don't think anybody could ever figure him out, if that's what you're getting at.''

"Fine. Point taken.'' Nemetz scratched his forehead briefly. "What would really help us figure out what happened would be if you knew if there was some kind of link—so far as you know—between Mr. Ullrich and the hammerheads.''

Corrigan looked out the window at the East River. Clearly the question disturbed him, Nemetz thought.

"I don't know exactly what you mean by a connection,'' Corrigan said after a moment. "But Fader produced a film about them. I didn't have anything to do with making it, though. It was entirely Fader's show.''

Nemetz was sure there was more to the story, but he was

just as sure he was scaring the shit out of Corrigan. He told himself he'd go easy on the first try.

"What kind of a film was it? A documentary?" Nemetz gave the questions a kind of perfunctory well-it's-about-time-to-go tone.

"No. Fader made the whole thing up, as far as I could tell." Corrigan chewed on one of his thumbnails for a bit, then added, "You've probably heard about it. It was the underground horror film the TV news people broke just before the attack."

Nemetz got out his notebook computer.

"That could be the link," Nemetz said, detaching his magnetic pen from the notebook's cover. "One of the other kidnappings involved a woman journalist who had done a series of stories on hammerhead frenzies in Pennsylvania."

"So what are you going to do?" Corrigan asked.

"Don't know yet, Mr. Corrigan. Unfortunately, we'll have to wait to find out." Nemetz started making notes to himself and became oblivious to his surroundings as he did so.

IV

About the time the last of his teeth fell out, Ullrich started hearing the whistling. At first it was the sort of high, keening sound Ullrich always heard when he took aspirin, but then it began to take on form and rhythm. After a while, it almost seemed to make sense to him. Clearly, he thought, it was some kind of language.

It had to be the language of his captors. So far, he hadn't seen who they were; he told himself it couldn't be the hammerheads, even though he could clearly remember the splayheaded form in the yellow light on the fire escape spraying gas into his apartment.

But from everything he'd heard, the hammerheads didn't kidnap people. They just killed them.

He paced his cell, slapping the palms of his hands together

from time to time. He couldn't tell how long he'd been there. Maybe three weeks now. But it was long enough for him to be sure that he was being microded.

He'd never bought into microding. To him it just seemed like another scam: you reprogram peoples' genes with viruses, and then get them to transform themselves into pop icons. BFD.

Worse yet, you couldn't really change a microding very well once you'd done it.

Of course, that hadn't prevented him from accepting some big money from one of the big companies for making an ad for designer geneware.

But what was happening to him was more than a transformation into a pop icon. All his skin had come off, replaced by a kind of gray pebble-grained leather.

His jailers slid a platter through the slot at the bottom of the door. It contained the chewy tofu they had been giving him recently, the blood-flavored kind. When he smelled it he couldn't help himself.

He drooled.

CHAPTER 5

Testimony of Timothy J. Wandel

I

Johnny held the big party in the penthouse to introduce his fall line. Ray-Lee had ordered all of us to show up half an hour early, wearing tuxedos. When I exited the elevator into the hieroglyphic-filled lobby, I was stunned to find a very human-looking Johnny Stevens welcoming everyone. He was total jones, without a single scale on him, and even he was wearing a tux. In fact, he looked a lot like he did the last time I saw him before he ran away, back when he was about seventeen, except his hair was shorter.

"Welcome, Tim," Johnny said. "Ray-Lee would like to see you. She's inside, by the runway."

"Fine," I told him, practicing the professional smile Ray-Lee had been teaching me. We shook hands, but there was something about his palm that didn't feel quite right—not quite sweaty the way a person's hands really are. It was a replicant, of course.

As I walked through the crowd, I wondered how many replicants he owned. I'd run into two of them. Each one was supposed to cost a couple billion plus. In the movies, they're cheaper to use than stuntmen, of course. That's why they were invented. But this was just business.

Unless Johnny was expecting some kind of security incident tonight.

For all I knew, he might be up at the high-security lab in Connecticut, plugged in to a relay station on-line to this replicant. But it was so good that most of the guests wouldn't know it was a robot.

Then again, it might just be part of the show. I remembered what Ray-Lee said that first night I had dinner with them, something about leavening for this recombinant-DNA, funanimal world.

All the curtains had been removed from along the perimeter of the hall, revealing a series of vestibules filled with Louis XVI side chairs. Off to one side, a classical guitarist was setting up his sound system.

Ray-Lee was wearing a yellow satin gown, something like the robe on the Statue of Liberty. The two people from the marketing department, Henderson and the stilt-microded Crawford, were already hovering beside her.

"Good evening, Tim," she said as I joined them.

"Hi."

"I was just running through the schedule again." She looked at her wristwatch. "The guests will start arriving at eight, the background music begins at eight-fifteen, and the show starts promptly at nine. Circulate until just before the show begins; then take your places in the elevator lobby to welcome any late arrivals." The Bronx Anubis appeared wearing an Egyptian-sort-of robe, carrying a Campari and soda. She took the glass and sipped at it. "And there will be late arrivals."

"Ya welcome," Anubis said under his breath as he stalked away, clearly irritated at her.

She smiled at us then, perhaps the most sincere gesture I'd ever seen her make. It was a smile that presupposed victory of some kind. "And remember, dears, don't even hint at what Johnny plans to say."

"Which is easy 'cause we don't know what he's going to say," Henderson told her.

"I know. But don't even hint." She smiled again and sipped her drink.

A little late, but in very large numbers, the guests arrived. Most of them were fashionably reconstructed—faces and bodies reminiscent of filmstars and Olympiads—though there were occasional joneses who looked old and frail and fabulously rich. Not wealthy, but downright rich. One group of them showed up dressed alike in the most expensive clothes I'd seen yet: a liquid-crystal fabric displaying moving patterns like the ads down at Times Square.

But this show wasn't about clothes.

It was about flesh.

"You're new here," a blonde Madonna said to me as she grabbed me by the biceps. Her hand more than went 'round my arm.

"Hi," I said, smiling.

"What's the big story tonight?"

"The boss has an announcement to make after the show," I told her. "That's all the more I know."

She pouted and let my arm go when Monica Sammler bounced up through the crowd and hugged me.

"Monica, how'd you get in here?"

"I'm covering the show for the magazine."

"Hey."

She looked at me sort of sheepishly, and I knew what she wanted to ask.

"I don't know what he's going to say, Monica."

"Okay. Let's get something to drink."

"I'm under orders to circulate."

"Then circulate with me."

Monica and I roved through the masses pressed into the neo-Egyptian hall while the guitarist got his sound system working and began to play Villa-Lobos. She introduced me to a bunch of conceited newspeople whose names I didn't catch, and then the show began.

The guitarist started playing some kind of flamenco riff,

and Ray-Lee announced, "Ladies and gentlemen, welcome to the Johnny fall collection." She faked an upper-crust British accent that dripped with suppressed lust.

A guitar flourish; the lights rheoed down and the spots came up on the runway, focusing on a woman wearing a mesh bikini. She was stunning—her hair tawny, her eyes almond shaped. But she looked as jones as the old people with the liquid-crystal clothes.

"Fall will be a season for subtlety," Ray-Lee continued in her husky received-standard English. "Except when warranted."

And then the woman in the swimsuit began to change color. By the time she walked to the end of the runway, her skin had gone beyond tan into the near-chocolate. She threw up her hands and bowed, a very Marilyn stance. Then she turned and began to walk back slowly, her skin color lightening with each pace. The crowd started to applaud, moderately, but firmly.

Johnny had a whole line of chameleon numbers ready—each one slightly more exotic than the others, culminating in a feathered couple who seemed to be making love standing up as their feathers pulsed through the visible spectrum. At that, the crowd went wild, and the guitarist played the most frenzied and hackneyed classical Spanish riffs imaginable.

Monica held on to my arm when the spots went out, leaving the hall in darkness as the guitar banged away to the conclusion of a kind of mutant malagueña.

Gradually the spots came back up and focused on Johnny's replicant standing in the middle of the runway.

"Ladies and gentlemen," he began, his voice sounding authoritative, almost like a newsman's, "you have seen a small indication of things to come. The fall will bring the most exciting—but subtle—changes of any of my seasons. Never before has technology allowed such a range of expression. And let me announce a spectacular breakthrough. Until now, no one has ever been able to completely reverse a microde design.

"Now, for the first time, we can offer a safe and thorough regression technique to the public. Developed during the last year in our laboratory by the chief of our research team, Dr. Antonia Salvatore, the Salvatore process will allow our new designs to be used to complement or replace any existing design.

"Let me add, ladies and gentlemen, that our most important discovery of the last year has an extremely practical application. We have found a means to use the Salvatore process on even the most unfortunate of recombinant programs. Ladies and gentlemen, I am talking about the hammerheads. And I am proud to say that we have turned over the formula to the United Nations today. We seek no profit—"

The crowd began to applaud; at first slowly, but then more enthusiastically. Johnny raised his hands, but it took several minutes for them to stop clapping.

"We seek no profit from this development," he said at last. "It is our contribution, our social contribution—a way of showing that we are committed to the improvement of the human condition. It is our belief that the hammerhead keiretsu combines cult, chemical dependence and microding in a very dangerous way. Within a few years, if allowed to develop without hindrance, they would soon control most of the world. We will take steps to assure that our retromicroding technique ends this danger, once and for all."

The crowd had trouble believing it, I guess—I know I had trouble believing that Johnny was saying it, and I had caught a few hints about it in the past couple of weeks—but the applause built on itself, a waterfall gaining momentum until it was overpowering.

They brought up the hall lights and turned off the spotlights, and Johnny left the runway and mingled with the crowd.

"I never realized your boss was such a humanitarian," Monica said.

I was so stupefied by Johnny's announcement that I'd almost forgotten she was standing beside me.

"Neither did I," I told her.

II

After the last of the guests had gone, Johnny called me over to where he and Ray-Lee were seated among the piles of empty plates and glasses.

"I want you to drive this replicant up to Connecticut tonight," he announced. "Ray-Lee has to stay here."

"I'm pretty tired," I said. I looked at my wristwatch. It was getting on toward one.

"You can sleep up at the guest house. Ray-Lee," he said, turning to her as she sat beside him on the love seat, "you take care of the shop, okay?"

"Yes dear," Ray-Lee smiled. She looked more dissipated than I'd ever seen her before.

One of the char force started vacuuming.

"I don't think I can stay awake a minute longer," Ray-Lee told him. Then she kissed him. He kissed her back; it had to be a good replicant if she didn't mind that.

"Why don't you use the guest suite down on the tenth floor, honey?" Johnny asked. "We'll escort you down."

"Okay."

"If I'm going to drive, I'm going to need some coffee," I said.

"No problem," Johnny answered. He got out his pocket phone and dialed up a cup of coffee in the kitchen of the guest apartment; by the time we dropped Ray-Lee off, my coffee was ready.

Johnny didn't say much as we took the elevator down to the basement garage. He handed me the keys and led me over to a small red Chevy with a dent on the driver's side.

"What're you staring at?" Johnny asked me.

"I just figured you'd have something a little more, um, upscale."

"I do. But we're going incognito tonight." He gestured toward the door.

I unlocked the car, got in and opened the passenger door.

Johnny got in on his side and undid his tie, just as though he were really there.

"Drive out to the delivery area and punch into the Manhattan grid."

I yawned then and shook my head.

"I wish to hell you could drive this thing."

"Replicants can't drive on a public thoroughfare. You know that. It's the law."

I drank some coffee, breathed deep, then turned the car on and drove out to the street. Once outside, I pressed the car's brain into action, and it steered us out of Manhattan using the city grid. It took us about thirty minutes to reach the Merritt Parkway, where the city guidance system ends. By that time, I was awake enough to drive on my own.

"Johnny, you there?" I asked.

The replicant nodded sleepily and turned to look at me.

"You're gonna have to talk at me if I'm gonna stay awake."

"Okay. You know where the lab is located?"

"Yeah. Branchville."

"And to get there, just watch for Route Seven and take it north."

"Okay."

"So tell me, what did you think about tonight?"

"D'you mean the new line, or what you had to say?"

"Both."

I tried to think of some kind of diplomatic response. "Well, I thought the new designs were pretty impressive." I finished the coffee, now gone cold at the bottom of the cup. "I don't know what the hell to make out of what you said about the hammerheads."

"I'm glad you liked the new stuff." He paused briefly. "You know, I think the whole idea of microding is right at the cusp of getting stale. If we hadn't come up with something like Salvatore's process, I don't think we'd survive. A lot of other companies are onto the same thing. But we're there first with the most sophisticated design."

"And you know what I think?" I asked. "I think this is the first real step toward making microding just another, everyday kind of thing. Like cosmetics used to be."

"It's more than that, Tim." He pounded his fist against the dashboard and smiled. "It's the first time anybody has shown how wide-open our time is. They used to say the twentieth century was the American century. So what the hell is the twenty-first supposed to be?"

He paused for a moment, and I said, "Post-American?"

"Shut up." He laughed. "It's going to be the time when we stop trying to hide the fact that we're part animal and start dealing with it instead. We're just scraping the surface with microding. We're at the threshold of something big—something really big. I can feel it." He put his hand out the window and moved it in the airflow.

"It's something as big as—civilization. I can feel it."

He leaned forward and fiddled with the sound system. A kind of ghostly rock song filtered out from the speakers. It sounded familiar; then I recognized it as the music that was playing the first time I'd seen his penthouse.

"What is that?"

"The Doors."

We let the music engulf us; after "The Crystal Ship," Johnny turned down the volume.

"I want to let you in on a secret, Tim." I could see him gazing toward me out of the corner of my eye. "Tonight we seeded the atmosphere with an aerosol-borne microde virus that will undo every hammerhead recombination on Earth. So no matter what they do, we've overcome. It's just a matter of time."

I couldn't reply for a while, letting what he'd said sink in.

"You sure it's going to work?"

"Absolutely. We've run successful trials."

We turned off onto Route Seven then, and Johnny programmed the sound system to skip a few tracks ahead. An evil-sounding sitar cranked up out of the night as the track began.

"The hammerheads are the biggest threat," Johnny said. "Bigger than communism ever was. Probably bigger than fascism." Then, very softly, almost as though he were talking to himself, he asked, "And you know why?"

"Why?"

"It's because they're trying to shunt us back along an evolutionary line we gave up half a billion years ago."

I wasn't sure if I was just tired or what, but I didn't really understand that at all.

"I guess I'll have to sleep on that, man," I told him.

"What I mean is, they've figured out how to use microding and organized crime to run countries in a new way. But I don't think they realize what that means." He paused to let that sink in, then changed to a slightly less serious tone. "You know, they really *do* worship the shark as a god."

"No I didn't."

"And if you try to remake mankind in the image of the shark, then you're twisting evolution into a new channel. That's what's really wrong with them."

The sitar-sound rose out of the speakers and transformed itself into the wail of an electric guitar as we drove over a hilltop.

I looked over briefly and saw Johnny swaying to the music, his eyes closed, looking—through the miracle of a billion dollars' worth of radio-operated robotics—as though he had transcended all his troubles.

"Doesn't that riff sound sinuous—like a snake?" he asked.

"Yeah, I guess so."

"That's the riff that finally made me realize what Morrison was going on about. You know, everything he wrote for the first couple of years was about the world serpent. And that's the riff that proved it to me."

I shrugged and kept my eyes on the road.

"Okay—just think about this for a minute," he said, hunching forward toward the dashboard. "The world serpent is the worm Ouroboros—it bites its tail to make a circle, and that represents something without a beginning or an end. Which is to say, eternity.

"And that's how—" He stopped speaking abruptly.

"And what?" I asked.

"Listen Tim, I've told only one other person this before. Maybe I shouldn't be laying this on you now. So please—don't tell anybody else I said this. You see, it's that riff that made me start believing in reincarnation."

"How can a single guitar riff in a single song from a century ago make you believe in reincarnation?" I nearly laughed at him.

"Well, it did," he said a little sheepishly. Then, more assertively, he added, "Did it ever occur to you that if you ever lived before, and you did something wrong, that you might have to make up for it in another life?" Before I could answer he rushed on, sounding more and more as though he were talking to himself—as though I weren't there or something. "And when I hear that music, it always make me realize that everything Morrison wrote was about the celebration of the lizard as the Earth power, not the power of love. And that that's what he did wrong." He turned toward me and asked, "Haven't you ever had a feeling like that?"

"No, I never did. I just don't believe in that stuff."

"I guess I shouldn't have said anything."

"No—it's okay. Really. Millions of people believe in karma. You can believe in it, too, if that's what you want to believe."

"I'm sorry, Tim. I thought maybe—you felt it, too." And with that he fell silent.

CHAPTER 6

RECONSTRUCTION OF EVENTS SURROUNDING THE "MICRODE CITY" INCIDENT

I

You don't have to talk to a lawyer," Elise Smythe told Corrigan as she got out the antique "Country Scenes" Kmart coffee service. "Just go down to Rutgers and talk to one of the computer trainers. It's only a ten-thousand-dollar fee. You'd pay more for a good meal at a first-class restaurant."

"Lisa, please. You know I had nothing to do with making Ullrich's film. I just worked for him at the the theater. I can't possibly be guilty of anything under the Mental Health Act." Corrigan looked up nervously at the cat-tailed clock on the wall.

"Fine. If you're so sure about that," she said as she pulled herself close to him on the sofa, "then please shut up about it." She looked him closely in the eyes. "Now calm down. Please. The cops will be here in just a few minutes, and then it will be all over."

"I hope you're right." Corrigan reached over to the table and got a cigarette out and lit it. "This is going to be the third time they've talked to me. Every time gets worse, Lisa."

"What do you mean, 'worse'?"

"Exactly that. I just feel more and more guilty. I don't know what it is. I've already told them everything I know."

"But that's what they're trained to do—make people feel

bad. Just tell yourself that. And besides, they're coming here. It'll be on our territory. We're going to be in charge."

"If you say so."

"And this time I'll be here with you." She smiled at him and leaned over and kissed him on the neck. He put his cigarette in the ashtray and hugged her.

Then the doorbell rang.

Corrigan put out his cigarette, got up and opened the door and let Nemetz in. A short man named Mfune, the New Jersey metropolitan affairs agent, followed Nemetz inside. Unable to think of anything else to do, Corrigan took their coats and hung them up.

"So, Corrigan," Nemetz said as he sat down on the Jean Royere sofa. "We wanted to tell you what we've found out so far, and see if it makes sense to you."

"I don't know if I'll be much help," Corrigan said as he sat down beside Lisa.

"Nevertheless, that's procedure in a case like this."

Nemetz and Mfune looked blandly at Lisa, and Corrigan introduced them to her.

Lisa felt uncomfortably awkward for a moment, and then slipped into a twentieth-century mode of thought and asked in a patently demure tone, "Would you like coffee?"

Nemetz looked over at Corrigan and then back at Lisa. Despite himself, Corrigan almost laughed out loud at her preposterous role.

Mfune accepted a cup of coffee rather gravely, though Nemetz declined. After waiting until she had poured the coffee for Mfune, Nemetz said rather embarrassedly, "Uh, miss, not sure you should sit in on this."

"Nonsense. I knew Fader as well as Eddy did. And I used to work for him, you know."

"In what capacity?" Nemetz asked, just a shade hesitant.

"I was a model for a number of ads he programmed."

"Ah." Nemetz looked over at Mfune. Both of them raised their eyebrows and nodded their heads from side to side. Ne-

metz seemed to recover some of his usual aura of pleasant sto-
lidity.

"Well, all right, then," Nemetz said, placing both his hands
on the priceless Formica coffee table before him. "To start at
the beginning, we've been aware for some time now that there
is some sort of gray space between the triads of the hammerheads and the normal world. Mind you, it's not what's left of
organized crime. It's something else. We haven't really been
able to pin it down.

"But we think Mr. Ullrich must have had some contact with
that realm, if you will, in order to make the film he made about
the hammerheads. Does that seem possible to you?"

Nemetz looked at them both, and Mfune focused on Nemetz.

"I don't know," Corrigan answered. He looked at Lisa.

She looked down at her coffee cup reflectively and added,
"I don't know for sure, either." She glanced across the table at
Nemetz. "But Fader always got hold of this really advanced
computer gear that nobody else in the business seemed to
have. Some of it he made himself, of course. He was famous for
that."

Nemetz got out his notebook and began to write in it.
Mfune nodded.

"And what about the firm Microde City?" Nemetz asked.

"Well, we both worked on the ad that Fader did for them,"
Corrigan said.

"As I said, I was one of the models," Lisa added.

Nemetz made a few notes in his notebook and looked up at
them again. "Did he—Mr. Ullrich, that is—ever give you any
indication that there might be some kind of connection between Microde City and the hammerheads?"

"Huh?" Corrigan said.

"What Eddy means, I think," Lisa murmured in a kind of
twentieth-century movie actress's voice, "is what kind of connection are you talking about?"

Corrigan looked at Lisa quizzically, and then back at Nemetz.

"Well, a connection. Business transactions or bribes or payoffs. Things like that." Nemetz stared intently at Corrigan.

"No, I never heard him say anything like that," Corrigan answered. "Did you, Lisa?"

"No."

"Did he ever talk about any of the owners of Microde City?"

Corrigan looked at Lisa. "He never talked to me about them."

"Well, he mentioned the woman who was the head of marketing when we were filming the Egyptian ad."

"And what did he say about her?" Nemetz asked, turning his penetrating gaze on her.

"He said she was a—very unpleasant person." Lisa gazed into her coffee cup to avoid making eye contact with Nemetz.

Nemetz sat back in the sofa, glanced briefly at Mfune, then said, "So, that's about everything I wanted to ask."

Then Mfune got up without saying a word and fetched his own and Nemetz's coats, and the two of them ambled out of the apartment.

"What in the hell was that all about?" Corrigan asked as he closed the door behind them.

"They weren't cleared to ask us what they wanted to ask us." Lisa shook her head, half in disbelief, half in disgust at the big buildup Corrigan had given the whole business.

"More like they didn't know what in the hell they were talking about." Corrigan got out and lit a cigarette. "That guy Nemetz really gets to me. He pops brain juice all the time, and I can't stand the way he looks at you after he does it."

"And I just thought he was impolite." Lisa put her hands on her waist gym-coach style and said, "You know, I bet I could find out what they were after. One of my best friends works for Microde City. She's at their lab up in Connecticut. I could ask her."

"Oh, yeah. Meryl what's-her-name." He couldn't hide his antipathy for the woman.

"Merril. Meryl Ellen Merril." She frowned at him. "Don't be like that."

"Like what?"

"Like that. You don't want me to find out anything, do you?" She gazed at him as he stared aimlessly into space. After a moment, she added, "Well I'm not going to try to solve any mysteries. I'm only going to see if I can find out what Nemetz was snooping around for this time."

"Now you're really scaring me."

"Eddy, you scare too easily." She pulled him close and kissed him.

For a time they sat there, until she realized that Corrigan had his head cocked to one side, as though he were listening for a sound only he could hear.

II

After what seemed like weeks, Ullrich's captors had turned on a dull red light in his cell. The vague shadow of his head, cast on the floor as he ate from his bowl, gave him the first hint of what he was becoming.

But he wasn't sure until his first new tooth broke through his gum.

It was sharp, serrated, triangular.

No human tooth had ever been shaped like that.

It was the tooth of a shark.

But the funny thing was—and he laughed inside himself until he could hear the laughter echoing in the silence between his heartbeats—he knew what was coming, and he wanted it.

III

Not even the blue sky and the incredibly warm weather could change her mood. Lisa reached the exit for the state highway that went up to the Microde City laboratory. She accelerated the little Izhevsk motorcycle through the curve and kicked it up to sixth gear. But even with the bike vibrating under her as she gunned it on the straightaway, she kept yelling at herself, arguing about Corrigan.

"He's getting worse, and you can't do anything about him," she hollered out loud as she cruised past the stands of bare trees on the Connecticut hills. Christmas and New Year's had been the worst. But in the couple of weeks since, he hadn't been much better.

And then, silently, she thought, "But I love him so much. What in the hell am I going to do?"

However, by that time, before she could think any more about it, she entered the town of Branchville, and its traffic-grid computer starting flashing holograms at her to get her to plug into its control programming. She ignored them—except for the glowing skull and crossbones that made her duck under the fairing—and rode to the small office Microde City maintained in the town. She parked the bike alongside a beat-up red Chevy and dismounted.

There was an elderly woman working as a receptionist in the office, and she seemed a little frightened to see Lisa saunter into the place wearing biking leathers. Lisa pulled off her helmet and shook out her hair.

"May I help you?" the older woman asked, her voice quavering.

"Yes, please," Lisa told her reassuringly. "I have an appointment with Meryl Ellen Merril. She's working out at the lab. The farmhouse, I mean."

"I take it you've been out there before, then."

"Yes, that's right. I worked in some ads for the company. Meryl Ellen is expecting me."

"I'll call her. Please have a seat." The older woman gestured toward a framework office chair, and then closed her eyes.

After a moment, Meryl Ellen's voice began speaking through the old woman's mouth.

"Hi, Lisa," Meryl Ellen's voice said. "We'll send a car for you. Just wait for a few minutes."

"Will my motorcycle be all right here?"

"Sure. The security force is all over town."

"Okay. See you soon."

The elderly woman closed her eyes again, opened them, and smiled at Lisa.

"I trust everything's in order?"

"Yes, thanks. They're sending a car around for me."

"That's just fine. If you'll excuse me, then, I've got some other duties to attend to."

The elderly woman closed her eyes again and sat quite still.

Lisa stared at the woman, noting the net of wrinkles on her face, the wispy hair on her neck. It had to be the best remote she'd ever seen—even better than the one used by Johnny Stevens, the owner of the company.

But he was supposed to be under death threats every day, Lisa reminded herself, so it made sense for him to spend the money on a remote for protection. This was just—well, conspicuous consumption.

IV

Gradually, during the next few days, the scraping and whistling sounds became sharper and clearer until Ullrich finally began to make sense of them.

They were words in a language he seemed always to have known.

"Triad," they whispered. "We are the triad. This is your matrix, your place. We have been waiting for you. When you are ready, we will tell you the great goal we share."

For the first time, he began to whistle back at them.
"Take me," he told them. "Take me now."
"We have," they answered.

V

Lisa felt she couldn't really say what she wanted to say to Meryl
Ellen because the cops might hear, so she concentrated on eating the *salade niçoise* and staring out at the Microde City estate
from the patio of one of the guest cottages. It was really an old
farm, complete with a barn and a farmhouse and several sub-
basements where they'd filmed some of the ads she'd worked
on.

Meryl Ellen had changed enormously since the last time
they had met; she had been microded into an Earth Mother,
nearly two meters tall and heavily built, and she seemed to eat
more than three times what Lisa could. Yet despite her size,
Meryl Ellen kept a certain grace about her. Lisa had to keep
reminding herself that this was one of her closest friends because Meryl was wearing a cream linen dress without a single
wrinkle on it.

Lisa almost automatically always hated women who could
manage to wear linen without wrinkling it.

And Lisa was having trouble keeping a conversation going,
too. Maybe she's picking up on my mood, Lisa thought. After
an awkward half hour of munching and mumbling, Lisa finally
got out a notepad and a pen and wrote on it: "Are we secure
from eavesdropping here?"

Meryl Ellen looked at Lisa bemusedly, then said, "Why?"

Lisa flipped over a new piece of paper and scribbled:
"Cops investigating Ullrich saw us yesterday and asked about
Microde City and hammerheads."

Meryl Ellen craned her neck to read the last message, then
pushed back from the solid oak table.

"Lisa, just leave this stuff here," Meryl Ellen said in a very
bland voice. "I'll have the char force clean it up later. Let me

take you on a little tour." Meryl Ellen gestured to Lisa to take
the pad and paper. Once Lisa had put them in her jacket
pocket, Meryl Ellen got up and slipped on her coat. They left
the patio and strolled along the gravel driveway, down the hill
to the barn. Once inside it, Meryl Ellen tapped an entry code
on a lock set in the concrete wall inside the entrance, and a
steel security door slid open.

"Right this way," Meryl Ellen said, and they both walked
into the antiseptic concrete room beyond the threshold. The
security door shut behind them with a rush of air. They took
an elevator down to the subbasement.

"There's a room here we can use," Meryl Ellen told Lisa as
they exited the elevator into a wood-paneled hallway. They
passed through an office suite and entered a small conference
room paneled in light oak and furnished with a clear plastic
conference table and matching chairs. Meryl Ellen closed the
door, tapped in instructions on a keypad set in the wall, then
turned to Lisa and said, "It's safe to talk now." She smiled nervously. "Why don't we sit down?"

Lisa sat down on the nearest chair, and Meryl Ellen took
the seat next to her.

Lisa hesitated for a moment, then asked, "Meryl Ellen,
would you mind if I smoked a cigarette?"

Meryl Ellen furrowed her forehead but said, "Sure. We've
got an ashtray here somewhere." She got up and walked over
to a translucent plastic credenza, opened a drawer and
brought back an ashtray with a built-in air cleaner.

"Go right ahead."

"Thanks," Lisa told her, getting out her cigarettes and
lighting one. "You know, living with Eddy makes it impossible
for me to quit." She inhaled deeply and blew smoke at the
ashtray. "Well. The cops came to see us yesterday. They asked
if Ullrich had ever mentioned Microde City or anybody who
worked there. One of them said they were looking into some
kind of link between Microde City and the hammerheads."

"What exactly did they say?"

"They were pretty vague. But it seemed obvious to me they weren't cleared to tell us something. So they asked these sort of general questions about the time I worked on the Egyptian ad, what was it like to work there, that sort of thing. And then they left."

Meryl Ellen rubbed her eyes with one hand and sat back in her chair.

"Lisa, there is no link between us and the hammerheads," she said at last, letting her hands drop to her lap. "I don't know where they come up with this stuff."

"Well, I just thought you should know."

"Thank you, Lisa. I'm grateful." Meryl Ellen turned and leaned her considerable bulk on the edge of the table and added, "We would do anything here to help get rid of them, in fact. Do you remember meeting the president of the company at the ad premier? Stevens?"

Lisa nodded.

"He's working on something to fight against them." Meryl Ellen closed her eyes and rubbed her throat, then opened her eyes once more. "You're not to tell anybody else that, though. All right?"

"Of course," Lisa answered. She gazed down at the translucent tabletop and through it to the concrete floor below, then looked up into Meryl Ellen's broad face, wreathed in brunette hair like some Renaissance vision. "Listen, Meryl, I have to talk to you about something else, too." She gazed down at their reflections in the tabletop momentarily.

"I don't know what I'm going to do. This is the third time the cops have seen Eddy since Ullrich disappeared, and it's driving him crazy. He's not doing his work. He even missed a big auction last week. I got a call from MOMA asking him to do an appraisal, and he hasn't answered it. I don't know what I'm going to do."

"Maybe you guys need a vacation."

Lisa took a final drag on her cigarette and put it out.

"That might help. I don't know. What I've been thinking is

that I should just leave him. He's becoming too dependent on me." She looked down at her hands for a few seconds, then gazed across the table at Meryl Ellen once more. "Actually, it's worse than that. It's like he's become an emotional black hole."

"Maybe you need to take a vacation from him."

"Maybe you're right."

Meryl Ellen glanced at her wristwatch and frowned.

"Lisa, thank you ever so much for telling me this. I can tell you need to talk some more, and you know I'd stay and visit longer if I could. But I've got an appointment coming up soon, and I can't miss it. I'm sorry. I'll have to take you back upstairs now."

"No—don't feel that way. I guess I shouldn't have said anything about Eddy." Lisa reached out and folded Meryl Ellen's hand in hers. "Forgive me," she said, realizing, to her own surprise, that she was almost ready to cry.

VI

Nemetz spent several hours of annual leave that morning with his lawyer going over his estranged wife's response to his suit for divorce. On the subway ride back to his own office, his mind started running through a fugue of recriminations. If only he hadn't said what he'd said on her birthday; if only she hadn't deliberately burned his father's Vietnam War medals; if only . . .

By the time he reached his own desk, he wasn't able to read an entire sentence, let alone the pile of disks and papers that had accumulated in his high-security in-box. For several minutes he made the effort of sorting through the detritus, and then he broke down and opened his bottle of phokus.

In half an hour, he'd separated the stack of circular memos from the action items. Then he accessed his computer search program.

He looked down at the computer screen, saw the blinking read-out, and pounded his desk.

"This is it!" he said out loud. His computer search had found a delivery-service receipt indicating that the Microde City lab in Connecticut had taken receipt of three hammerhead cadavers, shipped by a biological-supply firm in Ohio.

He sat back in his chair. So many of the things he'd picked up in the last five months since Ullrich had disappeared pointed in the direction of Microde City. Of course, when he'd talked to the people at the lab, they'd denied everything. But all the facts—right down to the number of hammerhead sightings in the vicinity of the Microde City lab and the company's Manhattan headquarters—pointed to some kind of link.

Maybe it wasn't quite as solid as he would have liked. Maybe he'd have to make a pitch to the interagency coordinating office to get anything done. Nevertheless, Nemetz told himself, this was the time to write a memo to the department's chief of liaison, Frederick Hamilton, to try to link up what he'd found out with what the feds knew.

Nemetz logged his computer to writing mode and started typing.

VII

It was the day of the cleansing ceremony.

The triad prepared him for it by commanding him to sit in the lotus position before the cell door, taking care to close his eyes. And then the door opened, and the salt water rushed in, and so they released him from the narrow room into a vast pool.

It recalled to mind something from his former life, when he had been the man called Ullrich. Somehow he had known about this sacred place, albeit only in a grubby, perverted, human way.

And at the bottom of the pool, past the limit of the light, he could hear the great one speaking.

At first he had trouble discerning what the great one was saying. He floated silently then and listened carefully, and at last he began to understand the words.

—You are commanded to move with the triad to dispose of the enemy, came the rumbling from below.

—The enemy has a fortress that we must destroy, because inside that fortress is the means to destroy us. You are among the chosen to bring about the destruction of the enemy. This is the great goal that you have been chosen to complete. Rejoice in your good fortune at having been chosen.

—If you perform well, then you shall be among the chosen who shall learn the greatest goal of all.

He swam deep, then, diving toward the darkness with a swarm of others in the triad, and for one moment of bliss he glimpsed the enormous, blue-gray outline of the great one in the shadows below.

VIII

"Nemetz, this is Hamilton," the deep, clipped voice sounded through the intercom. "I want to see you about this memo of yours right away." Hamilton's voice was calm, and Nemetz couldn't tell from the tone of the man's voice whether or not Hamilton agreed with the memo.

"I'll be there in five minutes," Nemetz answered. He keyed the security system to let it know he was leaving his cubicle, cleared his desk and tossed his workpad into the safe.

He looked in the mirror mounted on the wall near the entrance to his office suite, straightened his gold web tie, then rushed out.

As he waited in the elevator lobby, he tried to figure out what Hamilton would say. If Hamilton agreed with the memo, then they could start a full-scale investigation of Microde City's involvement with the hammerheads. If not, then Nemetz thought he'd have to try a different tactic. Maybe see if the Ohio state FBI office would look into exactly what kind of cadavers Benjamin Medical Supply was shipping to the Microde City laboratory. . . .

The elevator door opened, a couple of people exited, and Hamilton got in and pressed the button for the fiftieth floor. There was a group of people in the car from the statistics office he knew, and they muttered a few polite words about the weather before they exited on the forty-eighth floor. Nemetz was left alone in the elevator when it stopped at the executive offices on the fiftieth.

He got out and walked to Hamilton's office—an actual office, with Hamilton's name above the words "Chief of Liaison" on the door. With a little hesitation he pressed the knob and the door slid open.

Inside, an elderly woman sat at a desk typing. Nemetz wasn't quite sure if she were a remote—but then, sometimes it was hard to tell.

"The chief just summoned me," he told the woman. "I'm Nemetz, from the kidnappings division."

"Chief Hamilton is expecting you. Go right in." She gestured toward what appeared to be a real wooden door marked "Private," her blue shirtsleeve billowing as she moved her arm.

Nemetz opened the door and entered, stepping aside so the door could close automatically.

Hamilton was certainly an imposing figure, Nemetz thought as the chief stood to shake hands with him. It was the first time he'd ever actually met the fellow. Beyond the man's height, Nemetz thought, it was Hamilton's shock of white hair that made him look like some kind of twentieth-century president. "Nemetz," Hamilton said. "Good to meet you. Have a seat."

Nemetz lowered himself into an uncomfortable side chair across the desk from Hamilton.

"This was a well-written memo." Hamilton waved at the hard copy on the desk. "This business about the three hammerhead corpses being shipped from Ohio to this outfit's lab in Connecticut—what's the name?" Hamilton looked at the hard copy and read out loud, "Microde City. And your argument here is top-notch."

That was when Nemetz realized there was about to be a punch. Something bad was coming.

"But there are other things going on here that you don't have the clearances to pursue, Nemetz. I'm recommending a meritorious pay increase for you on the basis of this work. But at the same time, I have to order you to drop this case."

Nemetz clasped his hands together and said, "Could you grant me the clearances? I've got a real feel for what's going on here."

"Yes. I can tell that. But you know the way Uncle Sam operates. It would take months to get you the clearances you would need to pursue this. Frankly, I don't think we have that much time."

"So you're turning it over to the federal level entirely?"

"I can't go into it in any more detail with you. I'm sorry about that."

Nemetz looked around the office—the wall full of citations and presidential commissions, the dark-oak shelf of books, many in Russian—and realized how cramped a space it really was. Not even a window.

"I want you to understand that there is nothing prejudicial in the case going elsewhere," Hamilton went on, his tone almost fatherly. "If you are asked who is taking over, just say that I am. I know how the guys ask about these things. I daresay that should be all the explanation needed."

"All right." Nemetz tried to make that sound as positive as possible; he didn't think he succeeded.

Hamilton stood again and held out his hand.

"Thanks for taking this so well."

"Certainly, sir," Nemetz said as he shook hands. Hamilton walked from behind the desk and opened the door. "You'll see the paperwork on that step increase later this afternoon."

"Thanks."

Nemetz walked past the secretary, through the outer door and into the elevator lobby.

"You old bastard," he thought to himself as he pressed the elevator button. "If you're taking me off this case, you must be in this shit chin deep." As he rode the elevator back down, he started to rage against being deprived of his one chance to compensate for everything that was going wrong in his personal life, and he began to fumble for the bottle of pills he thought sure he'd put into his coat pocket.

IX

Only after months of training were they allowed to wear the shimmering clothing of the initiate and to participate in the kill.

Their set was unusual in the triad because it was made up of people who could remember their former lives to some extent. Most members of the triad could not.

So when the triad leader told them,—You are to lead us through an area you knew in your past lives, it meant that they were elected to an elite.

It was the first night of the year when the air remained near blood temperature, and the plan was to cause as much consternation as possible among the joneses south of the city without taking any reprisals. It was, in fact, the first part of a diversionary strategy, because the ultimate goal was a site north of the city. But that was months away yet, as the leaders kept saying.

—You of the chosen set, the leader told them after they had been given their initiates' clothing. You will cause as much property damage tonight as is possible. But you will avoid the police completely. You are to avoid fighting with the joneses. If you must kill, then kill, but only as a last resort. Now run.

And so they ran through a long tunnel, their path illuminated by red fungus spread along the walls, a light to which their eyes were particularly sensitive but which the joneses could hardly see. After many kilometers, they found the door that would open only to the touch of a triad member. Then they ran out into the humid night air, exiting into the countryside from a storm sewer.

Ullrich knew the place at once, though it seemed oddly distorted to him—both smaller and more hideous than he remembered it. They entered a warehouse district and, as decreed by the triad, they split up.

As he ran through the deserted streets, Ullrich threw stones at the few windows he found, joyously turned over trash cans and managed to climb a street-light and wrench the bulb free and throw it through the front windshield of a parked car.

It began to build within him. He raced down the street and the power increased in his chest. He felt invincible.

Ahead of him in the night there was a dog. He could smell it, and he chased after the scent. Running down an alley, he knew he was getting closer.

And then he saw the animal chained to a wall. The dog, a German shepherd, turned and stared at him. It reared and began to bark, straining at the end of its chain.

Ullrich's heart pounded and he charged the dog, leaping at the last minute as the triad had taught him, catching the animal's neck in his mouth.

It died instantly.

He lapped up a little of the blood from the gaping wound he'd made in the dog's throat, and then charged on.

At that point he began to throttle back. Tonight was only a diversionary effort, he reminded himself.

Running down another alley, he plunged abruptly into an open space filled with rows of figures made of white stone. At first he did not understand what they were, and then he realized that he had been in this place before in his former life. They were reproductions of a famous Roman sculpture—a man holding out one hand whose face bore an oddly accusatory expression—but he couldn't recall the subject's name. And that expression seemed to pierce the berserk bubble inside him.

Afterwards he gazed toward the building beyond the statues, and it, too, seemed familiar. Although he couldn't think why, he realized that he had to avoid harming anything in this place. For a time he rested there, trying to recall the name of the sculpture. But then he noticed a movement at one of the windows in the nearest building and so he ran off.

He tried to put the place out of his mind and to revel in the destruction of the joneses' world. But he kept thinking about it through the rest of the night, and at last, as he returned to the nest, he remembered that the statues were of a man called Caesar. He couldn't forget the accusatory look on the faces of the statues until the triad released the raw liver; and after he had gorged on it, he slept.

X

It was the first really sultry night of the year, and naturally there was a brownout in northern Jersey. That meant no air conditioning, of course. Although Lisa could sleep in the heat, Corrigan couldn't, so he got up at about two in the morning, got a cold beer out of the fridge, and sat drinking it and smoking a cigarette in the kitchen.

With both kitchen windows open, there was the faintest hint of a breeze. Corrigan thought about the exhibit he was supposed to work on tomorrow at MOMA; at least he didn't have to be there until ten. And then he told himself it was better not to think about it—better to try to empty your mind, Corrigan, and try to get back to sleep.

From the windows he had a view of a courtyard filled with reproductions of classical statuary. Their neighbor, Gregor Stefani, the Czech-Italian sculptor who lived on the first floor of the warehouse building, manufactured them for the garden set. Beyond the field of alabaster statues loomed the orangeish light and the distant gasohol smell of New York City, give or take a few other warehouse scents and some swamps.

There was a crescent moon that night, and though it didn't give off much light, it was enough to make the rows of statuary seem to fluoresce. But it was dim enough that, when one of the statues seemed to move, Corrigan thought at first that it was just the play of cloud shadow.

For a moment the figure hesitated, then Corrigan clearly saw it run off into the night. He could see that its head followed no classical proportions he had ever studied.

In fact, in the dim moonlight, its head seemed football-shaped.

He stubbed out his cigarette, got up from his chair very quietly and went into the bedroom.

"Lisa, wake up, honey." He nudged her shoulder gently.

"What is it?" she asked crankily.

"I think we need to call the cops. I just saw a hammerhead outside."

She sat bolt upright in the bed.

"Where?"

"It was down in the courtyard, standing in Stefani's sculpture garden."

"You're sure you saw it?"

"Absolutely."

They stared at each other in the sickly light of the alarm clock readout, and then Corrigan leaned downward and hugged her briefly.

"I'll call the cops," he said and got up and went to the phone. He had a sinking feeling as he input the emergency number on the keypad.

A standard police-emergency-services icon appeared on the telephone screen, and a synthovoice said, "Please state your name, address and the nature of the emergency. Thank you."

After Corrigan gave his name and address, he added, "I've

just seen a hammerhead outside my building. It looked like it might be casing the place. It may have noticed me at the window, and then it ran off.''

After a few moments of processing, the computer voice responded: ''We will send a squad car to your address within ten minutes. Please stay near your telephone and do not break the connection until the squad car arrives. This circuit is voice activated and, if you feel it necessary, you can request a human operator. Please hold. Thank you.''

''Goddamn it, the hammerheads could be in this place before I could even get a squeak out!''

''Shh, honey.'' Lisa joined him at the telephone screen. ''It'll be all right. Why don't you get some clothes on while I wait here.''

''Okay.''

The police arrived in just under ten minutes. They took the report seriously—Corrigan could see that in the way they wrote down what he said. He went outside into Stefani's sculpture court with them and showed them where he'd seen the thing. They took infrared photos as the sun started to come up.

''We've got about everything we can here,'' the head of the investigating team said after he finished taking the pictures. ''If you see any more hammerheads in the neighborhood, please let us know.''

''I will,'' Corrigan told them as he saw them to their car.

He stumbled back inside.

''Lisa, I can't take any more of this,'' he told her as he sat at the kitchen table. ''I feel like they're closing in on me. Like they've decided to do something . . . I don't know what.''

''Corrigan, can't you just shut up and put it out of your head?''

He looked at her intently; she seemed to be fed up with him. Then that look faded, and she seemed to regret what she'd just said.

''Eddy, I'm sorry I said that. I need to get some sleep before we have to get up for real. Let's go back to bed for two hours.''

He followed her to the bedroom and they lay down beside one another in the humid early-morning light. Corrigan couldn't get back to sleep, though. Just as he was about to drift into unconsciousness, a question surfaced in his mind: wasn't there something familiar about the hammerhead among the statues?

Maybe it was its posture, or the way it hesitated and looked back at the building over its shoulder. He couldn't figure out exactly what it was; but by the time he had put it out of his mind, something else about it would crop up from another untapped zone of his subconscious.

Corrigan thought back to the first time he'd ever heard of the things. There were a couple of sightings in Florida, he recalled, both of them treated as silly-season fluff until a news crew filmed a group of the things in lower Manhattan. Within a few months there were regular reports from all over the world about them. And after a while it became obvious that they weren't being used just to attack rival mafias. They were being used to destabilize everything.

Inevitably he recalled Fader's movie about them; he couldn't help himself. That film was like a curse—the sort of thing his Irish-Cherokee grandmother used to warn him about.

His eyes were wide open when the alarm clock went off.

XI

They slept in the red-lit days and ran in the damp, spring nights, until at last nearly three months had passed and it was summer once again. That was when Ullrich's set killed its first jones, and the smell of the blood and urine mixed with the scent of mud and wet tree bark at the site of the kill in New Jersey.

XII

That Friday, Lisa got home early from the last day of her consultancy with Davno and Morelli, the big Midtown interior-design firm. She had splurged and taken a cab home from Newark because they'd given her a bonus.

Corrigan wasn't there and she couldn't find a message saying where he'd gone; but then, that wasn't unusual anymore. So she slipped off her shoes and lay down on the sofa. As she lay there thinking about the last two months she'd spent with Davno and Morelli, she tried to be fair; but she couldn't be fair about such unpleasant people.

The phone rang and she answered it.

On the telephone screen, the logo of the Museum of Modern Art scrolled up to reveal a bland square-faced woman with spiked silver hair.

"Hello. May I please speak to Edward Corrigan?" the caller said.

"I'm sorry, he's not home just now."

That clearly irritated the spike-haired woman.

"I would rather have had the opportunity to speak to him in person. You, I take it, are his significant other?"

Lisa hadn't heard that phrase in years, and she was so taken aback at hearing it that she didn't answer.

"I regret to inform you, then, that we are terminating his contract with the museum for cause. If he wants to discuss it with me, he is welcome to do so. Good day."

Then the woman broke the connection, and the screen reverted to its flat gray color.

"Corrigan, what the hell have you done now?" Lisa asked out loud.

There was no question about what the call meant. Corrigan's contract with MOMA was their main source of income.

He'd blown it away entirely, and she'd just finished the only work she'd had in interior design in six months.

There was nothing she could do now but distract herself

from her anger. As quickly as she could, she went into the bedroom and changed her clothes, then walked stiffly into the
kitchen and started pulling cans from shelves at random, and
finally decided to prepare a particularly difficult Indonesian
sauce. After she finished making the stuff, she nearly broke
down.

For a brief moment, she considered calling her mother
—something she had refused to do for almost five years; the
last time they'd talked, she was just starting the work on her
doctoral dissertation.

It occurred to her then that she should make a *rijstafel,* so
she got out the self-warming server and filled one of the bowls
with the hot sauce. A few more sauces, she told herself, and
maybe I'll be able to talk to Corrigan in a civil tone when he
gets home. Then she got to work on the peanut-butter paste.

She didn't hear the door open. When Corrigan entered
the kitchen and said, "Hi," she turned around and threw the
entire server at him, sauces and all.

XIII

Only after Ullrich's set had killed several joneses would the
leaders reveal the greatest secret to them.

—There is a jones who is trying to kill us, the leaders said,
speaking in relayed choruses across the bottom of the seas.

—Instead, we are going to kill him. And after that, we will
create the new ecology throughout the earth.

—Throughout the earth, echoed the lesser ones, nestled in
their pools and estuaries around the world.

—The new ecology is the great secret, the leaders continued, and its inception will mark a new age. For we will domi-
nate the Earth, and our dominion will permit no creature that
walks upon the land. For the turn to the land was the turn to
wrong living. This must be expunged. Just as we must expunge
the wrong thinking still remaining within us.

—There is no right living without the new turning, and

there is no new turning without the returning to the sea. The false societies that jones has built upon the land will be replaced by the true civilization within the ocean depths. And we will accomplish that great return only when we kill the ancient gods that dwell within us!

—And we shall kill the ancient gods that dwell within us!

That was the chant they all took up until they could repeat it no longer, and then the lesser ones broke the surface of the water and screamed the battle cry.

CHAPTER 7

I

When you see the sign for 'Crofton,' turn right. Up there, see?'' Johnny pointed at a white marker. He was still sort of angry at me; I could tell by the kind of distant tone in his voice. But I didn't say anything then, figuring it was better to shut up and not raise the subject of reincarnation again.

"Okay, turn off here and stop by that mailbox," he said. "Close enough so I can reach the box from the car."

I made the turn, saw the rusty mailbox at the side of the road, and pulled over. Johnny reached out and put the flag up at the side of the box, then lowered it again. A van, parked about 20 meters up the road, flashed its headlights at us.

"Okay. We can go now. Just follow this road until you come to the gate. There'll be a guardhouse there."

"What is all this shit?" I asked him.

"Security. We could have hammerheads on us anytime now." Johnny chuckled. "And the goddamn Food and Drug Administration, too."

The road meandered through a hilly hardwood forest.

I don't know why I should remember it then, but for some reason the thought of Johnny and me visiting the science museum in St. Paul popped into my head. Thinking that talking about that might stop him from being quite so ticked off at me, I decided to mention it to him.

"You remember the time we went to see the dinosaur show in St. Paul?" I asked him.

"No."

"You said you wanted scales, just like *T. rex.*"

"I did, huh?"

"Yeah."

"Well, I guess I've outgrown that. I'm right in the middle of a new transformation. You'll see me in a couple days and probably know me right off."

"Really."

"You'll see."

The road came to a halt in front of a solid wooden gate, flanked by a New Englandy fieldstone wall. There was a small half-timbered guardhouse with mirrored windows. No guards came out to check us, though; instead, the gate simply opened automatically.

"You might as well stop at the guest house," Johnny told me. "Then I'll drive down to the lab."

"I thought replicants couldn't drive."

"Private property, isn't it?"

I pulled through the gate and stopped.

"You take it, then. I'm beat." I set the parking brake and got out. Johnny slid over to the driver's seat, and I walked around and got in on the passenger's side.

The seat wasn't warm. A robot had been sitting there, all right.

Johnny drove me up to a small cottage at the edge of a curve in the gravel driveway. It sat on a knoll looking down on a clearing filled with a white barn and a farmhouse.

"You'll find pajamas in the dresser in the bedroom that ought to fit you," he told me. "Help yourself to breakfast in the morning, and when you get ready, join us down at the farmhouse."

"See you," I told him as I got out.

" 'Night.' "

I shut the door and he drove off down the hill. For a moment I stood there watching the car's taillights, attempting to figure out if Johnny was really trying to prevent the hammerheads from changing the course of human evolution, or if he was so caught up in all the games he was playing that he couldn't tell reality from fantasy anymore. I couldn't figure it out, so I walked over to the front door of the cottage in the surprisingly bright starlight, found it open, and went inside.

It didn't take me long to find the bedroom, settle in, and go to sleep.

Small-arms fire woke me up.

II

No transition, no muzzy half-wakefulness; my eyes were wide open, and I sat up in bed.

Gunshots at close range always have that effect on me.

A heavy explosion rocked the cottage, and I fell out of bed into the space between the bed ruffle and the outside wall of the bedroom.

That's what saved me.

The next detonation blew out the bedroom window. If I'd been in bed, the shards of glass would have done their own microde number on me.

Automatic machine-gun fire answered the two bomb blasts, and I managed to roll under the bed. I looked out across the floor, and the whole cottage seemed wrong somehow; at first I couldn't quite tell why. Gradually it dawned on me that there wasn't a right angle left in the place. The whole structure was leaning at a 60-degree tilt.

I heard someone running down the gravel driveway, followed by the sounds of several other sets of feet. Then machine-gun fire opened up from somewhere near the gate.

It was answered by a kind of wordless screaming just outside the cottage. Somehow it didn't quite sound human. I heard the distinctive crunch of bodies falling down across the gravel, followed by the sounds of another set of feet running down the driveway toward me.

There was a pounding on the cottage wall.

"Anybody in there? This thing's about ready to collapse."

"Yeah!" I shouted. "Over here!"

"You okay?"

"Yeah." I rolled out from under the bed, avoiding the clumps of broken glass on the floor.

A very compact man dressed in dark camouflage fatigues stood looking in through the window frame. The frame itself was a trapezoid now.

"Let me get my shoes on," I told him as I slid them on. I grabbed my clothes off the chair and went out through the gap where the window had been.

"What happened?" I asked.

"We took missile hits. Come on with me. We're evacuating."

I followed him toward the shattered gate, looking back briefly over my shoulder. Down below the barn was burning, and by its light I could see several hammerheads lying dead on the gravel road beyond the contorted wreck of the cottage.

CHAPTER 8

RECONSTRUCTION OF EVENTS SURROUNDING THE MICRODE CITY INCIDENT

I

It was the day after the big argument between Lisa and Corrigan. He'd slept on the couch that night and had gone out the next morning without telling her where he was going, so Lisa called Meryl Ellen Merril and asked to meet her for Saturday brunch at a Midtown restaurant they both liked. Meryl Ellen was almost an hour late. In the meantime, Lisa downed three drinks while staring at the front page of the *New York Times* in the screen set in the bar.

Lisa realized only when Meryl Ellen arrived—as she stood up to hug her—that she'd had too much to drink.

"I've got to sit down," she said as she plummeted back toward her seat, landing at an awkward angle. "I didn't realize how strong these things were."

"And I've got to have coffee," Meryl Ellen told her. "That office party we had last night went too long into this morning." Meryl Ellen accessed the keypad built into the bar and ordered from it.

Lisa tried to ask Meryl Ellen the big question, but found herself crying instead.

Meryl Ellen put her enormous arm around Lisa's back and whispered, "What's the matter?"

"I'm sorry," Lisa told her. After a minute or so she found

she could actually say it out loud. "I've decided I've got to leave Eddy."

"Oh, I'm so sorry."

"Remember what I told you that time out at the lab?" Meryl Ellen nodded. "Well, he's been getting worse all summer long. Every other day now, he claims he's seeing hammerheads around our building. The cops practically live on our doorstep. And everything I say or do is always wrong."

"I'm sorry, Lisa."

Finally she managed to say, "Meryl, you're my best friend out here. Could you let me stay at your place for a month or so? I've got a line on a job with a gallery in Norwalk that starts October first, and after that I'll be able to get out on my own."

"Of course you can," Meryl Ellen answered without hesitating.

II

Some of the time Corrigan hardly noticed that Lisa was gone.

And some of the time, it seemed of far greater importance that he avoid being sucked into the enormous vortex swirling outside his apartment. It still wasn't clear how it was trying to trap him, but he knew he had to exert every effort to avoid being dragged into its maw.

That was the most important thing, he kept telling himself.

He let his computers carry out the basic business transactions and went off personally only to a couple of auctions or to make a few appraisals. The scary part was that he actually had to go out of the building sometimes, now that he didn't have steady money coming in from the museum.

Occasionally he felt that Lisa was being caught up in it, too, even though she'd left. There were nights when he thought about the danger she was in, and how it was all his fault, and how he didn't dare phone her.

But it was clear that the hammerheads were up to something.

He knew it, even if no one else would believe him.

Not Lisa, not the cops, not the newspapers.

Corrigan began to tell himself, "They're out to get you because you're the only one who's figured out that they're up to something. You're a genius, Corrigan. That's your trouble."

And then the phone would ring and he'd be too frightened to answer it, so he let the answering program take a message instead.

III

Nemetz got back late from lunch and stood dumbfounded for a moment as he stared at the blinking message on his desk computer:

TO: NEMETZ, KIDNAPPING INVESTIGATING DIVISION
FROM: HAMILTON, COORDINATION
MESSAGE: YOUR PRESENCE REQUESTED IN MY
        OFFICE AT 2:00 PM
SUBJECT: MICRODE CITY

It had been—what—almost six months since Hamilton had taken him off the Ullrich case.

And if he didn't get a move on, he was going to miss this chance.

He dashed out to the elevators, caught one right away, and entered Hamilton's outer office with a few seconds to spare. An extraordinarily attractive blonde woman wearing a long navy business dress stood in the waiting room, her back turned toward the secretary. She glanced around and looked at Nemetz as he entered the room, then smiled reassuringly.

Just at that moment, Hamilton opened the door to his inner office.

"Ms. Lenard, Nemetz, please come in."

They both entered the wood-paneled office and sat down in the armchairs Hamilton pointed to.

"Thank you for seeing me," the woman said. She half-smiled, as though she were involved in some kind of practical joke. "How secure are we from eavesdropping here?"

"Just a moment," Hamilton told her. He crossed over to his desk, tapped a keypad, and then sat down on the sofa facing both of them.

"We're quite secure now. Let me see," Hamilton said, brushing back his white hair with one hand, "have you two met?"

Nemetz shook his head.

"Let me introduce you, then. Ms. Lenard, this is Lieutenant Jay Nemetz of the hammerhead task force investigations unit. Nemetz, this is Ray-Lee Lenard, the vice president of Microde City."

"How do you do?" she said. Nemetz smiled and nodded back at her.

"I'd like to get right down to business, if I may," Lenard said. The smile had completely left her face. "As I said in my fax to you this morning, the security people we employ have warned us they believe there will be some kind of hammerhead attack against us tomorrow night. That's when we're holding the showing of our fall line at our headquarters on West Eighth Street, in the Washington Square high-security zone." She paused, as though to catch her breath.

Hamilton interjected, "Your fax seemed to imply there was some proximate cause for your, um, worries." Hamilton looked meaningfully at Nemetz, though Nemetz had no idea what kind of idea the old man was trying to transmit to him with that gaze of his. "This room is as highly secured as anything we've got. Please tell me why you think they're going to attack you tomorrow night."

"It's simple," she answered. "We're going to announce a major effort to eradicate the hammerheads."

Nemetz found himself chewing on his thumbnail.

"How do you propose to do that, if I might ask?" Hamilton nodded his head and smiled. Nemetz realized for the first time then why the old man didn't have his hair microded to its natural color: it gave Hamilton's rather weak features extraordinary gravity.

"Before I go into the details," the woman said, shifting in her chair, "you're going to have to promise that you'll protect everything I say as business confidential, and to embargo any public discussion of it until after we announce our plan at the showing tomorrow night. Agreed?"

"Certainly," Hamilton told her.

Lenard clasped her hands and tilted her head slightly to one side; Hamilton seemed to start, as though he recalled the gesture from a long time ago. "By way of background, I've got to tell you that we believe that part of the technology that produced the hammerhead microding was stolen from our laboratory three years ago. Our company's president, Mr. Stevens, has conducted his own research into how that particular microencoding program operates. You might call it his own vendetta against the hammerhead keiretsu.

"And at the same time, our laboratory has developed the first successful technique for completely reversing microding. It's a major breakthrough, and we're announcing it tomorrow night as well.

"It also means we can completely reverse the hammerhead microding."

She set her jaw and gazed briefly at Hamilton, glanced over at Nemetz, and looked back at Hamilton again.

"This is all rather extraordinary," Hamilton said mildly, "but I'm not sure that I'm the one you should be telling this to. Perhaps Lieutenant Nemetz should take you to—"

"No, I wanted to contact one of my father's friends about this." She smiled mischievously, then laughed.

Hamilton sat back in his chair, looking both puzzled and amused. Nemetz had no idea what was going on, and he started to get the uneasy feeling that he'd been using so much phokus, he couldn't understand anything any more without it.

"Oh, Ray-Lee, it *is* you, isn't it? You're such a tease,"

Hamilton said at last. Then he laughed, shaking his head theatrically. He turned to Nemetz and added, "Lieutenant, I used to work for Ms. Lenard's father in Washington. Many years ago, now. It was that new last name of yours that fooled me, Ray-Lee," he added, turning back toward her. "Oh, and the years probably had something to do with it as well."

"I was married, Uncle Fritz. And I wondered how long it would take you to catch on." She smiled, and then her expression phased into the somber. "So, Uncle Fritz, will you please tell the people who need to know about this? Okay?"

Nemetz was struck by the sudden intensity of Hamilton's gaze.

"It's very serious, isn't it, Ray-Lee? It's not a game."

"No, Uncle Fritz. It's not a game. It's *very* serious." She stopped smiling.

"All right." Hamilton thought silently for a moment, drumming his fingers on the yellow upholstery of his armchair. Then he looked up at Nemetz. "Lieutenant, I want you to start special surveillance on the Microde City headquarters. You'll have to work with the liaison group to set up special surveillance on their laboratory in"—Hamilton drummed his fingers on the chair arm once more—"in Connecticut. And please give me a status report by COB tonight."

"Yes, sir."

"Lieutenant, would you excuse us now? I have to chastise Ms. Lenard for pulling the wool over the eyes of an old family friend." He chuckled as he stood and opened the door.

Nemetz nodded to the woman and got up from his chair and walked out of the room. As Hamilton closed the door, Nemetz heard the old man saying, "Ray-Lee, you should have given me a hint it was you! I haven't seen you in almost twenty years. . . ."

Outside in the waiting room, Nemetz stood for a moment to catch his breath. His theory about Microde City had been wrong; they had to be working against the hammerheads, not for them.

Moreover, there was some kind of unusual link, however loose, between the firm and the federal government because Ms. Lenard had to be the daughter of a former director of the Federal Bureau of Investigation.

After all, everybody knew Hamilton had retired as deputy director.

IV

It was the night of the freeing of the great leaders.

He was among those chanting as they spun the wheels that opened the floodgates so that the great ones could swim down the river and back into the ocean, where they would initiate the mission. The half-moon glittered through the surface of the waters as they swam.

And when the leaders had gone, the entire triad followed after them, out against the tide. Within him the rage and joy rose wild in the realization that their enemies were doomed, and they chanted in unison as they went:

—And we shall kill the ancient gods that dwell within us!

V

Meryl Ellen walked into the living room carrying an opened bottle of wine and asked, "Anyone for a friendly cabernet?"

Meryl Ellen's boyfriend, Fowler, a giant microded to match Meryl Ellen's proportions, said, "Just give me the bottle. I'll drink it if no one else will."

"Oh, shush. Lisa, how about you?"

"Sure," she answered.

"I'm going to need a bottle of my own if I'm going to have to watch Stevens," Fowler said.

"Tut-tut. Such disrespect for our employer."

"I'd need more than that if it were really going to be him speaking," Fowler added, leaning back in his beanbag chair.

"But wine should do it, as long as it's just going to be a remote."

The two of them stared at each other for a moment, and Lisa began to get a cold feeling in the pit of her stomach that they were going to start arguing.

"We can talk in front of Lisa," Meryl Ellen said, nodding her head. She turned to Lisa and added, "According to the scuttlebutt at work, Stevens is having himself remicroded."

"But that isn't supposed to work very well, is it?" she asked.

Meryl Ellen smiled. "It's a new process he's going to announce tonight."

Meryl Ellen got out glasses and poured the wine as Fowler turned on the TV. He got up and adjusted the way the screen was hanging on the wall, then sat back down on his beanbag chair. Meryl Ellen settled beside him.

"We've got a choice," Fowler announced. "We can either watch the in-house, closed-circuit version, or the coverage from the Style Channel."

"Let's watch the Style Channel, Fowler," Meryl Ellen told him. "We already know the agitprop line in the office. I'd like to see what they've got to say." Fowler nodded and keyed in a command on the remote control.

A trim woman in a green dress appeared on the screen, standing in what seemed to be the colonnaded lobby of a very large hotel crowded with hundreds of people. Although she was speaking, the volume was off.

"Is that it?" Lisa asked.

"Uh-huh," Meryl Ellen answered. "That's the executive office, all right."

"Let's hear what she's saying." Fowler pressed the remote control.

"—Excitement is palpable here," the reporter announced over a background of augmented flamenco guitar music. "We've just seen one of the most spectacular fall lineups ever produced by the microding industry, and, yes"—she looked over her shoulder at a raised runway—"I believe that Johnny Stevens is about to say a few words." The camera focused over the announcer's shoulder on the figure of a man dressed in a tuxedo clambering onto the runway.

"Dammit!" Meryl Ellen sputtered. "We missed the fashion show!"

"They must be running ahead of schedule," Fowler said.

The camera cut to a close shot of Stevens, a surprisingly young-looking man with a winning smile. He began to speak, but the Style Channel didn't seem to have a working feed from Stevens's microphone. A watery, unintelligible sound came out of the speakers.

"Try the in-house channel, love," Meryl Ellen told Fowler. He was already fumbling for the remote control, and he keyed in a command that changed the channel and produced both Stevens's face and voice.

"—Our most important discovery of the last year also has an extremely *practical* application," Stevens was saying. "We have found a means to use the Salvatore process on even the most unfortunate of recombinant programs. Ladies and gentlemen, I am talking about the hammerheads. And I am proud to say that we have turned over the formula to the United Nations today. We seek no profit—" At that point the crowd began to applaud. Stevens held up his hands, but the people continued clapping.

"Was that it?" Lisa asked.

"I don't think so," Fowler replied. "I'm going to flip back and see what the Style Channel has to say." He keyed in the command. The screen blinked, and the image of the very trim woman reporter appeared, this time with her name, Janessa Fielding, below her.

"There you've heard it," Fielding announced. "A crowd enormously impressed by this surprise announcement by one of America's richest men." The applause appeared to be tapering off, and the reporter glanced back at Stevens, then again at the camera. "I believe Mr. Stevens is about to say a few more words. Let's see if we can't get that line to his microphone once more."

The camera cut away to Stevens, who appeared to be enjoying the applause. When the cheering subsided, he began talking again.

Stevens had uttered several sentences before they managed to get the microphone link working. At last the sound came on and he said, ". . . will take steps to assure that our retromicroding technique ends this danger, once and for all."

Stevens nodded his head briefly and flashed that smile again.

"Now that," Fowler said, "must have been that."

"Let's see what the announcerette has to say," Meryl Ellen told him, putting her forefinger to her lips.

The camera pulled away from Stevens, standing in the spotlight, and focused once more on Janessa Fielding. "In a statement that seems tantamount to a declaration of war," Fielding began, "Johnny Stevens, one of the world's richest men and president of the Johnny line of microencoding ware, has just said that he and his corporation have developed a formula that will combat the hammerhead mafia.

"I can only hint at the enormous impression he has made here. Seldom have I been so stunned by such an evening. More than a fashion show, I think we here at the Style Channel have actually broken a story of worldwide importance."

"Excuse me." Meryl Ellen grabbed the remote control and turned off the sound. "I'd forgotten how egocentric they can be on that channel."

The three of them sat in silence for a moment, absorbing what Stevens had just said.

After a while, Lisa asked, "Maybe I'm dumb, but why did he make an announcement like that?"

"That's just the way he is," Fowler told her.

"But isn't he afraid of the hammerheads? I mean, won't they really be trying harder than ever to get him now?"

"I don't think so," Fowler said. He looked uncertain and asked, "Is it all right to talk about it now, Meryl?"

"I'm not sure," Meryl Ellen answered.

"Well, it'll be in the news soon—if not tonight, then tomorrow morning." Fowler leaned over toward the coffee table and poured himself another glass of wine, then drank half of it in one gulp. "You see, Stevens had us release active retromicroding virus yesterday. It should already have started to undo the hammerhead microding by now."

"Fowler, I don't think you should say that—"

"Well, I did. And I'm glad it's off my chest."

VI

It was the night of the kill.

In the darkness his triad swam across the Hudson from the New Jersey shore to Manhattan. They began well to the north so that, without the greatest of efforts against the current, they reached the broad platform of Pier 40, scrambled onto it and immediately removed the launcher from its waterproof container. The triad then began to jog down West Houston Street, stopping half a block from the high-security checkpoint at Sixth Avenue only to load a missile and to blow the police building and the security wall into dust.

They charged through the rubble, darted through the traffic jam the attack had caused on Sixth Avenue, then proceeded up MacDougal to West Eighth. Once they reached Eighth, they spread out and sealed off the street at the three nearest intersections. The leader gave the sign, and they drew the three breaths that must be taken before the kill.

Then he aimed the launcher at the upper story of the old apartment building at the corner of Eighth and Fifth Avenue and exhaled.

The ritual complete, the leader nodded and they launched the missile. Above them fire exploded in the night. They loaded and launched a second missile that ripped into a back section of the upper floor of the building.

After that, they ran, always eastward, always toward the other shore, chanting, though their breaths were ragged.

—And we shall kill the ancient gods that dwell within us.

VII

Corrigan was restless. It was past midnight and he couldn't sleep. Of course, he had a bottle of prescription sleeping pills he could take, and he didn't have anything to do tomorrow, so he could sleep in if he wanted. . . .

But there was something outside he needed to see.

So he decided the only thing he could do was go riding. He got out of bed, put on his leathers, grabbed his helmet and gloves, and got out his bike.

Without any sense of where he was headed, he found himself riding along the approach to the Holland Tunnel. After he exited into Manhattan, he realized he was headed down toward the Soho quarantine zone.

Traffic was really bad, he thought to himself as he edged through the tie-up on Hudson Street and took an alley at random, hoping to get out onto Broadway somehow.

The twin mushroom clouds boiled up, somewhere just north of Washington Square, as he came out of the alley. Just for a second he wondered if this was the start of an atomic war or something, but then he realized the explosions couldn't have been nuclear. They were too small.

But they were bad enough.

He heard the sound of sirens and saw a police helicopter flying overhead.

Something clicked inside him. He pulled the bike over near a phone booth and hit the engine-kill switch. It was late enough that there wasn't a line in front of the phone.

He started keying in Lisa's number up in Connecticut.

After a moment a recording came on the line: "Due to

emergency conditions, your call cannot be completed at this time. Please do not attempt to place your call again so that we may process emergency calls to this area."

He hung up the receiver and got back on the bike.

VIII

Lisa had finally managed to get to sleep when the knocking on the door woke her up.

"This is Lieutenant Lopez of the Connecticut Highway Patrol. We are evacuating this building. Please gather your valuables and depart this building in ten minutes."

Lisa went to the door and looked through the security lens at a strapping man wearing the uniform of the highway patrol.

"What's going on, officer?" she said through the security microphone in the door.

"You folks work for Microde City, right?"

"Uh, my roommate does."

"Well, their headquarters building was just blown up in Manhattan about half an hour ago. So we're evacuating the entire area around their lab. Sorry, ma'am. I don't have time to talk much more. Me and the boys are sort of spread kinda thin."

She saw him nod at the security lens and walk off toward the next apartment.

Meryl Ellen opened her bedroom door, leaned out into the living room and asked, "We're being what?"

"You heard him. Evacuated."

"I'd better call Fowler." Meryl Ellen stalked over to the phone, put the receiver to her ear and shook it. "No dial tone."

"We'd better get dressed and get out of here."

"You're right."

IX

Corrigan was about fifteen minutes away from Branchville, Connecticut on Route 7 when he saw the missile coming in. The solid pack of clouds that covered New York City had broken somewhere near the state line, so he had a clear view of it. At first he'd thought it was a meteor. But then it changed its angle of approach and headed off toward the north, emitting an intense contrail on its way.

Seeing that put a chill down his back stronger than anything caused by the late September chill, so he pulled off onto the shoulder and parked his bike, letting it idle in neutral. After a few seconds he lost sight of the missile behind the silhouette of the hills. But before he could even think about where it might be headed, there was an enormous glare from beyond the horizon.

Thinking this one might well be a nuke, he killed the engine and dragged the bike down into the ditch, huddling as near to a narrow culvert as he could get. If there were going to be a shock wave, that was about the best he could do.

As he huddled there, pressed against the damp grass and the cement of the culvert, he recalled tapes he'd seen of Hiroshima. The images of the dead, the shattered buildings, and the mushroom cloud roared past his mind's eye. That's when he remembered something he'd read about how a nuclear blast emits a strong electromagnetic shock wave, just like the blast that destroys so much in its wake. But it's the electromagnetic pulse that destroys any kind of electronic equipment that manages to survive—computers, phones, TVs, radios—anything that happens to be on when the bomb goes off.

Corrigan wondered if any of the phones would be working should he get through this. A moment later, he had the strangest feeling—almost like déjà vu—that all this was going to be repeated again at some point in the future.

Then the sound of the explosion engulfed him.

CHAPTER 9

TESTIMONY OF TIMOTHY J. WANDEL

I

As far as the hammerheads were concerned, the attack was successful, I guess: They killed Johnny.

They would have gotten Ray-Lee, too, if she had stayed in the penthouse, because the missiles they launched gutted the three upper stories of the building on West Eighth.

But that was only for the moment, of course.

Because the retromicrode virus worked.

In retrospect, the virus probably worked better than Johnny figured it would. But it wasn't perfect by any means; a lot of hammerheads just got sick and died, many of them right in New York.

When the virus hit and the hammerheads started dying or retroing and the swarms began to fall apart, there were financial panics all through the Pacific Rim. Most of the crank and dust cartels operated by the swarms imploded, and that brought down a lot of narcotics-based economies. I guess you could call it germ warfare, but it wasn't anything like the movies. The religious right split over whether Johnny had shown that microding could be used for good or not, and the media started running a lot of stories about how the hammerheads had kidnapped people, microded them and then brainwashed them.

Things started falling apart for me right then, so I didn't have much time to pay attention to all that.

II

There is nothing I hate more than a funeral. But there I stood, on the deck of a yacht in Long Island Sound, listening to the droning of a family departure counselor as he delivered a eulogy. Ray-Lee, dressed in a flowing black dress, released Johnny's ashes onto the surface of the water when the man finished speaking. It seemed to happen at a breakneck speed, as though it were all on fast forward.

When we got on shore and were walking toward our cars, four heavyset joneses approached Ray-Lee. I was walking beside her and stopped when she did.

"Are you Ray-Lee Lenard?" one of them asked. He had a constricted mouth and tight little eyes.

"Yes, I am."

"I have a summons here from the New York State Environmental Protection Agency. You are required to appear at a public hearing on the eleventh of this month at the address stated in this writ." He handed over a folded document that was several pages thick.

"What is this?" she asked as the men walked away. Absently, she turned and passed it to me.

I opened it and read through it quickly. It looked to me as though she was being charged, as the head of Johnny, Ltd., and associated firms, with deliberately releasing an active recombinant virus into the atmosphere.

"I think we'd better get hold of the legal department quick," I told her as we got into her car.

"You call them for me, okay?"

I sat down beside her in the backseat and accessed the phone.

III

For what Johnny had done, you'd think the feds and the U.N. would've been grateful.

Instead they started hitting us with a series of legal actions. About two months after Johnny died, we had to sell the ruins of the penthouse to pay for legal expenses. After that, Ray-Lee dragged us into meetings with lawyers as often as she had us working on the microde trade. On one of those occasions, when we were meeting with Maurice Golob—the very high-priced attorney the company had hired to handle the state-level cases against the company in New York and Connecticut—Ray-Lee's phone rang.

She picked up the receiver and listened, gazed around at the cheap synthowood office we were working out of, and then muttered something quietly several times. Her face grew pale and her forehead puckered right between her eyebrows. She slammed down the receiver.

"What happened?" I asked.

She didn't answer for a moment. "The feds have just charged us with environmental conspiracy. I'm cited specifically."

"Who was that who called?" Golob asked.

"Your office," she told him.

"Just calm down, Ray-Lee. I'll talk to them."

He smiled reassuringly, but when he phoned his staff, he wasn't smiling anymore.

IV

The second Thursday in December, I got into the office a little late and found everybody still working for the company—except Ray-Lee—standing in the reception lobby.

"Are you Mr. Wandel?" a scowling man asked.

"That's right," I told him.

"Sign that form and I'll give you your severance pay."

"What the hell?"

Henderson turned to me and said, "They've closed us down."

So I signed the form, and the sour-faced guy from the government handed me an envelope with a check and a bunch of memos inside it.

Meryl Ellen Merril insisted that we have a drink before we went home, and she took us to a bar in Midtown, a kind of mirrored barrel of a place with a picture window looking out over water tanks and rooftops.

We had lunch and sat drinking beer into the afternoon. Before we knew it, it was dark outside, and the lights from the city chased their reflections back and forth among the mirrors. By that time the happy hour crew had arrived—mostly a jones crowd.

It was my turn to go to the bar and tell the waiter to bring us another round, but when I got up I found my balance was a little off. I looked up and noticed an enormous creature with long blond hair standing in a mirror in front of me, dressed in a shred-satin suit with an expensive European cut. Somehow I knew it was me, but at the same time, I couldn't recognize myself. All the while the joneses were milling about below me.

Meryl Ellen stood up and put her arm around my waist.

"Need some help walking?" she asked. I couldn't answer right away, and she said, "Whatcha lookin' at?"

"I don't know," I told her. "I don't seem to recognize it." I turned and hugged her. Nothing around me seemed real, not even my own reflection, and I felt terribly alone and lost. "Meryl Ellen, hold me. I need to be held."

And after that we got maudlin.

Very maudlin.

CHAPTER 10

RECONSTRUCTION OF EVENTS SURROUNDING THE "MICRODE CITY" INCIDENT

I

The morning sun was shining directly through the cracked windows of the high-school cafeteria and Lisa had to squint as the scrawny, bald man from the state civil-defense office held up his hands to get the crowd's attention.

"We've completed the preliminaries, everyone," he said. "I don't have any good news to tell you. We've determined that a guided missile hit the Microde City lab outside of town at about 1:20 this morning. It was not—I repeat, not—a nuclear weapon. There is no sign of radiation out at the site. Instead, it was a very powerful conventional weapon."

"Anybody survive?" someone asked.

The bald man licked his lips and rubbed one hand across the front of his red plaid shirt. "I'm sorry to say that no one survived." He looked down at the floor.

Several people around her began to cry, and Lisa, too, felt as though something had just been pulled out of her.

"This is the hard part, folks," he said, looking over their heads. "I've got to ask for volunteers to come and help us identify the victims. It's about all we can do for 'em now."

Lisa couldn't stand it inside the high-school building any longer, so she put on her coat and began to walk through the crowd. Meryl Ellen, whom she had forgotten about somehow, touched her arm.

"Where are you going?" she asked.

"I—just have to get some fresh air."

"You okay?" Fowler asked, looking over Meryl Ellen's shoulder.

"Yeah." She smiled, and the effort set off a muscle spasm in one of her eyelids. Then she turned and made her way through the crowd and out the heavy steel doors into the blue shadows and brilliant sunlight.

She sat down on the steps outside the entrance to the cafeteria. The cold stone beneath her jeans and the white and faint blue of the sky seemed to suggest that there was still something real about the world, and that was the kind of reassurance she needed just then.

After a few minutes, when she had nearly dozed off despite the chill autumn air, a news-service van rolled up and the driver rolled down his window and asked, "Is this where they evacuated everybody last night?"

"Yeah."

"Would you like to be on TV?"

"No."

The driver turned to talk to someone else inside the van, and that's when Lisa heard the motorcycle. It was the distinctive stuttering sound of an Izhevsk 150. She looked down the street and saw Corrigan riding slowly toward her.

And then he saw her and dropped the bike and ran toward her while trying to take off his helmet.

"Lisa, you're okay," he said, panting as he neared her.

She stood up.

"Yeah, I'm okay," she replied, using as even a tone as she could muster. Oddly enough, she found that she was sort of happy to see him, though at the same time she couldn't help feeling scared that he would try to do or say something completely deranged.

"I had to find out how you were," he said, fishing his cigarettes out of his jacket pocket and lighting one, then stuffing his gloves and pack of cigarettes and lighter back into the same pocket. "I couldn't get through on the phone. And I waited most of the night by the roadblock. They just opened it a couple of minutes ago." It seemed to her that he was about to say something else, but he just inhaled on his cigarette and then blew smoke out the side of his mouth.

"Jesus, Lisa, I'm not thinking. D'you want a cigarette?"

"No, thanks. I quit."

"Oh. . . . That's good." He tossed his cigarette on the sidewalk self-consciously and crushed it out with his boot.

He looked down at the sidewalk and asked, "Lisa . . . can I give you a hug? Just to see if you're real?"

She couldn't help herself; she laughed a little at him, and told herself she needed a hug. She nodded.

As they stood there hugging one another, the video crew got out of the van and filmed the two of them for international satellite broadcast.

II

He collapsed in the night while running to join the triad assembling in the north. When he awoke, he found himself sprawled on a ledge in a storm-sewer conduit that looked out onto a body of water bounded by decaying brick buildings. Early-morning sunlight cast long shadows on the water nearest the conduit, and the thought occurred to him, though it seemed somehow alien and out of context, that he was looking at a stretch of the East River.

He remembered that view.

That was when he noticed the corpses bobbing in the water. The East River was full of the bodies of hammerheads. Of his own kind.

And then the fever struck him again and he vomited. After that he closed his eyes once more.

III

Ray-Lee Lenard wore a black silk pantsuit, and as they sat across from each other in Hamilton's waiting room, Nemetz thought he'd taken a little too much phokus that morning. He couldn't stop looking at her, and she clearly felt uncomfortable around him. At last Hamilton summoned them into his office.

"Ray-Lee, Nemetz," Hamilton said, gesturing toward the guest chairs as he closed the door behind them.

Lenard stared down at the *New York Times* on Hamilton's coffee table, featuring a front-page picture of the half-ruined face of Johnny Stevens's remote android peering out from the shattered concrete of the Microde City laboratory.

"Please turn that off," she told Hamilton, who leaned over and touched the contact switch at the upper right-hand corner of the paper. It switched to digital gray.

"Ray-Lee, let me say again, right at the outset, how sorry I am about what happened."

She nodded, her lips drawn.

"You know I'm retiring this week," Hamilton continued, smoothing his gray hair, "and when I'm no longer on active duty, Nemetz here can act as your point of contact with the force."

Lenard nodded. "Uncle Fritz, I asked for this meeting because I want you to pass my comments to Washington," Lenard told him. "Not that it will shake things up at the NSC, where they really need to be shaken up. From what I've been able to piece together, they couldn't figure out that a missile had been launched against the United States in time to respond to it. At least, in my father's day, the Pentagon used to be allowed to handle things like that."

She folded her hands.

"But I'm not here to complain. I want you to know some things that I hope Washington can use. To begin with, I have to give you a little background." She fell silent and rubbed her hands together.

"Johnny Stevens and I were both equally disgusted with the current administration and its inability to do anything about the hammerheads," she continued. "And when it was clear that we ourselves could do something about them, we decided to go ahead on our own. It was a big chance, but we took it.

"We knew that it was illegal to release live microding virus. We knew it was dangerous. The papers already have some figure of twenty thousand hammerheads killed by the retromicrode virus. We figured it might be quite a bit higher, in fact." She stopped speaking and gazed at the coffee table.

"Ray-Lee," Hamilton said after a moment, "I'm not a lawyer." The old man folded his own hands and then stared at them as he continued to speak. "And that's what you need. The government never authorized your activities, and it can't provide you any form of support now."

"Listen, I know that," she said, smiling faintly. "For what it's worth, my lawyer thinks we can fight off most of the legal attacks. But I know how the FBI will chew on this, and that's why I want you to know why we went ahead and did what we did. I'm sorry I didn't tell you about this earlier. Maybe we should have." She let out her breath, almost sighing. "But I'm not sorry we did it."

Hamilton nodded and said, "I think I understand, Ray-Lee."

"We both felt a real responsibility about this," she added. "Whoever started the hammerhead keiretsu used our patents. If it's the last thing I ever do, once the smoke clears on all this, I'm going to get the person who did that."

Hamilton's phone rang, and he got up and went to his desk and answered it. After a moment of talking in tones so quiet that Nemetz couldn't hear what he was saying, Hamilton put down the receiver and told them both, "I'm sorry I'm going to have to cut this short. We've got a meeting with Interpol coming up. Ray-Lee, thank you. It was good to see you again." He licked his lips almost uncertainly. "Keep a stiff upper lip. I know you're as brave as your father ever was."

"Oh, I don't know about that," she said, smiling faintly to cover up the fact that she looked nauseous. She got up and Nemetz followed her out the door, thinking to himself that whatever happened to this woman, it was going to be so far out of his league that he'd never have action on it again.

He escorted Lenard to the elevator lobby.

"I'm sorry about what happened," he told her as he pushed the call button.

She didn't answer, so he stared at his shoes to prevent himself from locking onto her eyes. The whole time they waited for the elevator, she never said a word. She just kept folding and unfolding her hands.

IV

Three weeks after the missile attack on the laboratory, Lisa got her first salary deposit from her new job at the art gallery in Norwalk and moved out of Meryl Ellen's apartment into an efficiency only a few blocks away from work. It was just in the knick of time, she thought. The news stories about the government lawsuits against Microde City made it seem likely that Meryl Ellen was going to be hauled off to jail before very long.

Although she'd never worked in a gallery before, she took to the work naturally. And she loved the sense of peace that having her own apartment—no matter how small—gave her. Just to have her books out of the Val-U Storage out on Route 7 made everything she'd been through worth while.

After about a week, though, she started to feel she ought to be doing something more than just working and living on her own and not thinking about Corrigan. All right, she told herself; maybe there's an undertone of guilt there, too. After all, she owed Meryl Ellen quite a bit.

And as she sat there one Thursday night, closing out her second week on the job, she picked up the phone and called Meryl.

"Hello," Meryl Ellen said, sounding very tired.

"Hi yourself. It's Lisa."

"Oh it's good to hear a friendly voice. It's been an awful day."

"What happened?"

"I was served with a subpoena. I've got to go to a hearing in New York. The lawsuits are breeding faster than yeast in a brewery."

"Well, Meryl," Lisa said, shaking her head, "what could they do to you?"

"I don't know yet. And neither does our lawyer. At the very worst, we might all be charged with wrongful death over all the hammerheads who died after—after we let the virus loose."

Not knowing what to say, Lisa told her, "I'm so sorry."

Meryl Ellen paused, and it sounded as though she were trying to catch her breath. Then she said, "Listen, Lisa, thanks for calling. Unfortunately, I'm afraid I have to go. We're working a lot of overtime right now, trying to patch things together so we'll have money enough coming in from the research division to pay for all the legal bills and trying to rebuild and everything. It's a good thing you called when you did; otherwise I would've been out the door already."

"Well, if you need to talk, call me."

"I will. And thanks again."

After she rang off, Lisa sat there thinking about the way she'd lived for the last year or so. It seemed as though time had speeded up, somehow, and that it had spun her and Corrigan apart, and then slowed down and given her back her life again.

A couple of days later she called Corrigan. He wasn't in, but she left a message on his machine.

The next night, when she got home, he'd left a message on her machine.

"Lisa, thanks for calling me," his message said, "but I don't want to talk to you. I just can't be your friend now. I'm sorry. Good-bye."

She didn't cry after she listened to the recording, though for a moment she felt like it. Then she smiled and almost laughed, remembering how goofy his hair always looked when it was tied back and sticking out from under his motorcycle helmet.

V

Ever since the night he'd spent in the ditch thinking he was going to be nuked, Corrigan had started reading the newspapers again. It was something he hadn't done in years.

After that he decided to really make some changes in his life. For one thing, he quit smoking, though there were plenty of times when he still wanted a cigarette. Then he stopped trying to figure out what his hunches meant. Those hunches were just a mental black hole, he decided, and they never did anything good for him.

Finally he managed to put Lisa out of his mind.

Since then he'd had a real string of luck in getting special projects from museums, so reading the paper in the morning was a luxury—the only time he really had to himself. The rest of the days and nights turned into blurs of indexing furniture and pricing it and writing descriptions of the pieces for catalogs.

One morning he saw an article in the *Times* about the hospital camp that the federal government had set up in Brooklyn to house the retromicroding hammerheads, and it occurred to him for the first time that he ought to call them and see if Ullrich was one of the survivors. As it happened, he was working at the Brooklyn Museum that week, so he thought he'd call during his lunch break.

After a morning of checking through seemingly endless

file drawers in search of something like a modern indexing system for various early-twentieth century vases, it was time to knock off for the midday break. He stopped by the cubicle they let him have for an office and called the hospital, and told the computer voice on the other end that he was looking for Ullrich. The computer asked where Ullrich had been born, and when; Corrigan couldn't quite remember the date, but recalled that Fader had been born in Battle Creek, Michigan.

To Corrigan's surprise the synthovoice said, "Yes, there is a Mr. Ullrich, who was born in Battle Creek, Michigan, who is recuperating in this facility."

"Well, can I visit him?"

For a moment the line remained silent. Then the computer replied, "All patients at this facility may be visited. Visiting hours are from nine A.M. to eight P.M. Thank you."

He rang off and walked down to a fastsushimi place, sat staring out the window without being able to tell what he was thinking about, then finished eating and went back to work.

It was past seven when he left the museum and took the subway down to the hospital; it was so late he'd toyed with the idea of taking a cab, but circling around the unsafe zone in central Brooklyn would have been just too expensive. So it was nearly eight by the time he got to the enormous rehabbed warehouse that served as the main hospital building.

He had to go through a brief security check at the entrance, and they made him give up his jackknife and the personal-security blister he wore on his belt, but then the guard very politely told him to take the elevator up to the fourth floor and go to ward three.

As he got off the elevator and entered a lobby filled with pink plastiform furniture, a synthetic voice announced, "Welcome, Mr. Corrigan. Please take the main corridor to your right to find ward three. Also, please note that there are less than ten minutes of visiting time left. Thank you."

Corrigan nodded and walked down the hall, past rows of

exposed pipes, until he found a door marked "Ward Three." He opened it and entered a vast room divided into separate cubicles by soundproof panels.

He found Ullrich stretched out in a rotobed, his face covered with a personal viewscreen mask.

"Fader," Corrigan said, jostling the man's shoulder.

Ullrich pulled the viewscreen from his head, revealing a face vastly widened into a kind of vicious caricature.

"Son of a bitch," Ullrich said. He got up and put his hands on Corrigan's shoulders. When Ullrich tried to smile, Corrigan saw he didn't have a tooth left in his mouth.

"It's good to see ya," Corrigan told him. He couldn't think of anything else to say.

Ullrich sat back down and looked away, then rubbed his face. Corrigan realized the man was crying.

"Hey, hey," Corrigan said, thinking his voice sounded lamer than it ever had. He couldn't think of anything else to do, so he sat down on the bed next to Ullrich and put his arm around Ullrich's shoulder.

After a moment's pause, Ullrich answered in a hoarse voice, "I'm okay."

"Jesus, you're a rotten liar, Fader."

"I know it."

After a bit, Corrigan got up and sat in the plastiform chair opposite the bed. They sat there for a while, searching for something to say to each other. Chimes sounded overhead, and the hospital synthovoice announced that visiting hours had ended.

"Listen, Eddy," Ullrich said as Corrigan got up from the chair. "You're the first person who's come to see me since I've been in this place. I'm sorry I'm such a mess, here." Ullrich looked down and added, "They've got me under sedation, so I'm not much good to talk to now, but if you'd come back every so often until they let me out. . . ." His voice trailed off.

"Sure, Fader. I'll be glad to."

Corrigan shook Ullrich's hand and left, feeling more at

ease than he had in a year. Somehow it seemed to him that life had come back to a place where it would allow him to just live again. As he rode the elevator down to the lobby, he found himself whistling Bach's Second Brandenburg Concerto, a sign that he was happy in a way he hadn't been in a long, long time.

VI

Ullrich's therapist, Dr. Sladky, told him it would take at least six months before his head started to look normal, but it seemed to him as though that was just a superficiality. Inside, he wasn't sure if he'd ever be the same.

He was grateful that somebody like Corrigan would stop by as often as he did. Sometimes they played cards together, sometimes they watched TV (but only the comedy channels), and once in a while they just talked.

One evening about a month after Corrigan had started to stop by the hospital, they sat watching TV together.

"Say, Eddy," Ullrich said, "would you mind if we turned that thing off? I'd just as soon go for a walk, if you don't mind."

"Whatever you say." Corrigan touched the remote control and the picture vanished. They got up and left the TV room.

"Did I ever tell you what it was like?" Ullrich asked as they walked out into the hall.

"What what was like?"

"You know."

"Fader, you haven't said much about anything, dude."

Ullrich looked down the long, gray corridor and then back at Corrigan.

"Well, it was like waking up and having the opposite of amnesia. I don't know what you call it. Not déjà vu, that's for sure. Suddenly I had, like, a whole other set of memories inside my head. And there was a new language, too, but most of it was way up there"—he waved one hand over his head—"like a dog whistle."

Ullrich had said just about everything he could think of to say, so they walked along without talking and stopped at a window that looked toward Manhattan, glowing in the twilight.

"So, what were they trying to do, Fader?"

"Take over the world."

"Take over the world I know. But there was something more than that. There had to be."

"It's hard to explain it. See, what they wanted . . ." Ullrich scratched his head where the hair was starting to sprout again. "Well, they were going to change the whole planet. There was something about removing all the animal life from the continents. Everything was going to go back into the sea. And we were the exalted ones. We were going to destroy everything. . . . "

Ullrich's voice trailed off, and they walked along for a few paces. Then Ullrich stopped again.

"I know this sounds nuts. But I wanted it more than anything. And it sort of made sense at the time."

"Well, they scrambled your brains, Fader. They did that to everybody they got hold of."

"Yeah. There's a couple more hospitals like this one full of people whose brains are so badly scrambled they can't bring 'em back to anything near normal." Ullrich punched his right hand into his left palm. "Those are the ones I'd like to be able to help."

"Jesus Christ, Fader. I don't think I ever heard you say you ever wanted to help anybody before in your life."

"Yeah, well, I used to think I was a pretty tough jones." Ullrich clasped his hands behind his back and gazed down toward the end of the hall. "I guess I took a big hit because of it. Maybe if I hadn't made that goddamn movie about the hammerheads, I wouldn't have gotten in trouble with 'em. And then this guy Stevens saves my life, and a whole bunch of other people's lives, and gets killed for it. And I was one of the people who was tryin' to kill him. So go figure."

"Yeah, well, I've thought about it a lot."

"Me, too." Ullrich pounded his fist into his palm again. "So all I can think of is trying to do something to help out. I don't even know what. It's kind of like there's this armed memory unit inside me that's going off, telling me to do something good for a change."

"Huh."

They walked back to Ullrich's cubicle. Then the chime rang, and the synthovoice announced the end of visiting hours.

"Time to go," Corrigan said.

"Thanks for stopping by," Ullrich said. For some reason, he was overwhelmed with gratefulness and, instead of just shaking Corrigan's hand, he hugged him and slapped him on the back and told him, "Thanks again, man."

Corrigan walked back to the entrance to the ward with him and said, "So long."

Ullrich watched Corrigan walk away past the rows of pipes and electrical conduits and started thinking there had to be something he could do to pay off his debt to Johnny Stevens. It wasn't like he'd known the guy, or anything; but Jesus Christ, how he owed him. That's when it occurred to him that he ought to make a film about what Stevens had done and the rehab program the government had set up.

And the hardest part, he realized, would be to explain to people who had never been hammerheads what a wonderful thing it is to be a human being.

CHAPTER 11

Excerpts from the Testimony of Elise Smythe before the Senate Intelligence Committee

I first met Johnny Stevens when I worked on a series of advertisements for his company. In one of the ads, I actually appeared as a model. I was the only jones in the middle of a crowd of creatures transformed into Egyptian gods and goddesses. Of course, Johnny's own genetic costume was really much stranger than the new Egyptians', but that's another story.

Johnny always struck me as an incredibly well-read person, and maybe that's why he wasn't afraid to hire people who were clearly running the gauntlet of the Mental Health Acts.

Thinking back on it, it seems to me that the National Mental Health Act was the central, driving factor in the whole era that produced Johnny Stevens and the Microde City crew. I didn't think much of it at the time, of course, but then I was either working on my doctoral dissertation or recovering from writing it during those years, so I was simply too preoccupied to notice.

One of the members of that circle was Fader Ullrich, who produced the ads for Johnny. Ullrich was a horror artist in those days, though he's more famous now as a writer under his own name, Nils. Back then, of course, production of any sort of film or book or comic that could be labeled as "horror" by the

National Standards Review Board meant running the risk of legal action.

If you've seen the ads that Fader produced, especially the ones dealing with the microding looks inspired by Egyptian myths, then you can see that Fader had a way of making even something as routine as microding seem—well, darkly glamorous.

And when I think back about it, that conceit seemed to be the driving force behind the last collection that Johnny designed. Once he had the Salvatore process to reverse any microding at all, Johnny suddenly had a kind of freedom he'd been lacking before. Everyone knows he started out by designing microdings based on all sorts of pop icons, but that last collection was entirely based on the concept of a new mutability that he called "the chameleon approach."

It would have been interesting to see what kind of advertising campaign Fader would have developed for that line. Maybe working on it would have helped him evolve more as an artist. I don't know. It's pointless to speculate about that sort of thing.

But what happened about that time prevented Fader from continuing with his work in advertising. You must understand that we never got along very well, and he was never a close friend of mine; but it was clear that Fader became much more distant than he had been. Distant from everything and everyone.

A—mutual friend told me later that Fader had become fixated on the hammerheads right about then, and he produced a film about them that must have been too near the truth for the keiretsu.

In those days the hammerheads were pretty much a mystery to us all. Of course we knew they were more than just a microding fad among members of gangs, but we had no idea at all about what they were preparing to do.

But because of Fader we found out they didn't want anyone getting too near the truth about them. It wasn't very long after he started showing his film that he disappeared under very mysterious circumstances.

And with Fader's disappearance, and Johnny's death, and the collapse of Microde City, the whole school of art that was starting to develop around that axis came to a halt. My own life disintegrated as a result, I should add, and it's taken me several years to put it back together.

All in all, I'd say I was one of the lucky ones.

CHAPTER 12

TESTIMONY OF TIMOTHY J. WANDEL

It seems funny now, but I didn't find out that Ray-Lee had been arrested until after I got home and heard it on the news one night. Eventually she got fined, spent six months in jail, and had five years' probation with several thousand hours of unpaid "socially contributory" work tossed in. But she was lucky—she got no mandatory therapy.

I wish I'd been able to attend Ray-Lee's trial, but I didn't have the time. They did call me to be a witness at a pretrial hearing, and I keep trying to tell myself that what I said on the witness stand then helped Ray-Lee. But that was all I was able to manage. When the company was dissolved, I didn't have a job anymore, so I did a crash course in writing résumés.

Worse yet, one of those memos in the envelope that the guy from the government had handed me was an eviction notice. They were seizing my apartment as part of the company's assets, and I had a month to get out.

At least I wasn't charged with being an accessory, like some of the surviving research people up in Connecticut.

For a couple of weeks I thought I'd be able to land some kind of full-time writing job. I had three interviews and got one offer. It paid well enough, but there wasn't any housing allowance, so I had to turn it down.

About then my friends Alice and Moustapha called me to say they were moving to Vancouver. I lied and told them things were going okay for me. After we said good-bye, I stared at the phone in my apartment for a couple of minutes. I had one less place to stay if I wanted to remain in New York.

Sometimes you just can't escape home at all. There wasn't any way I could stay where I was. But then, there wasn't anything keeping me there, either. So I called my sister, and she said I could crash with her for a few weeks until I got on my feet. After that I did a little free-lance work for Monica over at *Scope* magazine. I earned enough to buy a bus ticket and headed back to Minneapolis.

I don't think I've ever felt as wasted and crumpled up and thrown away as on that bus ride. A lot of the time I kept blaming myself for getting sucked into the whole thing, and then it occurred to me that maybe microding had made us think we could outrun all of our problems, death and the hammerheads included. I'm pretty sure that escape was part of what was going on in Johnny's head when he started his work on bioengineering; and it was probably inside me, more than I figured.

The first night on the bus, I barely slept at all. I'm too tall now to fit comfortably into one of those things. Maybe that's why I had this strange dream-memory, somewhere before a bleak February dawn in Ohio, when I was in a kind of hallucinogenic state near sleep.

All of the dream had a sort of quicksilver sheen to it, as though I were seeing it played out in a mirror. It started out with the droning voice of the chairman at Ray-Lee's pretrial hearing: "Regarding the purpose of that firm's release of active microde virus . . . " On and on the chairman muttered, while our lawyer pushed me forward to stutter a few words about Johnny's humanitarian efforts.

And then I was going through an endless series of job interviews conducted in mirrored rooms where giant versions of myself seemed to be asking all the questions.

I left one job interview through a silvery door and, without warning, found myself in the dimly lit lobby of the St. Paul science museum. Right in front of me stood Johnny, about age ten. And off to one side, glistening in a greenish light, loomed the dinosaur models. All the perspectives were distorted. Johnny was in his element, and I wasn't.

It came to me then as a kind of a three-o'clock-in-the-morning, bus-ride revelation that the time we went to the St. Paul science museum was a pivotal moment in Johnny's life. After that, he started creating a dreamworld that eventually redefined him and everybody else. And once he was gone, the rest of us were left to live in little pieces of that dream.

You know, that's one hell of an epitaph.

PART
TWO

CHAPTER 1

EXCERPTS FROM THE TESTIMONY OF TIMOTHY J. WANDEL

I

Nine months to the day after he died, my cousin called me. I was out biking around the lakes district that particular Saturday morning in June, trying to force the horrors of my stupid job working as a recording engineer out of my system, so I missed it when it came. By the time I got back to my apartment, the light on my answering system was blinking.

I was standing in the yellow-tiled kitchenette, looking out into the back alley with the towers of central Minneapolis looming not far away, when I hit the button and heard Johnny's voice for the first time in all those months:

"Tim, this is Johnny calling. If you're getting this, then I'm dead, and the computer is transmitting this after it thinks it's safe for you to get this message.

"I've got a favor to ask of you.

"It's more than that, really, Tim. In fact, there's an awful lot at stake. You're about to win a major lottery in Europe, and when they contact you about it—probably within a few hours of your getting this call—then I want you to phone my lawyer. They have a Minneapolis office, so you can try reaching them there, too. I'm not sure where you'll be when you get this, so I'll give you both numbers." He read them twice, and I wrote them down.

"And that's it for me for now. There's going to be a high-speed transmission after this, so you might want to turn off the sound when I'm done. As soon as you can, take the recording cube out of your phone and put it in a vault. And so I guess that's it. Say good-bye to my mother for me, if you see her. Tell her I've tried to make up for a lot of things—things I did in the past. And remember, nobody gets outta here alive." His voice seemed strangely detached as he said that—even for him—and then the high-speed garble started and I turned off the sound.

"Good God!" I said as I sat down on the floor and leaned my sweat-soaked hair into my rickety wire-frame kitchen chair. I thought I'd put Johnny's death behind me, but the phone call twisted me up like a washcloth and forced all the memories back out in front of me.

I must have sat there in a stupor for several minutes, thinking back about the days when I'd lived in New York working for my cousin. Even if it was only a recording, hearing his voice again worked like some kind of time machine for me; the dull present receded and the vivid past played out before me once again.

Then the phone rang.

"Yes," I said, loud enough to voice-activate it.

"Is that Timothy J. Wandel of Minneapolis, Minnesota?"

"Yeah." It sounded like an ad, and I couldn't keep the resentment out of my voice.

"You have just won the Euro-jackpot sweepstakes of seventeen billion dollars! Aren't you excited, Mr. Wandel?"

"Oh, boy, I'm excited," I managed to say, wiping the sweat from my eyes.

II

I guess I should have known not to win the lottery. No sooner had my bank's automatic teller confirmed that the money had been deposited in my account than the Internal Revenue Service called. They took half of the $17 billion right off the top.

But then I hadn't entered the sweepstakes of my own volition in the first place.

My philosophy of life has always been to go take a shower when things get this intense, so I did. I must have been in there for an hour or so. When I finally had had enough, all I could think of was that long showers were the only real advantage I had gained by leaving New York and going back home. In Minnesota, at least, there is no water rationing.

Maybe I was still in something of a daze, but it was already going on nine when I finally left my building and headed down to the subway. Friends of mine were playing a gig at one of the riverfront raves; it didn't promise to be a great Saturday night, but I've had worse. And now I could actually afford to splurge a little.

"So make it a celebration," I told myself as I walked down to the station. I tried to whistle, but my spirit wasn't really in it.

Time always seems to stop for me in subways, and it kind of vanishes completely when I'm actually riding a train. So before I knew it I was walking out of the Minnehaha Falls station and past the art nouveau apartment buildings crouching on the edge of the park, their sound-shielding fluorescing a little in the night across their curving stonework.

In the park itself there were sound-shield projectors all along the perimeter of the rave zone for the under-eighteen crowd; I avoided it and marched along to the brutalist concrete entrance to the slidewalk that led down to the river. There was a really good smart bar down there, even if it was a city-owned operation, and that was when I figured I'd drink something that would do my brain some good. I usually don't go in for that kind of thing, but then it's not every day your dead cousin calls you and lays a few billion bucks on you, just to make life extremely complicated.

Looking out through my reflection in the windows, I could

see that there were a lot of very expensive cars driving in the same direction that I was headed, ready to pay the parkboard that $100 parking fee just for the status of it.

At last the slidewalk delivered me to the wood-paneled bar with its expansive views of the Mississippi gorge and the high-rises across the river in St. Paul. It seems every movie they make in this town features the place, but it is a nice scene—the river's about a kilometer wide at that point and the bluffs are 60 or 70 meters high. And there, 100 meters below me on the levee, where the swirling color and fluorescing curtains emanated from the sound-shield generators surrounding the beach, was the rave.

"Tim," a woman at my side said rather insistently. I looked around. Standing behind the bar was a vaguely familiar person.

"Don't you remember me? I'm Christa Lennon."

"Christa." It took a few more nanoseconds, but my brain stopped being overcome by her body and reminded me that we'd gone to high school together.

"So what are you doing here?"

"It's a summer job. I'm a grad student at the U by day."

I sat down on one of the bar stools.

"So what do you have for somebody down on his luck?"

"Well, I can recommend this new stuff from Russia, uda-cha. But it doesn't really bring you luck, like they say in the ads—just synchronicity."

"How can any smart drink give you luck?"

"I told you, it's not luck. The human brain ties events together in the universe, and that's synchronicity. It just seems like some of that is what people call lucky."

"I'll try one."

"It'll make for an interesting night."

So she gave me one of these things—mixed into some kind of orange shake—and I drank it. It tasted good, but it didn't seem to do anything special for me.

Christa had some other customers, and I let her take care

of them while I finished drinking the thing. By that time I remembered why I had forgotten Christa: when I'd finally gotten up my nerve to ask her out on a date in eleventh grade, she'd told me she was gay.

So I left her a tip and walked out of the bar and down the sprawling staircase. Through the sound-shields and the cool, humid air, it sounded as though there were some enormous concert being held on the moon, loud enough to be heard on the south side of Minneapolis.

I could see the band playing on the dais in the center of the dance area, a kind of miniature Rock of Gibraltar rising up from a mass of writhing dancers. It occurred to me then that maybe I didn't need to shake so much as just sit and look at the moonlight on the river for a bit, so I flashed my VIP pass and entered the zone, assaulted by the sound, and headed down another series of stairs to one of the riverboats tied up at the levee.

The boat I chose had a bar facing southward toward New Orleans and the Caribbean and the Magellanic Clouds and other invisible destinations, and so I boarded and sat down and ordered a beer. As I drank it, I watched a police boat cruising upstream. Suddenly the deck reared up and glassware and bottles crashed to the floor.

So did I and just about everybody else in the place.

III

Something with the mass of a small submarine had rammed the boat and driven it part of the way onto the shore. I found myself folded around a sofa and a couple of other people where the couch had lodged against the railing, looking out at the hole where a picture window had been.

"Excuse me," I told the couple I had been tossed against, and then I jumped through the hole onto the squishy sand. There was the sound of something thrashing in the river. I backed away from the boat. The couple I'd fallen on top of followed me out through the window, and, a little dazed, walked past me toward the stairs.

The police boat sounded its siren at that point and shone a searchlight on the partially capsized boat. I saw something swimming agitatedly out in the river—something at least as big as a porpoise.

But no porpoise I knew ever rammed a boat like that.

A police helicopter swooped in over the bluffs and hovered above the shore, casting its searchlight on the water. The music stopped behind me. I backed up the hill to where I could see the grayish white thing in the green water of the Mississippi recoiling from the light. The helicopter moved out across the river, turning and following the thing downstream.

When the 'copter was half a kilometer from the rave zone, a man leaned out from it and fired a rifle into the water. The shot echoed through the river gorge, and then the man shot again.

At that point the thing in the water breached. For a moment I could see the outline of its head illuminated against the night by the 'copter's spotlight, something like an enormous cross. The marksman shot again, and part of the head splattered like a rotten pumpkin.

"What in the hell!" somebody muttered behind me.

There was no doubt in my mind about it. A giant hammerhead shark had attacked the boat I had been sitting in.

More than 2,000 kilometers from the sea . . .

Past an extensive series of locks and dams . . .

Through some of the most closely monitored waterways in the world . . .

Gazing down at the shore, just to make sure it was still there under my feet, I admitted to myself what I'd seen. It wasn't a pleasant thing to have to do. Because after Johnny released the virus that destroyed the hammerheads, some of the people who survived the process claimed there were even more radically microded hammerheads—they called them the "great ones"—still in the sea.

They were right.

The great ones had survived.

And they were mad enough to attack me on a boat on the Mississippi.

The word "vendetta" formed in my brain.

IV

The cops moved in and closed down all the raves and yacht clubs along the river, and I got caught in the crowd. As we were shuffling up the stairs, I noticed for the first time that a lot of the people around me were very high microde. Green seemed to be the dominant skin color for maybe a third of the crowd that night.

Giving up any hope of meeting my friend who played lead guitar for the band, I fished my phone out of my sleeve pocket and tried to access my home system. There wasn't any response. I shook the thing, and noticed only then that the LED was dead. It couldn't be a dead battery, I told myself. But then what else could go wrong with a phone? There was nothing to it but to hit the self-repair button and forget about it till the morning.

The subway stations were crowded beyond belief, and it took two hours before I got home. When I entered the kitchen, I saw that my answering unit was flashing. I shut the front door and walked over and pressed the access button.

"This is Bill Ligoth," an unusual, reedy voice said. "I'm with the Minneapolis office of the law firm of Golob, Westerberg and Macintosh that represents the estate of Johnny Stevens, and I've been asked to represent you. Please call me tonight regardless of the time. Without being melodramatic, the message I've gotten from the New York office says that time is of the essence." He gave his number and rang off.

I looked at the clock on the unit; it was just past midnight. For a moment I debated calling in the morning, but then I figured I wouldn't sleep until I found out what this was all about. So I had the unit access Ligoth's number.

A woman answered the phone; I told her who I was and asked to talk to Ligoth. After a moment, he came to the phone.

"This is Bill Ligoth."

"Uh, Mr. Ligoth, this is Tim Wandel returning your call."

"Oh, I'm glad you called now, Tim. We were going to try to stay up for your call, but my wife says she's feeling a little poorly. Now let's see. According to the instructions we got from our New York office, you're to bring in some kind of high-speed recording for us to work on. Now tomorrow—or rather today, seeing that it's past midnight—is Sunday. We go to church in the morning, so we'd be able to see you at noon, if that wouldn't be inconvenient."

At first I didn't realize he'd asked a question and then I said, "Sure. That's fine."

"Come over to our Lake Street office. We're in the Nicollet Circle Building, Suite 1100. And before I forget, according to the New York office, your cousin left instructions that, should you ever receive any recorded message from him, you are to disconnect all your computer equipment and store any computer recording cubes you have in—Hang on a minute, I'll have to read this to you." I could hear him rustling through some papers. "You're to store your computer recording cubes in an EM-73 grade vault. Do you know what that is?"

"Sure. You use them in professional audio-video work. I've got one here in my apartment."

"Well, that's what I'm supposed to tell you. I must confess I don't know what to make of it."

"I'm not sure either, but I've got some ideas."

We rang off then, and I grabbed all the recording cubes I could find, including the one in the phone, and tossed them in a gray-metal vault by my home editing gear. And at that point I flopped over on my bed without turning out the lights and slept.

V

It was a sultry morning, and my shower was wearing off as I biked up to the Nicollet Circle Building. I decided I could afford the insured parking lot under the building and pedaled down the entrance ramp and pulled into one of the rental cubicles, popped a $10 coin in the slot, and took the key with me.

An art deco elevator took me up to the eleventh floor and left me to stare at a mural, painted in twentieth-century, depression-era style, of lawyers at work in the courts, with the Supreme Court looming prominently at the center. Underneath the picture of the Supreme Court were a pair of dark wooden doors leading to the offices of Golob, Westerberg and Macintosh. I opened one of the doors and entered.

An elderly man wearing a shirt and tie was seated in the oak-paneled art-deco waiting room reading a newspaper. I knocked on the opened door and he looked up.

"Are you Mr. Wandel?" he asked in that unmistakable reedy voice.

"And you must be Mr. Ligoth."

"Bill. That's right. Come in, please, and shut the door."

He turned off his newspaper and sat it down on a table and led me through a labyrinth of passages to yet another wood-paneled room filled with shelves of hard-copy books.

"I've got an engineer coming in a few minutes to help us with that recording of yours."

"You know, you didn't have to do that. I work as a recording engineer." I swung my backpack onto the table, opened it, and took out the vault that contained my memory cubes.

"Oh. Sorry. I didn't know that. But at any rate, we're going to have to take some extra security measures, and she's bringing in equipment to do that."

"Okay."

He sat down opposite me at the table. "Just to help me get acquainted with what the parameters of this case may be, let me ask a few questions. At the outset, let me say that I know a bit about your cousin. One of our firm's more famous clients, in fact. We tried to keep his company afloat after he was killed, you know. But when all was said and done, unfortunately, we were only able to get reduced sentences for the people the government charged."

"Well, if you release active microde virus and it kills lots of people around the world, it's bound to get the government in trouble. And that means they're bound to go looking for scapegoats," I said.

"I take it, then, that you don't have a very high opinion of your cousin's work."

"I wouldn't say that. He was just the biggest risk taker there ever was, is all. I guess I'm pretty lucky I wasn't thrown in jail with the rest of them."

"Why is that?"

"Well, I worked for him. He hired me out in New York about a year ago, and I worked in his marketing department, right through the attack and up until the company went under."

A look passed across Ligoth's face that made me think he was about to berate microding as the work of the devil when a buzzer sounded.

"That must be the engineer. Excuse me." Ligoth got up and left, then returned a few moments later accompanied by a woman who looked as jones as could be except for the cockatiel feathers growing out of her otherwise bald head. She was pushing a small cart loaded down with electrical equipment.

"Hot one today, isn't it?" she said.

I nodded and looked longingly at the million dollars' worth of gear she had on that cart.

She turned to Ligoth and asked, "Do you have your own security system in this room?"

"Yes, we do," he answered.

"If you'd turn it on, I'd like to run a few tests."

Ligoth walked to a cherry-wood credenza, opened a drawer and adjusted the keypad inside it. The doors to the room slid shut automatically.

"That's it," Ligoth said.

The woman turned on a sensor, punched a keypad a few times and nodded.

"Can I have the memory cube?" she asked rather abruptly.

Ligoth turned to me and said, "If you'd be kind enough to give her the cube . . ." I opened the case and handed it to her, and she popped it into the intake on the top of the cart.

As she fiddled with the equipment and watched her readouts, Ligoth said, "Now remember, we need a copy of the cube and a complete hard copy of the text."

"Don't worry, pops. No sooner said than done."

Ligoth suppressed a scowl.

After a moment, the woman said, "Well, part of this is text, and a very short bit at the start is audio. Do you want to hear the audio while I'm printing?"

"No, we'll wait," Ligoth told her. "Just let us know when you're done."

I would just as soon have listened to whatever was on the recording, but instead sat there across the table from Ligoth, tapping my fingers against the cherry-wood surface.

After ten minutes or so, the woman finished.

"We're done," she said. "It'll still be printing for a few more minutes, but you can listen to the audio now. Just press the audio-play pad and you're set."

"Thank you very much," Ligoth said, getting up from his chair. "Let me show you out." He walked to the credenza and opened the doors and then escorted the woman into the hall.

I didn't want to play the recording without the benefit of the security system, even though, as far as I could tell, it had been transmitted to me without any protection. So I got up and looked at the printer in action. It was quietly spewing sheets of genuine paper out into a plastic containment area.

Sheafs of chemical formulae and graphs and a series of what looked like deep-sea navigational charts flashed by as I watched.

"Well, I guess we should listen to the audio," Ligoth said as he entered the room. I looked up at him and he asked, "Is it done printing yet?"

"Not quite," I said. "Why don't you turn the security system back on and we'll listen to it."

He did so and then sat down in a reproduction Chippendale chair.

When the doors had closed and Ligoth nodded his head, I pressed the keypad.

Johnny's voice issued from the speakers built into the top of the cart. "Tim," he said, his voice sounding tinny because of the speakers, "you are surely listening to my voice under some of the most bizarre of all possible circumstances.

"As I record this, you're working away at the presentation of our fall fashion show, and you really don't know much about what we've tried to do. Now, undoubtedly, you know a good deal more about it. But you've got to believe that not even I know everything.

"There are some loose ends that only Ray-Lee could clean up easily. If she is still alive, contact her at once. You should have the money to be able to do that now.

"But whether or not she's still alive when you hear this, you've got to take some of the lottery money and start a research study of everyone who's successfully retromicroded from the hammerhead state. There must be several thousands. What you must do is to find out everything you can about the warlords, the real leaders of the hammerheads. Because we may not have reached them with our retromicroding virus.

"This is probably all ancient history to you. But do these things for me.

"In the meantime, I've tried to take care of you. And so I have to ask you to take care of the people I'm responsible for.

If you're listening to this, you know I just didn't have time to do the job."

He paused for a bit then, and both Ligoth and I thought the recording had finished. But just as I was about to press the keypad, Johnny's voice started once more.

"Tim, the text I'm putting in this message is from our files on the hammerheads. Make sure that the FBI gets a copy as soon as possible. Of course there's the chance they've got it already. But if you can, ask Ray-Lee about whom to give it to. So, until we both break on through to the other side, good-bye, man."

This time I checked the readout, and that was indeed the last of the audio recording.

"You'll have to explain some of that to me," Ligoth said.

"Well, the most important thing to do is to get hold of Ray-Lee Lenard," I told him. "I think she might still be in jail in New York."

"That was your cousin's—uh—paramour. Am I right?"

"Who knows? They lived together, if that's what you mean." I couldn't help sounding rude.

"You're not being very helpful, Mr. Wandel."

"I'm being perfectly honest with you. I have no more an idea than the man in the moon about whether they loved each other."

He gave me a look that suggested he realized at last that he was getting in too deep. "All right," he answered. "I take your point. Let me call New York and see what we can find out."

VI

Ligoth and I made a deal: he'd phone New York and make copies of the printout of the document Johnny had sent us, and I'd go down to a take-out Ethiopian restaurant on Lyndale Ave. to bring back lunch for both of us. When I returned,

Ligoth came to the door looking as though he'd just seen a car run over a dog.

"I've been reading the manuscript," he told me as he locked the door behind me. "It's . . . very disturbing."

"What do you mean?" I asked as we walked back to the consultation room. He gazed over at me and then looked down at the floor. I don't think I've ever seen anybody before with that kind of mixture of confusion and unease on his face.

"There's a lot more than what's been in the news," he added. We entered the consultation room, and he turned on the security unit as I unpacked the food. When the doors had closed, Ligoth said, "That thing that was killed in the river last night must be one of the warlords your cousin wrote about in the essay we received."

"That's what I thought as soon as I saw it break the surface."

"You mean you were there when it happened?"

"That's right." I finished setting the plastic serving pods on the table. "And I started thinking right away they were after me, and maybe a few other people their street punks didn't manage to kill besides. But that's not the kind of thing you tell your lawyer right off the bat."

"No, I suppose not."

"So let me have a copy of this thing to read."

He pushed one across the table at me and I sat down, opened the plastic container and started to eat as I read. The first section of the printout was a series of diarylike entries that Johnny had written about Stanislav Karnovsky, one of the first partners in Johnny's firm. Karnovsky disappeared with a number of the company's files, and the police turned up evidence that he'd either been kidnapped by, or had gone to work for, the hammerheads. It took me a while because it had been so long ago, but I recalled hearing about Karnovsky when I worked for Johnny.

Unfortunately there wasn't much more there than I remembered having heard.

There was a second section—written by several people who had worked at the Microde City laboratory in Connecticut—that was something like a history of the hammerheads. I don't know where they got their information, but they claimed that three East Asian mafias (that had been famous for shark fetishes since the Middle Ages) seemed to have had some part in creating the hammerhead kereitsu. At the end of the section, they claimed that the triad gangs that started appearing a few years ago in the industrialized countries were only the foot soldiers in a bizarre war; that the generals were microded even more radically and had the ability to transmit on radio frequencies from organs within the bulging lobes of their heads.

The conclusion echoed something Johnny had told me once, just before he was killed: "We believe the hammerhead keiretsu intends to change the ecology of the Earth," the authors wrote, "and thereby to eliminate intelligent life on the planet's surface. The purpose behind this remains obscure."

Beyond that the paper contained a computer file on the retromicroding formula Johnny had used on the hammerheads. There was also a long paper on centers of hammerhead submarine activity in the major oceans and an assessment of what the hammerheads would attack next, by country.

I had finished reading and had been staring into space for a while when Ligoth cleared his throat.

"It's a rather remarkable document, isn't it?"

"Yeah." I couldn't help thinking about the last time I saw Johnny alive, the night I drove him up to Connecticut just before they killed him.

And then I reminded myself that it had only been his replicant that I'd seen that night.

But that replicant made it seem to me as though it had really been him—more like the person I grew up with than the pangolin creature he'd become, lurking in his Egyptian temple above Manhattan. Still, he'd been as distant as ever that night; though as we drove up to the Microde City lab, it seemed as though he'd been trying to break through some kind of barrier and tell me how dangerous he really thought the hammerheads were. Maybe, if I hadn't managed to get him ticked off at me about his believing in reincarnation, he would have told me more.

I looked up from the typescript at Ligoth. He was staring right into my eyes, so I stared back and said to him, "You know, I'll bet the original files were destroyed when the hammerheads blew up the Microde City lab."

"That's where your cousin died, wasn't it?" Ligoth asked, raising his eyebrows in a courtroom gesture he must have learned fifty years ago.

I nodded. Just then I didn't have a lot to say.

VII

Ligoth gave me the fax he'd gotten from Maurice Golob, the head of the law firm, and then shuffled off to try to have the New York office locate Ray-Lee Lenard. My head was so full of what Johnny had found out about the hammerheads that I had to read Golob's fax three times before I could make sense of it. The thing was written in a style that bounced between the abstract and the legal—it sort of reminded me of the time I tried to read Kant when I was in college.

What the fax said was, in short, turn off all your computers because Johnny Stevens sent us a time-delayed message warning that the senior partners of the hammerhead keiretsu are waiting to screw up the world economy by jiggering with international computer operations.

That was when I finally figured out how one of the great ones had gotten into the upper Mississippi. They'd reprogrammed the lock-and-dam system from inside their own heads.

Maybe it was a trial run before they started trying to blow up the financial centers around the world; 1929, anyone?

VIII

I waited for a couple of hours at Ligoth's office, mostly spent looking out the windows at people on the streets below. It turned out that Maurice Golob was playing golf with the attorney general of the state of New York and some retired federal government bigwig. Ligoth said it was all part of their effort to get Ray-Lee paroled. At a little after six o'clock, we got a call saying that Golob had gotten the attorney general's agreement to start parole proceedings for her.

"I want to talk to her," I told Ligoth. "Can you arrange that?"

"I'm sure we can. She's in a minimum-security facility." And he started pressing keypads and calling in favors in Albany and Manhattan.

IX

When the word came down that I wouldn't get to talk to Ray-Lee until Monday afternoon—Ligoth said that was the next phone-access period at the prison—I made sure he had my number and told him to call me whenever we could get through to her. Once I got outside the door of Ligoth's office, it seemed as though I'd finally managed to get something like a piece of popcorn kernel unstuck from between my molars. Just the guy's voice rubbed me the wrong way.

The heart of Sunday night opened before me without a chance to do anything. I thought about who might want to go get something to eat and then go and get smart. It was a short list—most of my best friends are musicians, and they were working. So I figured I'd call my old drummer, Syd Baltic, who was between women and gigs. And then I realized why my subconscious had picked him: he was once a Ph.D. candidate in microding technology. We had a lot to talk about.

Even though it had managed to repair itself, my phone is one of those cheap ones that doesn't work too well inside buildings, so I got my bike out of the garage and walked over to the park in the circle, where Nicollet and Lake go underground, and phoned Syd.

"Syd, it's Tim."

"Hi." He didn't sound too cheerful.

"Doing anything for dinner tonight?"

"Naw."

"You wanna go and get something to eat?"

"I can't, man. I don't have the money."

"Don't worry about it. You're not going to believe this, but I just won a lottery."

"You what?"

"I just won a lottery. You wanna come help me celebrate?"

"It's gotta be someplace that'll let me come inside."

"So how about the beer garden at Lake Calhoun?"

"Okay. You're buying."

"See youse."

Syd always has problems getting into restaurants nowadays because he's a centaur. He's the most radical creature I know. When I came back from New York for the first time in nearly nine months, I could hardly believe it when I saw him. If he'd had something like that done at my cousin's company in New York, it would have set him back a hundred million, easy. But he had some contacts in the boutique microding labs in Minneapolis, and one of them did the job as an experiment to see how well it would turn out.

It turned out pretty well, I'd say, but Syd hasn't held down a job since the scope-music fad fizzled out during March.

So I biked down the western length of Lake Street to Lake Calhoun, parked in a secure garage and took a seat outside the beer garden entrance to wait for Syd. As I did so, I watched the people blading along the perimeter of the lake and the crowds in the garden itself. I used to think that people here were more normal than in New York, where the subway cars are crowded with the microded. But there were just as many creatures here now, less than a year after Johnny introduced the technique that would retro any microding procedure.

Syd galloped up. He was wearing a Costa Rican woven vest, shades and Conan-style earrings.

"Hi."

"Hey, guy. Congratulations on winning the lottery. How much did you get?"

I told him.

"Jesus Christ on a crutch! You're rich, Tim."

"Not for long. The IRS already took its cut, and the rest of it will be gone before you know it."

"What do you mean?"

"My cousin arranged all this before they killed him. And he left me some unfinished business."

Syd thought about that for a moment, tapped his lower lip with one finger and said, "This sounds like it requires a lot of beer."

"You could be right." We walked through the gate and a mother jones sort of woman with a beehive hairdo—ninety if she was a day—escorted us over to a table at the far side of the garden where we had a great view of some shrubbery and a number of high-rise apartment buildings, but absolutely not a hint of the lake.

As she placed our menus on the white plastic table she said to Syd rather caustically, "Young man, that's a really rad microde job."

"Thank you."

She leaned back, frowned and crossed her arms and considered him closely.

"I don't think I've ever seen one like you before. Why would you want to do that to yourself?"

"I'm just a mythological kind of guy, ma'am."

"Hmm." She walked off shaking her head.

When she was out of earshot, Syd leaned over and said,

"More living proof that these social-security jobs should be given to robots."

"It's just another old mother jones, man."

About then the waiter rolled up and we punched in our order—a pitcher of beer and four large pizzas—and it rolled away humming to itself.

"Syd, listen. I've got a bunch of stuff I've gotta talk to you about."

"Such as?"

"Well, for starts, I don't know how he did it, but my cousin Johnny arranged for me to win this lottery."

"What was he trying to do, beat the inheritance taxes?"

"No. He left me a message saying that he figured there was a chance he was going to be killed, and he asked me to make sure that he succeeded in eliminating the hammerheads."

"But everybody knows he did, so what's the sweat? Take the money and run."

I scowled and counted to ten. "The problem is he didn't get rid of all the hammerheads."

A waiter rolled up carrying the beer and two glasses, sat them on the table, and spun off toward another rendezvous with the thirsty.

"They killed one of them last night in the river. I was there."

Syd poured the beers in silence, then pushed mine toward me.

"Here's to you," he said and then drained his glass. I took a couple of sips of mine.

"Syd, I think the hammerhead they killed was trying to get me first."

"So tell me, where's the body?"

"The cops have it. It was in the afternoon vids."

"You know, I can think of a couple of really unpleasant possibilities. . . . " He leaned back and looked at the clouds and switched his tail across his chestnut flanks, then poured himself another beer. "Johnny released an all-vector Hirschorn microding virus," he said in the kind of tone a graduate teaching assistant uses to set up a word problem. "And, from what you're telling me, it apparently didn't affect some of the high hammerhead muckety-mucks. So that means they must have changed their basic genetic structure enough so that no virus could affect them.

"What I don't understand," he went on, "is how they would eat. I mean, how they would live. If you do that to your genes, it seems like it would be real hard for you to digest the kinds of proteins and sugars and carbohydrates the rest of the world survives on."

It was beyond me. I only have a general-studies degree and a master's in journalism.

"So listen, Syd, I want to hire you to work on a project with whoever we can get from Johnny's lab to finish the job."

"How much are you willing to pay?"

"Damned if I know. More than you're making now."

"It's a deal."

And after that I sat fascinated, watching Syd finish off three entire large pizzas by himself.

The guy eats like a horse.

X

After dinner, Syd and I drank a couple of smart drinks that were something like coffee with lecithin and a lot of sugar and a few other upper-brain stimulants; and after about five minutes, we both realized we didn't know what the hell we were getting into with Johnny's legacy. And then the stuff wore off. We both really needed to sleep immediately, before what was left of our brains turned to ash.

I was home by about eleven o'clock, and the next thing I knew, my phone was ringing and my alarm clock showed it was 2:30 P.M. I'd slept through the whole morning.

When I got to the phone, I turned off the video.

"Hello?"

"Tim, is that you?" It was Ray-Lee Lenard.

"Hello, Ray-Lee. How are you?"

"I'm scared, Tim. They told me they were letting me out on parole. And then they told me why."

"I'm scared, too, I guess."

"So what are your thoughts about this?"

"I'd like you to come out here, Ray-Lee. But only on land. Don't fly. I'm worried about them reading the computer ticketing system and making your plane crash. Bring as many people as you can from the Microde City lab."

"Why don't you come out here instead? Wouldn't that be simpler?"

"I don't think I could live comfortably out there. For a lot of reasons." I didn't want to sound paranoid over the phone; worse yet, I didn't want to give away any more than I already had to whatever hammerheads might be listening. "Give me your credit-account number, and I'll wire you some money."

"Okay."

"And arrange to call me on a high-security scrambler this evening and let me know what you accomplished. Call me at ten your time."

"I don't know how much I can get done by then, Tim."

Her voice sounded genuinely uncertain; it was something I'd never heard from her before.

"Try your best, Ray-Lee. Johnny left a message for me asking us to try our hardest."

She didn't answer right away, and I guess it was a good thing I didn't have the video on.

"I'll call," she said at last, her voice strained. Then we said good-bye.

For some minutes I sat there trying to chase down my thoughts. It proved futile; my mind wanted to go in several directions at once. There wasn't much more I could think of, so I turned on the video and accessed the Radical Centrist channel. That was one of the pleasures of life here, I had to admit; I'd never even heard of that channel in New York. I went through their menu and watched a show put together by a private research group about the hammerheads. Afterward I made a mental note to myself to contact them to see what they could tell me.

CHAPTER 2

EXCERPT FROM "PUBLIC INTELLIGENCE" PROGRAM: "THE SIGN OF THE SHARK (4/17)"

A man in early middle age with a very angular face and an oddly twisted nose, seated at a light-oak desk, gazes into the camera as the "Public Intelligence: The Sign of the Shark" logotype fades out.

"Good evening," he says in a surprisingly deep voice, smiling slightly. "This is Doug Janssen for Public Intelligence. Tonight's program focuses on the goals of the hammerheads, long touted as the most dangerous criminal organization in history.

"Research conducted for the Public Intelligence Foundation indicates that there is much more to them than crime. Before the Microde City incident, which ended their control over millions of people who had been restructured as their land-assault troops, the hammerheads controlled a number of drug cartels and organizations for laundering money." Behind Janssen the image of a hammerhead warrior plays briefly on the screen and fades out.

"In our view, the hammerheads arose as a result of the decades of deconstructing society that began in the twentieth century. Microding only opened the door to the expression of one of the grammars of behavior programmed by evolution into every human being."

Janssen turns and the camera follows him, a world map inset fades in behind him against a light blue background.

"Interviews of those who have survived the retromicroding, conducted by both governments and nongovernmental organizations alike, indicate that there was some kind of quasi-religion taught to those who became hammerheads. Syncretistic in form, this religious training seems to have been based on the belief that all land-based life was somehow evil and had to be eliminated."

Janssen turns his head toward the world map, where red check-marks appear across the continents. "As shown on this map, the distribution of hammerheads was not uniform. Could that be an indication of not only where the organization had its headquarters, but also of hammerhead religious shrines? . . ."

CHAPTER 3

TESTIMONY OF TIMOTHY J. WANDEL

I

I went out for a walk after I ate brunch. When I came back, my sister had phoned and was recording a message on the answering system.

"Tim, this is your sister Abby. What's this about you winning a lottery? It's in all the vids—"

I picked up the receiver and canceled the message system.

"Hi, Abs."

"Tim, what do you mean by not calling me to tell me you won seventeen billion dollars!"

"Things happened."

"What could possibly have happened to—" She stopped speaking. A couple of possibilities must have occurred to her, such as her ability to phone every time I and my ex-girlfriend were, well, being romantic, back when we were living together before I moved to New York.

"Anyway," I said, "the taxman has already taken half of it, and I suppose the state will call real soon to say they're taking their bite."

"Well, you should definitely buy a house. They're the safest investment."

"All in good time." It took me about twenty minutes more

to calm her down after that. Abby's really a good person, but she's always had the ability to feel slighted by anything.

After that I worked on a letter of resignation for my job. Just because I happen to know a little about video and I like working in TV doesn't mean I have to go through life dealing with the bunch of arrogant doofuses who ran the station I was working at. Of course, I'd only intended it as a temporary job until something good came along. Good riddance to bad garbage; that was the tone I took.

By the time I finished and transmitted the letter, it was almost time for Ray-Lee to call.

The phone rang and I answered it.

"Hello?"

"Hi. This is Ray-Lee."

"Good. Hang on while I get the scrambler circuit going."

"Don't bother. I couldn't get access to one. At any rate, expect me tomorrow on the high-speed train. It looks as though I can get only one of the people who used to work at the lab, and only for a limited time. We've got to talk about how much money we can spend, and then we can decide what to do."

"Okay."

"I'll see you then."

"Bye-bye." She hung up and I sat staring out the window at the birds flying in between the trees, silhouetted against the darkening sky.

II

All right—it might have been Tuesday, but I was no longer employed and I had decided to sleep in. Nevertheless, about half-past nine my doorbell rang. I rolled over in bed and hit the security system. The monitor showed Syd standing in front of my door, still wearing his shades.

"Just a minute, Syd," I said into the mic. I untangled my

feet from the sheets, put on a pair of gym shorts, and walked out and opened the door.

"Have you seen the vids this morning?"

"Syd, I haven't even looked at a cup of coffee yet."

"Well go brush your teeth. I'll make coffee. There's no time to waste."

"What the hell are you talking about?"

"The bloom. It's in the Pacific and it's killing everything."

"Back up a minute."

"It's gotta be something the hammerheads made. Now go get cleaned up, and I'll show you what I'm talking about." He ambled inside, turned around carefully and shut the door, then backed out of the entryway and headed for the kitchen, his hooves clicking against the linoleum floor.

"What are you staring at?" he asked, looking at me over his shoulder.

"You really don't fit in a one-bedroom apartment very well, do you?"

"So hurry up before I break some of your valuable china."

I went into the bathroom and cleaned up, then walked out to the living room wearing my gym shorts and drying my hair with a towel.

Syd had sort of curled up by my desk, reading the morning papers off my computer.

"So what's going on?" I asked him.

"Eat some breakfast and let me get through the press-service reports, okay?"

I did as I was told. When I had finished off a couple of doughnuts, I walked back into the living room and looked over Syd's shoulder at the computer screen.

"Syd, no more stalling. Tell me about it."

Syd shuffled away from the desk a bit and looked at me. "There's some sort of bloom spread across about five hundred hectares of the South Pacific. The Australians have taken samples of it, and it isn't quite like anything else on Earth."

"How so?"

"It doesn't use the same amino acids to make DNA that everything else on Earth does."

"Something like the kingfish the cops killed in the river, huh?"

"Exactly right."

"So I guess the next thing we need to do is get a genetic assay done on the hammerhead corpse."

"Tim, you read my mind."

"And your mind tells me you're going to need money to do this." I rubbed my face, trying to figure out how much this was really going to cost. "Tell you what—I'll transfer, let's say, twenty thousand dollars into your account after I get dressed. Meantime, try to find out where the body is."

Syd nodded and turned back to the computer, and I went into my bedroom and put on some clothes.

III

The cops had taken disposition of the hammerhead corpse. After their forensics people had gone over it, they gave it to a zoology lab at the university. It took Syd most of the morning to find out who was in charge of the thing and then get permission to examine it.

Fortunately, Syd still had friends in graduate programs in biology.

One of them agreed to get us into the laboratory where the body was stored, and by lunch time we were exiting the subway station on the West Bank. We stopped at a taco stand long enough for Syd to buy half a dozen burritos; he polished them off before we got across the Washington Avenue Bridge and finally found the laboratory building that contained the thing.

A medusa was waiting for us on the steps.

Syd trotted up to her and said, "H. W., this is Tim."

"Hi," she said, turning toward me. I couldn't help noticing how realistically the snakes writhed in her hair.

"Hi," I said. "What's the H. W. stand for?"

"Please—I hate my names. I've used initials since I was in high school."

"Listen, H. Dub, what's the occasion?" Syd asked her, pointing at her head.

"I've got to see my thesis adviser today. This seemed like the only reasonable thing to wear."

"You mean you're not microded?" I asked.

"No, it's just a wig." She smiled at me, then looked at both of us and said, "Let's get going."

H. W. took us through a series of security doors, then down to a subbasement in a very rickety freight elevator. The elevator car made so much noise we couldn't talk.

At last the car stopped, and the woman led us into a half-lit hallway.

"Can we get a cellular sample of this thing, H. W.?" Syd asked.

"I don't think so. I don't have access to the containment vessel it's in."

"So how about any of the genetic assay work that the cops did?"

"It shouldn't be any trouble to get a printout of that for you."

"That would help a lot," I said.

She turned around and nodded, and the snakes on her head seemed to shimmy even more vehemently than normal.

For a moment we stopped while H. W. opened the cipher lock on a metal door marked "Lab 140," and then we crowded inside to gaze at the dead thing lying in its long refrigerated coffin. The door closed behind us, and for a time we stood in the dim room, staring at the corpse that was illuminated by a greenish fluorescent bulb in the freezer case.

"I'll get the lights," H. W. told us, and we heard her walk back toward the entrance and fumble around looking for the switch.

"This thing was a man once," I said, more or less to Syd.

"Whatever it was, the Minneapolis police department did

an excellent job of cracking open its braincase,'' Syd answered. ''And look at that kind of looping organ inside the shattered lobe.'' Syd bent down to peer intently at the remains of the hammerhead as H. W. finally switched on the lights.

''That organ must be the radio-transmitting device,'' I said.

''How do you know so much about it?'' H. W. asked.

''My cousin made them possible.''

''What?'' She stared at me in disbelief.

''My cousin was the guy who also tried to destroy them,'' I told her. ''Maybe you've heard of him. His name was Johnny Stevens.''

Syd and H. W. hesitated for a moment, but then they ignored me and started talking about what the genetic assay showed. As they did, I withdrew into my own thoughts as I stared at the seven-meter monster in the icebox. The body was the color of toothpaste.

While I stared at the thing, I thought back to the night when Johnny announced to the world that he had perfected the means of reversing the hammerhead microding, and for the first time it occurred to me that it had all been show business. No matter how evenly he presented himself that night on TV screens around the world, no matter how undramatically he had spoken on the recording he'd sent me—he was out for revenge.

They'd taken his dream and he wasn't about to let them keep it, even after they'd killed him.

''Tim, did you hear what I said?'' Syd asked.

''No—uh, sorry. What?''

''This thing has the same kind of amino acids as the bloom in the ocean.''

''In a way we sort of knew that before we ever got here, didn't we?''

''Yeah, I guess so.''

And after that H. W. led us out the way we'd come in, her hair writhing the whole time.

IV

When all was said and done, we really hadn't gotten very far. Through the last of the afternoon and most of the evening, Syd and I worked through a series of ways to undo the microding that had created the great ones. My computer just didn't have the capacity to run the problems, and I wasn't set up to interface with any of the research nets that would allow it. So Syd finally went home, and I decided to drink a beer and watch an old movie on TV.

It was some antique adventure flick, and as I switched the computer over to television reception and went out to the fridge for a bottle of brew, I heard a car pull up in front of my building. The car door slammed. Just as I opened the bottle of beer, my security system bleeped, so I went to the console and pressed the button. A woman's face appeared on the screen.

"Let me in. It's Ray-Lee." Even after she said that, I almost didn't recognize her. Her face seemed drawn.

"Come on up to the fifth floor," I said into the mic.

I pressed the button again to let her in and the screen went blank. Then it occurred to me she was probably carrying a fair amount of luggage, so I went out into the elevator lobby. The elevator doors opened with a thunk, and Ray-Lee, lugging a medium-sized suitcase, stepped out onto the worn beige carpet.

"Can I carry that for you?"

"No. It's not heavy," she said, clearly having trouble with it. I held the apartment door for her, and she slid the suitcase inside.

"It's good to see you, Tim," she went on, sounding strangely sentimental. She never used to sound like that when I worked for her. In fact, most of the times I could recall, she was either shouting at me or somebody else to get something done.

"It's good to see you, too," I lied, suddenly feeling quite uncomfortable in her presence. "I didn't know exactly when you'd be getting in. Otherwise I would've reserved a hotel room for you."

"You wouldn't mind," she said, staring into my eyes, "if I stayed here tonight, would you? I won't be any trouble."

"I suppose." The discomfort vectors in my brain were chasing up to the asymptotic.

"Can I give you a hug?"

"Sure." She came close to me and hesitated for a moment, and then she kicked the front door shut and surrounded me. She buried her face in my T-shirt, and then turned to one side. She was wearing a faint perfume.

"I missed you, Tim."

"I'm sorry I wasn't able to testify for you at the trial, Ray-Lee."

"Yeah. I got your letter."

"There just wasn't any way I could stay in New York any longer. I ran out of money and I couldn't get a job."

"I know." She nodded.

And then to my total amazement, she looked up at me, pulled my head down toward her, and kissed me.

For a long time.

V

About four o'clock in the morning, Ray-Lee shook me until I woke up. I opened my eyes and looked at her, snuggled beside me, covered with both a sheet and a blanket.

"What."

"Tim, can I talk to you? I'm nervous."

"What time is it?"

"I don't know." She sounded frustrated. "Listen, Tim, there are a lot of things I need to tell you."

"Okay. But I can't guarantee I'm conscious."

"There's a secret I need to tell you. I've never told anybody else. Not even my lawyers."

I propped up my head by turning my pillow on end.

"Ray-Lee, I don't understand a thing you're saying."

She put both her hands on my chest.

"I'm talking about Johnny and why he did everything he did."

"Okay."

She licked her lips and leaned toward me. "He thought he was the reincarnation of Jim Morrison."

"What?" She completely lost me with that one.

"The 1960s rock singer. From The Doors."

"Oh. That Morrison."

"There was something in The Doors' music about a lizard king, and that's what Johnny wanted to become. So when he reached the point where he could transform himself, he did."

I closed my eyes, and I could visualize my cousin in his scaly splendor, seated in his Egyptian temple on West Eighth Street, just as I saw him there for the first time after he'd microded himself.

Opening my eyes again, I told Ray-Lee, "You know, he always looked more like a pangolin to me."

"He wasn't satisfied with that creation, either. That's why he decided to revert to his jones state just before they killed him."

"Ray-Lee, he told me a little bit about it. But he made me promise not to tell anybody else."

"But he's dead, Tim. It might be important if you told me what he said."

I wasn't really in a sufficiently wakeful state to think about the ethics of the situation. I just said, "He told me he believed in reincarnation, and that he had to make up for something he'd done wrong in another life."

"But you never realized he thought he was the reincarnation of Morrison—is that it?"

"Yes, Ray-Lee, that's it. I'm stupid that way, I guess."

"Tim, I'm sorry. I didn't mean it to sound like that."

"It's okay. I'm just tired and grumpy—that's all."

I gazed briefly up at the dim ceiling, thinking that Johnny

was sadder and weirder then I ever figured, and then turned back to Ray-Lee.

"Tell me another secret."

"What other secret?" She shivered when she said that.

"Why did Johnny release the retromicroding virus when he did? Did he have some warning the hammerheads were going to launch the attack against him that night?"

"No. We didn't have any warning." She shivered again. "It was just—" She pulled close to me and hugged me; and though she didn't make any noise, I could feel her tears on my chest.

There was nothing I could think of to say that would help, so I just kissed her and stroked her hair. After a long time she fell asleep again; and after a while I shut my eyes and, really bewildered, finally reverted to unconsciousness, too.

VI

Ray-Lee was already out of the shower and reading through my computer files by the time I woke up. I found her nursing a cup of tea, hunched over the ramshackle wooden card table I used as a desk.

"Good morning."

"G'morning." She looked up from the computer long enough to flash that smile of hers at me. It was a smile I have never really been able to get out of my mind since the first time I saw her at my cousin's place in New York. Somehow her smile seemed very southern in the early-morning light in my shabby apartment. And then she turned back to the computer.

"I guess you've found where I keep everything."

"It's funny," she said without looking up, "but there is stuff in this message from Johnny that I've never seen before."

"That's the way he always was. He hid things from everybody all the time."

"Well, in his own way, he was very security conscious."

That struck me as a strange thing to say, and her tone was

something like some bureaucrat speaking. I took it as a hint that she didn't want to talk, so I went and made a couple of pieces of toast.

"You want some breakfast?" I asked from the kitchenette.

"No thanks."

So I wolfed down my toast and jam with a glass of milk and hit the shower. As the water was rushing down over me, I started wondering if there was something Johnny was still managing to hide from us.

At one time, I used to wonder if he hadn't made up the hammerheads as some kind of experiment, abandoned the whole thing in boredom after a time, and then destroyed it when it went wrong. That would have been like him. But after reading the stuff he'd put into his sort-of last will and testament, I was sure he didn't have anything to do with creating the hammerheads. The mafia organization that stole his research was a thousand years old if it was a day.

But there had to be something else. If Johnny had hidden things from Ray-Lee, the only woman he had ever stayed with for more than twenty-four hours, then there was something else.

That's just the way he was.

VII

We invited Syd over for a working brunch. Ray-Lee cooked a sort of Szechuan sloppy-joe, and when she brought out the incredibly aromatic stuff in a big aluminum bowl, Syd smiled enormously.

"I guess the first item of business is to find out where we are in all this," Ray-Lee said as she sat the bowl on my white plastic table. "You both have to realize that I'm not able to do it on my own—to do what Johnny asked us to do, I mean. At least I've learned that much." I got up to help her pass the plates, and she waved me away.

"And then I'm going to call one of my father's old friends

who lives out in the suburbs here," she added, stirring the contents of the bowl with a wooden spoon. "We'll need her to help us deal with the government."

"What did your father do?" Syd asked.

"Oh, among other things, he used to run the CIA."

Syd gulped.

"He did what?" I couldn't believe how squeaky my voice sounded.

"It's not such a big deal," she said with the utmost sincerity as she scooped the steaming stew onto a couple of slices of bread she placed in the bottom of my three soup bowls, each one of which came from a radically different set. "He started out as a lawyer with one of the big satellite-communications companies that went bust at the turn of the century. Then he worked for the FBI for years and years. After my mother died, he took an early-retirement option and got out.

"And after that, he managed to use all his connections and wound up in government again. That's all."

Syd and I glanced at one another, not really sure what planet we were on.

"So, what was it like, Ray-Lee?" I asked as she passed me my bowl.

"What do you mean, growing up in Washington?" She handed Syd his bowl. "I didn't like any of the kids I went to school with. They were the most incredibly boring, stuck-up people I've ever seen. So I took summer classes, got out of high school early and went to college in New York."

She served herself and sat down on my best chair, the one made out of bentwood. "But I enjoyed talking to my father's friends. And I've kept in touch with some of them. They've all tried to help me from time to time. I guess it must be their way of trying to apologize for what happened to my father. . . . " She gazed down at her lunch, somehow lost for a time. Then she looked back up at us and smiled.

"So what did happen to your father, Ray-Lee?" I couldn't help but ask it.

"It's a very sad story, Tim. Would you mind if we didn't talk about it right now?"

I nodded and took a spoonful of the sloppy-joe mix.

"Woman, this is wonderful," Syd said, his mouth still full.

I nodded in agreement as the taste exploded in my mouth.

"Thanks," she said, seeming very subdued.

VIII

After lunch Ray-Lee allowed me to put the dishes in the dishwasher while she made iced tea—just as she had the first time I met her, a little less than a year before. And then she took over, just as she did at meetings in the marketing department of Microde City.

"It seems to me there are two lines of approach to this business," she said, balancing her glass carefully as she sat down on one of the big pillows I'd bought to act as sofa substitutes. "The biological approach should be our job. But there is clearly an electronic one, and that's the one we should have the government work on."

"What sort of things do you have in mind on the electronic front?" I asked her. I looked over at Syd, who had spread out over most of the tiny dining-room floor and was leaning his head on a pillow in the living room.

"Jamming them before they try to destroy the world economy, for instance," she said.

"How about trying to figure out what they're up to first?" I asked.

"What did you have in mind?" she answered back.

"Well, for instance, trying to decode their messages. Like in World War II." I was thinking of a movie I'd seen a couple of weeks before about the Ultra decoding machine the British invented to use against the Germans.

"The problem with that, man," Syd said, "is that it'll take a lot of time. I'm not sure what the bloom down in the Pacific is supposed to do, but it seems to be growing out of control. We've got to do something fast.''

"You're right," Ray-Lee told Syd. "But we may be able to get something out of monitoring as much as we can of their broadcasts. I'll recommend that to Auntie Martha when I see her.''

Syd and I looked at each other, not sure whom she was talking about.

Ray-Lee saw we were puzzled and added, "That's my father's friend who lives out on Lake Minnetonka.''

"In the meantime," Syd told her, "we've got to start getting lab space. And I'll be the first to tell you I have no idea how much this is going to cost.''

"Syd," I told him, "why don't you start calling people about that after lunch and find out.''

"Okay.''

"And I'll call Auntie Martha and see if we can't come out for tea this afternoon," Ray-Lee added. I noticed she was looking distractedly out the window, as though she were thinking about something wonderful. Perhaps a pleasant memory from childhood had crossed her mind, I thought.

IX

Martha Battenberg lived in a nineteenth-century palace overlooking a secluded bay on Lake Minnetonka, some 40 kilometers from the central city. Ray-Lee and I took a cab out there; it was expensive, but Ray-Lee kept telling me I could afford it.

What's more, it took almost an hour to get there. At last the taxi driver stopped in front of a gate for a private road, and Ray-Lee called her Aunt Martha on my phone. Moments later the gate opened. We drove for another couple of kilometers through heavily wooded, hilly country, until we came to a wrought-iron gate marked "Battenberg." I paid for the ride and we got out.

You couldn't see the house from the road—but most of the houses (if you could use so common a word to describe them) around there were built that way. Ray-Lee had to make another phone call before we could get in, and then we walked up a deceptively steep hill for about half a kilometer along a cobblestone drive. We still couldn't see the house for the trees when we were met by a young woman wearing what Ray-Lee later told me was called a frock dress. She looked like something out of a historical vid.

"You must be Ray-Lee," the woman said, "and you must be Ray-Lee's friend. Welcome to Battenberg house."

"Are you Martha's granddaughter?" Ray-Lee asked.

"That's nice of you to think so. No, I'm just a robot."

"Oh."

The robot turned and walked away, and we followed.

"How rich is your Aunt Martha, anyway?" I asked, leaning close to Ray-Lee.

"I really don't know. But that must be a billion dollars' worth of robot walking ahead of us."

"At least."

Then we came to the top of the hill and saw the house.

It was a kind of pseudo-Persian monstrosity made of white brick and thickets of carved white stone along the columns that supported the veranda. A very suntanned, gray-haired woman stood by the front entrance, shielding her eyes from the sun to look at us.

"Auntie Martha!" Ray-Lee shouted, running past the robot and off the flagstone path, finally reaching the porch and embracing the old woman.

Both the robot and I stopped a few meters from the veranda watching the two of them hugging each other and whispering and laughing. At last Ray-Lee turned toward me.

"Auntie, let me introduce you to Tim Wandel. He's Johnny's cousin."

"Tim, come here so I can look at you," Martha said. Her voice carried as though she had been trained as a singer.

I walked up to the veranda, and she shook my hand.

"Let's walk around to the back, and we'll talk." She must have caught some sense of my anxiety about talking in the open about the great ones, because she added quickly, "We've got a security system there, you see. Won't be any trouble at all to use it."

It seemed to take nearly an hour to get around to the back side of the mansion, especially when we stopped to watch hummingbirds working through a patch of hollyhocks in one of the side gardens. And then we rounded a curving wall and saw the immense grounds leading down a broad hill to an inlet of the lake. Off in the distance, I saw there was a pontoon-fence stretching across the mouth of the bay to keep the tourists out.

"Elena," Martha said to the robot, who had followed us, "please bring the tea service out here to the patio."

"Yes, ma'am." The robot bowed slightly and left.

"Tim, would you open the umbrella on that table, please? I'm not tall enough to do it myself."

"Sure." I fooled with the thing until it popped open on its own, and we sat down in its shadow.

"There's usually a nice breeze here in the afternoon," Martha said. "But not today."

"Auntie Martha, it's so much nicer here than in Washington."

"Child, when it gets hot here, it can be just as humid as Washington."

We watched ducks flying overhead, and then the robot wheeled out the tea service. Martha made something of a production of serving the tea herself, carefully splashing ice cubes into filled glasses and handing them to each of us. She also put a plate of cookies on the table, then dismissed the robot.

"I like to have private conversations here, you see," Martha told us as she opened a kind of fuse box set under the white marble tabletop. "There. We're secure. Now tell me what this is all about." She smiled, and her eyes sparkled in a way that made me think her gray hair was faked.

"You probably know a lot about the hammerheads already," Ray-Lee began.

"I know a few things," Martha replied. She took a sip of her tea and added, "But I've always felt there was much more to them than merely a narcotics ring that went around transforming its lower echelons into some crazy excuse for a boogeyman. They're not just some yakuza prank—they seem to have an intimate relationship with organized crime leaders, of course, but they've got their own hierarchy, and they seem to have some kind of ideology behind them unlike any mafia I've ever heard of."

"That's for sure," I said. "And talking about their hierarchy, that thing that rammed the party boat on the river—you heard about that?—that was one of their bosses."

"I rather thought so," Martha told me. "But what are these radio transmissions of theirs all about?"

"How did you know about them?" I asked.

"If you read the scientific journals, you find out about the most amazing things," Martha answered. "I can only assume that the U.S. government and the United Nations have known about them for some time."

"That's where we need you to help us, Auntie Martha," Ray-Lee said.

"How, child?"

"Johnny assembled a lot of information on them. Some of it's about the transmissions. The people in Washington need it urgently. But if I were to present it to them, they'd see I was convicted in the Microde City trial, and they'd shred it."

"And there's a group called Public Intelligence that's doing research on them," I added, "and we might be able to work with them, too."

"Well, now, I don't really think very much of this so-called Public Intelligence Foundation. They're really a bunch of mystics in disguise." She paused and tapped one finger to her lips. "But what I gather is that you want me to talk to people and get things stirring—is that it?"

Ray-Lee nodded. Her face looked older than Martha's just then. That's stress for you.

"What you have to keep in mind," she said as she got up from her seat, "is that the hammerhead mafia is more sophisticated at black propaganda than most countries on Earth. They're good enough at it to conjure up visions of a nuclear war and have people believe it, if need be. That means the sooner we get started, the better.

"So let's start calling people. There's no time to waste." Martha smiled, grabbed her glass and headed toward the door.

CHAPTER **4**

The "Public Intelligence" logotype fades into a view of Doug Janssen wearing shorts and a rugby shirt, walking down a gangway onto the deck of a small submarine at anchor in a crowded harbor.

"Today we're coming to you from San Diego harbor," Janssen says as he turns to the camera. "This is the APS *Čapek,* our newly acquired research submarine. I will be joining our crew of researchers for the next several weeks to explore the areas of the Pacific Ocean that seem to have the strongest emissions of microwave radiation caused by hammerhead swarms. Joining us now is Patricia Allegro-Daumier, the head of our research team."

A tall black woman with golden blonde hair, dressed in a tie-dyed T-shirt and jeans, steps into the picture.

"Hello, Doug," she says, her voice containing the barest hint of a French accent.

"Welcome, Patricia. Tell us where we're going and what you expect we'll find."

"Well, Doug, there are three principal swarms of the hammerheads, one in the North Atlantic, and two in the Pacific. We're going to investigate the largest of them, which is located several hundred kilometers from the Japanese islands.

"One of the main goals of our expedition is to determine whether the creatures are using machinery to generate these transmissions, or whether they have created some—well, 'natural' is a difficult word to use in this case, but it's what I mean. You see, there is evidence that they have developed a natural radio device, perhaps based on the restructuring of the kind of organ that allows an electric eel to produce a lethal shock."

"And what about their social organization—will we be able to find out anything about that?"

"We hope so," she answers, nodding her head vigorously. "We're going to conduct the first full-scale monitoring of their broadcasts, and we've got a top-of-the-line supercomputer on board that we hope to use to understand what they're broadcasting. . . . "

CHAPTER 5

TESTIMONY OF TIMOTHY J. WANDEL

I

After she made several phone calls—none of the people she wanted were available, so she left messages—Martha fed us incredibly well and summoned a taxi to take us home and put the tab on her account. Both Ray-Lee and I ate so much that we napped on the way into town and woke up only when the cabdriver stopped the car in front of my building.

As we walked across the street a man wearing a baseball cap with a vid-network logo on it came up to us from behind a parked van.

"You Tim Wandel?" he asked.

I felt Ray-Lee stiffen underneath my arm, and I said, "Yeah."

"I'm with Vid International. We understand that you have material on the hammerhead threat that you've passed to the U.S. government. Is this related to your cousin's role in creating them?"

It was such a stupid combination of ideas I couldn't think of anything to say.

"We have no comment," Ray-Lee told him, and she hurried forward, dragging me after her. The reporter shouted something at us, but by then we were entering the apartment building.

"I don't know how that could have happened so quickly," Ray-Lee said distractedly.

"Well, there's obviously been a leak somewhere." Where there could have been a leak, however, I really couldn't guess.

We took the elevator upstairs, and Ray-Lee starting squeezing her hands together as I unlocked the door.

As soon as the door opened, she rushed inside; and by the time I closed it behind me, she was already on the phone.

"Martha?" she said nervously into the mouthpiece. "Yes, we're at Tim's apartment now."

I could hear the distant sound of Martha's voice coming through the earpiece of the receiver but couldn't make out the words.

"Listen," Ray-Lee continued. "We were just hit up by a newsman in front of the building." She paused to listen. "Yes, that's right. There's already been a leak of some kind, and this guy was trying to tie Johnny into it as the man who created the hammerheads." She listened again. "Thank you, Auntie. I'll ring off now. Thanks again for a wonderful meal. Good night." She hung up.

"Auntie says she'll call people and tell them there's been a leak." She crossed her arms and looked out the windows.

"I don't like this, Ray-Lee."

She turned back toward me and said, "Neither do I."

II

It was four A.M. again. I woke up slowly, not quite sure where I was at first. Ray-Lee lay with her back toward me, and in the perpetual city-twilight that filtered through the shades, I could see she was tapping her hand against her hip.

"Ray-Lee?"

"Yes," she said softly.

"What's the matter?"

She rolled over and looked at me.

"You know what I think?"

"Huh."

"I think the hammerheads themselves must have dumped some version of Johnny's message on some of the press. God only knows how they would have changed it."

"But you never know with the government types, do you?"

"What do you mean?"

"Well, every other day it seems like there's been some big leak in Washington or Moscow or Berlin."

"But people in Washington wouldn't really have anything but Martha's word about Johnny's message."

I put my arm across her stomach reassuringly and said, "Well, Ligoth might have given it to the FBI already. I'll have to check with him in the morning."

"I didn't think about that," she answered. And then she looked away from me.

"Why don't you try to go back to sleep?"

"I don't think I can."

She got up, and I slowly shook my head against the pillow and closed my eyes. It seemed that there was something else going on inside her besides what she'd been willing to talk about. Whatever it was, I seemed entirely irrelevant to it.

Besides that, when it came to understanding whatever inner Vietnam she was going through, I didn't have a clue.

There was so much that was going on around me that it seemed time was rushing past before I had a chance to grasp its meaning. Still, there were a couple of things it occurred to me I could do that would improve things. If I could somehow get Ray-Lee out from under the weight of her conviction and imprisonment, that would certainly help, I thought. I wasn't sure quite how to do that, but I resolved to try.

Nevertheless, I had a strange feeling that nothing I could do would really help her. I can't explain where it came from any better than by saying it was just something about her

—maybe the way she curled up when she went to sleep—that convinced me of that.

III

At seven-thirty, the phone rang. I got up to answer it and heard Ray-Lee singing in the shower. That seemed a positive sign, I thought.

"Hello, is Ray-Lee Lenard there?" a young-sounding baritone voice asked.

"Uh, yes she is. Who may I ask is calling?"

"Fowler Ward."

I told him to wait and went into the bathroom.

"Ray-Lee, there's a phone call for you. A Fowler Ward."

"Oh, thank God," she shouted over the hiss of the shower. "Tell him I'll be right there. And introduce yourself. He used to work for us in genetic design. Ask him when he'll be here."

So I walked back to the phone and passed the messages. Ward told me he planned to stay in Chicago for two days and wanted her to meet him there. Before I could ask him what it was all about, Ray-Lee came rushing out of the bathroom wrapped in a towel.

"Fowler, I thought you'd never call," she said as she took the receiver away from me. "Chicago? What for?" And then she listened carefully.

"Well, I guess so," Ray-Lee went on, turning to look at me in a questioning way. "I'll call you back with the specifics," she told Ward, and then she wrote down some numbers on a notepad.

"So what was that all about?" I asked.

"I'm not sure. Fowler wants me to take the train down to Chicago to see something he's noticed there. That's all he would tell me." There was an edge to her voice when she said that.

"What in the hell does that mean?"

"I told you I don't know." She said it crossly, and then she looked down at the floor; maybe she was embarrassed by her tone of voice. "He wants me to go down this afternoon." She glanced up and then walked back to the bathroom.

"Well, should I go along?"

"No, Tim," she told me as she stopped at the bathroom door. She looked over her shoulder at me and added, "I think it'd be better if you stayed here."

When she closed the bathroom door behind her, I confess I felt jealous.

IV

The next several days for me were studies in irrelevancy. I talked to the lab in the far outer 'burbs that Syd had decided offered the best contract, then approved the deal and paid for it. After that I had nothing more to do, while Syd starting working eighteen-hour days. At one point I called Martha Battenberg for an update, only to be told by her answering service that she was out of town.

I even phoned my sister and went over to dinner at her place.

Several times I almost looked up the number for the Public Intelligence Foundation, but then I backed down. I couldn't risk running afoul of Martha. We needed her help, and I didn't want to do anything that would alienate her. Somehow it seemed to me, for all her fortitude and obvious strength, that Martha was sensitive in the extreme about anything she considered mystical.

So I never phoned them.

All the time I had this sort of queasy feeling—very much like I'd felt when Johnny's company collapsed and I didn't have a job or a place to live any more in New York.

Big things were happening all around me.

Yet it didn't seem to me like I was accomplishing anything at all.

Of course I was right in the middle of things, I kept telling myself. And of course I had to let the others do their parts. My job was to keep Syd plugging away at the research and to draw in all the talent I could to put what Syd learned into action.

At least that was the theory.

There wasn't anything else to do but try to get some exercise. So I spent Thursday afternoon biking. Oddly enough, I found myself tracing the route of the oil-crisis riots. There's a monument commemorating those who died down on Lyndale and Thirty-sixth. It's a brass etching of the burnt-out nineteenth-century frame buildings and twentieth-century gas stations that used to stand there; they've all been completely replaced with computer-generated art nouveau apartment buildings now. It's funny, but I've lived here most of my life and I've never noticed that thing before. It's a kind of a French-looking bas-relief on the side of an office building; I guess I've always thought it was just an ad and ignored it.

When I got home there was a message from Ray-Lee saying they were taking the noon train back from Chicago and would be in about four-thirty. I looked at the clock readout in the phone and saw I had fifteen minutes to get to the train station. I turned around and ran to the subway. Amazingly enough, I got to the platform just as a train arrived and made it to the central hi-speed terminal only about five minutes late.

I saw Ray-Lee standing in the lobby next to a giant of a man I'd never seen before.

"Hi, Ray-Lee," I called as I hurried over to them.

"Hello, Tim," she said, raising her right hand in a small wave. "Do you remember Fowler?"

"I guess I don't."

"No, I don't think we ever did meet. But my fiancée mentioned meeting you, I think."

"Who's that?" I asked.

"Meryl Ellen Merril," he answered.

"Oh, really." I smiled. I remembered partying with Meryl Ellen once or twice when we worked in New York. "How's she doing?"

"Terrific. She got a job with New Age Pharmaceuticals."

The name of the company meant nothing to me, but I said that was great and then helped them carry their luggage back to the subway.

On the train going back to my place, we had to squeeze in among the rush-hour crowd, Fowler towering over everybody else. As the train reached its highest speed and the rush of the air and noise of the wheels was greatest, I leaned over to Fowler and said into his ear, "What were the hammerheads up to in Chicago?"

At first he looked at me as though I'd been speaking a foreign language he didn't understand. Then he glanced to one side, thinking for a moment.

Leaning over toward me, he said, "They're in the lake, and they're getting ready to frenzy."

V

We turned the corner onto my street and noticed this big crowd halfway down the block. As Fowler, Ray-Lee and I got nearer, we realized the people were standing in front of my building.

"Excuse me," I said as we came up behind a man with a backpack standing on the sidewalk. "What's going on?"

He glanced at me and shouted, "Here he is!"

The crowd turned toward us, and someone turned on a portable spotlight and aimed it at us and people started talking at me all at once.

"I'm John Norton, NBC News. Can you tell us, Mr. Wandel, what is the meaning of the computer message your dead cousin had transmitted to you?"

"BBC World Service—your cousin's—"

"I'm from Public Intelligence and we'd like to know—"

And then the rest of the questioners drowned themselves out.

"I can't hear what they're saying," I shouted to Ray-Lee and Fowler.

"Tell them you have no comment and keep pushing through until we get inside," Ray-Lee shouted back.

I started to tell her, "They have a right to know," but she had already begun butting through the crowd with Fowler in tow, and I don't think she heard me. At any rate, these people weren't interested in her.

There was a momentary lull in the shouting so I held up my hands.

"I don't have much to say, so please be quiet and listen." I moved to the front door of the building and climbed on the stoop, then turned around toward them. The spotlight followed me all the way.

I started talking, not really sure what I was going to say, but certain that I'd lose any ability to say a word if I didn't start soon.

"Listen, I don't have any prepared statement or anything. But people have a right to know. My cousin left a series of documents for me that I received just a few days ago. They show that not all of the hammerhead organization was transformed when he released the virus that eliminated their foot soldiers. We're working with the United States government to try to get to the bottom of it. And that's all I've got for you for now." I swallowed, turned around and fumbled to open the door.

Ray-Lee was standing inside the inner door, frowning.

"Come quick," she said. Fowler was holding the elevator for me, and we crowded inside it.

"You shouldn't have told them anything," she sputtered once the door had closed and the car started to ascend.

"But Ray-Lee—people need to know this."

She was clearly angry at me and wouldn't even look me in the eye.

After a moment, Fowler said, "Maybe he's right, Ray-Lee."

She looked up at Fowler with an expression of apparent

boredom that, for her, meant a special kind of fury reserved for inanimate objects she had stubbed her toe against.

VI

I fed them some microwaved Mexican stuff I had in the fridge. Between mouthfuls, Fowler explained that he'd recorded a lot of radio broadcasts coming from beneath Lake Michigan. He'd even picked up one lengthy transmission from the shore of the Chicago River at Michigan Avenue.

"If they're that thick in the Chicago and Minneapolis waterways, they're about to launch some kind of attack," Fowler told us as he paused between burritos. "At least that's the way I figure it."

When we finished eating and I was clearing the table, I looked out the window to the street below and saw there was still a crowd down at the front entrance to the building.

"Jesus Christ," I said. "They're still here."

Ray-Lee leaned around in her chair, and Fowler got up and looked from across the table.

"I gave 'em a statement. What more do they want?"

"Blood," Ray-Lee said quietly.

"Always the optimist, aren't we," Fowler remarked as he sat down.

I took the dishes into the kitchen and started rinsing them off in the sink as the phone rang.

"I'll get it," I told the others. I picked up the receiver on the yellow counter behind me.

"Hello," I said.

"Oh, hello, Tim," said a very mature woman's voice that I didn't recognize. "This is Martha Battenberg calling. I have a friend of mine from Washington who's just flown in to see you. Would you mind if we came over this evening?"

"I wouldn't mind, Martha, but you should know that we've got a crowd of viddie people camping out on the doorstep. They don't look like they're ready to go away."

"The press corps, eh? Don't worry, we'll take care of 'em. We'll be over about eight."

"Okay."

We made coffee and played hearts to kill the time. I lost big; if we'd been playing for money, Ray-Lee would have gotten every cent I had left.

Just a bit before eight, we heard a particularly wicked-sounding car drive up. I was sitting closest to the front window and looked down at the street to see an old red Chevy two-seater pull up, puffing smoke—which, when you come down to it, is hard to do in a gasohol-powered vehicle. It dieseled after it was shut down, too. A woman with a beehive hairdo covered in a psychedelic-print scarf got out, accompanied by a short, bald man.

The woman charged into the crowd of thirty or so still hanging around the entrance.

"Whadda ya mean, standing around here?" the woman shouted. It was Martha's voice.

"Come look at this," I said to the others.

"What is it?" Ray-Lee asked.

"Come here." They crowded behind me.

"I'm the landlady of this building," Martha continued, "and if you di'n't know it, this is private property." She was laying on the South Minneapolis accent with a trowel.

"But we're the press, ma'am," one of the viddies said.

"So what're you hanging around here for?"

The man answered something we couldn't hear.

"I am giving you five minutes to get off this property before I call the cops," Martha said. "You shoul'n't have been here this long." And then she slammed open the front door and dragged the bald man inside with her.

We were waiting for Martha in the lobby when the elevator door opened.

"Hello, child," she said to Ray-Lee, squeezing her hand. "Let's get inside and I'll introduce you." Martha put an arm around the rather wizened, bald man standing beside her in the elevator doorway.

"That was a bravura performance," I told Martha on our way into my apartment.

"Well, we'll see how bravura it was if and when they disperse," she told me as she undid the scarf from around her head.

Once inside, Martha went over to the front window and gazed out at the crowd below.

"I'll give them five minutes, and then I really will call the cops." She turned around to face the rest of us and added, "Now then, this is Will Hjortshoj, from the National Security Council." Hjortshoj was surprisingly short—not quite as tall as Martha, in fact—and wore a baggy olive jumpsuit and a hippack.

Fowler and I shook hands with him, but Ray-Lee stood back and didn't say a word.

"This is Ray-Lee," Martha said at last.

"Ah, of course," Hjortshoj added, nodding his head a little too vigorously. "Would you mind if I sat down?" he said as he plopped onto one of my folding chairs. "Now, Martha has briefed us on what you have, and it fits with a lot of information that's coming into us at the White House." He smiled reassuringly at us; I noticed he had several metal teeth.

"The president has authorized me to talk to you about how we could cooperate on this. Let me say right at the outset that we need your help. You have clearly got a lot of expertise in this area."

"I just told the press corps that we were going to cooperate with you, if you haven't heard it yet," I told him.

"I'm happy to hear that." Hjortshoj nodded his head again. "Now what I'm going to say I want you to keep quiet about. It's not classified, but it's sensitive. You know how serious this business is, so I'm trusting you not to mention this to anyone outside this room.

"We've been monitoring these transmissions from the

oceans for some time. And we're very concerned about them. Yet our sense in Washington is that the most immediate threat is from this growth that seems to be spreading across the South Pacific. Is that your estimate?"

We all looked at each other, a little puzzled, and then I told him, "I don't think we've gotten that far with it yet."

"But, you know, the transmissions aren't confined to the oceans," Fowler added as soon as I finished speaking. "I spent the last two days in Chicago, and there are transmissions from Lake Michigan and the Chicago River."

Hjortshoj nodded again and pulled a pocketwriter from his hip-pack and started making notes.

"At this point," I told him, "I think we're farther along with the chemical analysis of the hammerheads that weren't affected by the retromicroding virus."

"And what have you found?" Hjortshoj asked.

Ray-Lee and I looked at each other. We both wanted to talk in private—that much was obvious.

"We're not really ready to go into that," Ray-Lee said after a few seconds.

"Maybe you should tell us what the government's ready to do," I added.

Hjortshoj nodded his head vigorously, as though he were agreeing with everything we said.

"Yes, well, we'd like you to continue working on the chemical end of things. We're prepared to provide government status to the entire effort. That way there is no possibility of an environmental lawsuit."

"We need help in getting samples of the Pacific bloom. Can you take care of that?" I asked.

Hjortshoj nodded. "Oh, of course."

"There's one other thing I need from you," I told him. Now was the time to try one of those ideas I'd had about how to improve things. "I want you to get presidential pardons for everyone who was convicted for working for my cousin."

Hjortshoj paused a moment and looked right at me for the first time that evening. He had amazingly pale blue eyes.

"I'm afraid I'm not authorized to discuss such things."

"I want you to get authorized to do so."

"I'm going back tonight, and I'll bring it up tomorrow."

"It's a fundamental requirement for me."

Hjortshoj nodded faintly, then typed on his pocketwriter. Then he glanced at his wristwatch.

"Too bad we couldn't have signed a contract on this tonight," Hjortshoj added. Then he got up and said to Martha, "All right, then. We're off to the airport." Pausing briefly, he added rather vaguely, "We'll be in touch."

I opened the door and escorted them out to the elevator, and Martha pressed my hand warmly.

"I'll stop by tomorrow morning if that's all right," she said. When I nodded, she added, "I'll call beforehand."

Back in the apartment, Ray-Lee asked me, "Do you always do these things without talking to anybody else about them first?"

"There are some things I won't compromise on."

I looked out the window to see that Martha and her charge had reached her car. None of the viddies were left; she'd succeeded in chasing them all away.

"I'll let Martha work on him all the way out to the airport," I said to Ray-Lee.

VII

We put pillows together for Fowler to sleep on in the living room, and then Ray-Lee and I retired to the bedroom. When I closed the door and turned to face her, she was looking into space while chewing at her thumbnail. Several layers of emotions seemed to be playing across her face, none of them happy.

"Ray-Lee?"

She looked up at me. "I'm really very upset," she said softly.

"Why?"

"Tim, when you make a big demand of somebody, as you just did of that man from the National Security Council, you've got to talk to other people about it first."

I couldn't answer her right away, but finally I managed to say, "I want to set things right, Ray-Lee. What better way is there to do it?"

"There are plenty." She left, heading in the direction of the bathroom.

I got ready for bed and lay there for a long time. At last I got up and walked out into the living room. Ray-Lee was seated at the table in the dining nook, silhouetted against the yellowish glow of the streetlights coming through the front window.

Fowler was snoring faintly on the living-room floor.

I walked over to her and said, "It's time to go to sleep, Ray-Lee."

"I'll be along presently," she said softly, nearly whispering.

Her tone suggested it was senseless to discuss anything with her, so I walked back to bed and went to sleep.

VIII

The phone was ringing, and although my alarm clock showed it was ten o'clock in the morning, I would have kept on sleeping if someone hadn't decided to call. I rolled over in bed and picked up the receiver.

"Hello," I croaked.

"Is this Tim?" It was Martha Battenberg.

"Yes," I said, clearing my throat.

"Have you seen the news this morning?"

"Afraid not."

"You should turn it on. Several hundred hammerhead sharks have beached themselves and died in California. It occurs to me that you might want to have someone take tissue samples of them to find out if they're real sharks, or the microded kind."

"I'll get the news on right away."

"It doesn't get much more interesting, does it?" She paused, then added, "May I please talk to Ray-Lee?"

"Hang on." I put my hand over the receiver and called for Ray-Lee. She didn't answer. "Sorry. I guess she's gone out."

"Well, please have her call me when she gets back."

"Um, Martha?"

"Yes?"

"Do you think we've got any chance at all of getting the pardons I was talking about last night?"

"I don't know, ducks. Those are hard things to get taken care of."

"It doesn't look good, then?"

"I couldn't say that either. This is one of those administrations that could do anything."

For a moment I felt like a real idiot, and then I decided I couldn't let it stop there. "Would you talk to people about it?" I asked her.

"Oh, I already have. Not that it's going to do much good. I'm too far—and too long—out of the loop. But we'll see. Forgive me now, I've got to go."

We said our good-byes and hung up. I sat on the edge of the bed thinking that I might have damaged more than my extremely new relationship with Ray-Lee when I asked for those pardons.

CHAPTER 6

**EXCERPT FROM "PUBLIC INTELLIGENCE" PROGRAM:
"THE SIGN OF THE SHARK (4/29)"**

The show's logo fades to an interior shot of a white room on board the *Čapek*. Two men stand over the dissected body of a seven-meter hammerhead, each holding onto the dissecting table against the shifting of the ship.

"Hello, Doug Janssen here aboard the Public Intelligence Foundation's research submarine, the *Čapek*. We're running against a rather choppy sea today, and our autocam is having some trouble compensating for it. Our apologies if the picture isn't as good as it ought to be."

A sharp wave hits the ship and both men fumble briefly against the dissecting table, while the enormous dissected corpse on the table shifts awkwardly in front of them.

"Let me introduce one of our marine biologists, Dr. Jeff Flying Eagle."

The autocam moves in on Flying Eagle's broad face.

"Thank you, Doug. We've come upon a group of dead hammerheads at sea today. All told, we found eighteen corpses floating within an area of about four hectares. We've examined this one," he says, gesturing with one hand at the white and gray of the bisected body before him, "to see what happened.

"The results are disappointing, and quite similar to the

Public Intelligence examination of a group of hammerheads that beached themselves in California yesterday. We see no evidence of physical disease of the type that sometimes causes whales to beach themselves. Moreover, there is no evidence of a struggle—no wounds—nothing to suggest that these creatures were killed, either by others of their own kind or by, for example, dolphins. I should add that we do know that dolphins, on occasion, will attack sharks, but that does not appear to have occurred here.''

''So what's your best guess, Jeff, as to what happened?''

''Well, we've got to keep in mind that we're dealing with creatures that were once human beings. They've gone through radical microding, and that's bound to have a profound psychological affect on them.'' Another heavy wave lifts the ship, and the two men grasp the table for balance. ''I believe there's some psychological dysfunction at work here. . . . ''

CHAPTER 7

I

All the news channels were full of some new crisis in Central Asia. I couldn't follow any of it—to me it seemed nothing but a series of claims and counterclaims. And nobody said a word about beached hammerheads in California.

I tried to call Syd after that, but he wasn't in. So I left him a message asking him to try to get tissue samples from the things on the coast.

After that I finally went out to the kitchenette and fixed breakfast, and that's when I noticed Ray-Lee's note attached to the refrigerator with a magnetic clip.

It read:

Gone fishing—chuckle, chuckle!—R-L.

What the hell did that mean?

I couldn't help myself. At that point I stomped off to take my shower, feeling acutely jealous and blaming myself for having caused Ray-Lee some kind of acute anxiety. And since both she and Fowler had apparently left together, I started blaming myself for having driven her into his arms, and thereby ruining his impending marriage. . . .

That sounds irrational, I know. But that's the way I felt right then.

After I got dressed, Syd called me back.

"I got your message and tried calling you a little bit ago," he said.

"Guess I must have been in the shower."

"Yeah—I figured I'd try right back. Anyway, I called some friends out in California in the meantime. They're looking into the hammerheads that washed up there."

"Great." I thought for a moment and caught myself chewing my lower lip. "Listen, Syd, I've got nothing else going. Why don't you let me ride out with you to the lab today?"

"Sure. I'm about to leave, in fact, so I'll be by in a few minutes—if that's okay."

I was waiting on the front stoop, admiring the sculpture of the north wind on the building directly across the street from mine, when Syd drove up in his rehabbed minivan. The sound of some kind of scope-rave mix was emanating from his car radio as I got in.

"What's that playing?" I asked him as I was entering the van. He'd removed the front seat so he could fit, which meant that I had to frog-walk to get into the backseat.

"Just the radio. I was scanning on the way here and caught this. Listen—it's got the five beats of scope, but then there's a rave-revival underbeat."

"Interesting. Listen Syd, take the interstate. I'll pay the fee."

"Okay." So he drove down to the Thirty-sixth Street entrance. I forked over the $200 entrance fee and off we went.

"Boy, this is great," Syd told me as he put on the automatic pilot and we accelerated. "I love speed," he added.

I looked over at the speedometer and saw we'd hit 100 klicks an hour.

We followed the tollway out to the state highway that follows the Minnesota River valley. It's pleasant hill country—though nothing like the ancient mountains and buttes of the upper Mississippi—and we were listening to this incredible music sung by somebody from Senegal all the way.

At last we saw the billboard for the research center—"Belle

Plaine Gasohol Genetics—We're Here to Make Sure Your Home Is Warm"—and turned off the highway. Syd pulled into the driveway and circled the building, one of those stressed-concrete things from the turn of the century constructed just before the art-nouveau revival started, and for a brief moment I caught sight of the interurban train running across the bridge in the distance.

Syd parked the car and turned off the radio.

"It's almost hot enough to be Senegal," he said.

"I guess." Now that we'd stopped, the heat radiating up from the asphalt was almost unbearable. We staggered indoors to our lab space.

It was cool inside and musky.

"What is that smell?" I asked.

"They're working up some kind of high-content, alcohol-producing hay."

"I suppose they think they can replace the Middle East oil fields."

"Don't laugh. They might."

Our lab was in a high-security tank, something like a small submarine lurking in a subbasement. We had a long ride down to the place in an incredibly quiet elevator.

Somehow we had both fallen silent, so I asked Syd, "Figured out how the warlords managed to eat?"

"You mean to digest normal food?"

"Yeah."

"Not really. But I guess it isn't exactly as big a deal as I thought at first. You see, they could just make different sugars."

The elevator halted, and we left it to wander through a long yellow corridor until we reached our lab space. Syd played with the cipher lock until the outer door slid open. Once we were inside, it slid shut behind us.

Syd told me as he switched on the computer, "What seems to be the most important part of their genetic design is that they've replaced the four standard amino acids with different aminos, and then changed the configuration of their cell walls. I don't think any virus could infect them." He started typing into a computer workstation, swatting his back with his tail nervously.

"So here's a display of what their altered DNA looks like."

On the overhead screen, a multicolored swirl appeared.

"Syd, what does it come down to? Can we undo this the way Johnny undid the other microding?"

"No."

I exhaled slowly, then asked, "So what do we do?"

"We have to design a completely new kind of virus to fit a completely new form of life."

After a while, I asked him, "So how much is that going to cost?"

"I've done some figuring, and it comes to about eight billion."

"In other words, just about everything we've got."

Syd flicked his tail a few times and said, "Maybe even a little bit more."

"Great. Just great."

II

After we left the lab, Syd drove a few kilometers out of the way to look at a horse farm. We left the exurban research and office parks and came into a fairly flat stretch of farm country dotted with ancient oak trees. Syd braked to a halt at the side of the road and hunched over the steering wheel, gazing at a group of chestnut-brown horses grazing at the top of a gentle hill.

"It's funny," he said.

"What's funny?"

"Well, I knew there would be some psychological effects with this kind of major microding."

"Yeah? Like what?"

He smiled and looked out across the fenced-in meadow.

"I don't want women anymore," he told me. "Fillies are more like it for me."

"Well, they are beautiful." One of the horses turned its head and looked toward us.

"Time to go," Syd told me, and he drove off.

I turned the radio on. There wasn't any music.

"—avoid the interstate system," the radio announcer was saying. "To repeat our top story, the entire city grid is down. Avoid the interstates, and try to use public transportation if you can. . . . "

"Something big must have happened," Syd muttered, almost to himself. He reached over and turned up the volume.

"We're going to go to—" the announcer said, and then his voice disintegrated into faint static.

I pushed the scan button, but there didn't seem to be anything to pick up.

"Sounds like something else just happened, too," I added.

III

If you sneak into Minneapolis from the southwest and avoid the main streets when the interstate system has completely collapsed and the subway has suffered some kind of fatal computer malfunction, it is possible to get where you're going in your lifetime.

Just barely.

Actually, it took us something like three hours to get back to my apartment through the worst traffic jam I've ever seen in my life. You'd think we would have done a lot of talking about the virus, but we both seemed to be fighting headaches all the way. Just putting up with the constant fits and starts of the traffic kept us from even thinking about anything other than where we were headed.

We finally got back to my street in time to see two guys break open the hood of a car with a defective security circuit in order to stop its horn from honking.

As we parked, one of the guys—a real, honest-to-God jones of a plumber if ever there was one—turned to me and said rather sheepishly, "Damn thing's been going off for the last four hours. The wife coul'n't stand it anymore."

I nodded at him and Syd and I went up to my apartment. Ray-Lee opened the door for us.

"Martha wants us to come out to her place right away," Ray-Lee told us as soon as we were inside.

"We've just driven through the traffic jam from hell," Syd told her. "You're nuts if you think we're going to drive out to Lake Minnetonka when it's like this."

She nodded and said, "It's like this all over the Northern Hemisphere, not just here."

Syd lay down on the living-room floor, and I plopped down on one of the big pillows.

"So what does she want us out there for?" I asked.

"Right after all this started, she called to say we should get out there as soon as we could." Ray-Lee sat down on my director's chair. "And I don't really know what's going on myself."

"It's gotta be the hammerheads," I told her.

"I know." She nodded.

Silence grew around us, while the sounds of the car horns roared in the distance.

"So where's Fowler?" I asked at last.

"I don't know," Ray-Lee said. "We went downtown to the library, ate some lunch, and then I came back here to sleep. I haven't seen him since then."

"This is not a good sign," I told her.

Syd started snoring. He'd gone out like a light when he hit the floor.

CHAPTER 8

I

I knew something was wrong when I started having dreams about committing suicide.

What I couldn't figure out was why it should be happening to me.

True enough, as other people have already testified before this committee, I used to run with the 'heads. I mean to say, I was kidnapped and transformed by the hammerheads.

But I was one of the lucky ones. When the great retro took place—that's what we transformees call the release of the retrovirus that returned us to human form—when that occurred, I survived. My senses were more or less intact, too. A lot of the transformed didn't do that well, you know.

What's more, I'd done a lot of things to get my head into a happier, healthier state than the one I used to be in. For instance, I quit using a nickname that I'd used since I was in grade school—because that name represented all the stupid things I used to associate with being "cool." After that, I deliberately tried to focus my esthetics on living things, healthy living things, instead of—well, instead of on the hammerheads.

So when I started having the dreams, I went back to the hospital in Brooklyn where I recovered from the great retro. My doctor, Harry Sladky, was visibly worried by what I told him.

When he asked me about them, I told him I wasn't having just a single dream. "There seems to be a cycle of them," I told him. "First, there were dreams of throwing myself off a cliff into the sea. And then there were dreams about blowing myself up with a bomb.

"And in that one, I was always inside some big building—I couldn't really tell if it was a skyscraper or what—and it was in the middle of the workday and there were thousands of people in the building with me. And then there's a cycle where I jump out of an airplane without a parachute."

"You're not alone, Nils," Sladky told me. He had white hair and bushy eyebrows, and he brushed his hair back with both hands from time to time. "In fact, you're the fourth case like this I've seen this week. Now is there anything that might have set this off that you can think of?"

"Like what?"

"Have you broken up with a girlfriend, for example."

I had to count to ten before I could tell him I didn't have any girlfriends. "I haven't gone out on a date since I was released from the hospital, doctor," I said. "I'm still too ugly."

"Young man, that's the only stupid thing you've ever said to me. You're almost back to normal." He looked carefully at my face. "Your eyes are completely normal. Inside another couple of months, your cheekbones will be as good as before the transformation."

"I'm not ready to go out and get rejected yet, doctor."

Sladky nodded slowly.

"That may be part of it, Nils. I'm not sure. The best course is to run some tests." He looked at my file and couldn't find a paper he was looking for. "Nils, forgive my failing memory. Did you find a job yet?"

"I've been working on a new film. I got a grant to do it."

"Why, that's wonderful news. Why didn't you tell me earlier?"

"Gee, well, I had this other problem on my mind."

"Yes, um, there is that. Would you be free for us to run

some tests on you tonight? You'd have to stay here at the hospital.''

"Okay.''

II

I had a lot of errands to run that afternoon, and after I finished
them I ate a forgettable dinner and took the subway to the hospital. They gave me a private room to sleep in—filled with
monitoring equipment—and a group of technicians spent a
couple of hours getting things set up. I called the two people I
was working on the new film with to let them know where I was
in case they needed to reach me.

That night I had a new nightmare. I dreamed that my
hands and legs had been cut off somehow. For some reason I
couldn't have them microded back.

I know that sounds stupid, but that was part of the nightmare—it had its own logic, and I couldn't escape from it. My
goal was to destroy myself and my enemies at the same time. It
was never clear to me who the enemies were, but they were the
ones who had destroyed my limbs.

And suddenly I found myself swimming, and I managed to
grasp my enemies and pull them under with me into the water.

At that point I woke up covered in sweat. It was six-thirty in
the morning, and a technician—a young woman with dark-
brown hair—came rather hurriedly into the room.

"Are you all right?" she asked. "I heard the alarm and
came as quick as I could.''

"What alarm?''

"There's a stress alarm with this equipment. It just went
off.''

"Well, I guess I'm okay. I just had another nightmare,
though.''

"Try to write down what it was about," she said, handing
me a pocket typer. I noticed she was wearing an ID pin that
said her name was Belabrosky.

"Okay." I took the typer and wrote a description of the dream.

As I did that, she started reviewing some of the gear that surrounded me. After a few minutes, she excused herself and left.

Although the nightmare was more or less fresh in my memory, I found it extremely difficult to write about. I managed to get out a few lines describing it, but they didn't carry any of the immediacy of the experience. If the Mental Health Acts hadn't been declared unconstitutional, I probably wouldn't be able to tell you as much about it as I have already. But in many ways, this nightmare was much worse than what I've described. While I could remember the others I'd had and could talk about them with relative ease, this one left me feeling sick and guilty.

Dr. Sladky came in at seven and ate breakfast with me. As we ate, he plied me with questions about the dream, and I explained what I could about it.

"This one was really the worst so far," I told him as we were drinking coffee. "It makes me feel like I'm a little kid who's done something wrong."

"Well, Nils, I'm afraid this is beyond me. The tests show only that your brain structure is not yet entirely back to normal. And that may be part of the problem." He thought for a moment and brushed his hair back with both his hands. "I tell you what I'm going to do. I'm going to refer you to some other people who have been looking into the psychological changes you have all gone through as a result of the great retro."

"So, what d'you think they'll do?"

"Well, there are a number of things they could try. There are drug therapies—very good ones—for this kind of thing. But I'm not sure if they'd help you right now. It's your brain structure and your brain chemistry that may be the problem."

That's all the more Sladky told me, but he referred me to a group at Columbia-Presbyterian—got an appointment for me later that day, in fact, and sent me on my way. As I left, I kept thinking to myself how lucky I was to be covered by the Trans-formee Recovery Act. Without that it would have taken me about 500 years to pay off all the medical bills.

Now I understand that not everybody would have been grateful to find out their brains weren't the way they're sup-posed to be, but somehow it reassured me. Maybe the most famous part of the hammerhead microding was the organic transceiver growing from both lobes of the brain. That's what was in those vaults of bone jutting out of the heads of all the triad members who stalked the sewers and back streets of the world. And it kept us all in touch with the great ones—the hammerhead leaders who had already transformed themselves into the living semblance of great sharks and who lived perma-nently in the oceans.

But as far as I can remember, the warlords never com-municated with us directly, even though I believe they must have been able to do so.

We always took our orders from triad leaders—I suppose you could call them lieutenants, for want of a better term. They were the ones who had direct contact with the warlords and, without exception, they were also the ones who either died during the great retro or—if they survived—who have never recovered psychologically.

So as I walked away from the hospital toward the subway entrance, I couldn't help but think that the warlords were try-ing to get through to me. There wasn't much left of what they'd done to my brain, but it was more than enough for what they had in mind.

CHAPTER 9

TESTIMONY OF TIMOTHY J. WANDEL

I

The vids came back on line about eleven that night. Syd was still sleeping on the living-room floor—Ray-Lee had already gone to bed—and I was reading a book about general semantics when the system came fully to life.

"—Greatest computer net breakdown in history," the newscaster announced as the screen winked into life. "Reports from world capitals now indicate most services have been restored in Western and Central Europe and North and Central America. Asia, however, remains down."

A phone call came in then, so I lowered the sound.

"Hello. Is this Tim?" It was Martha on the line, but there was no video to go with the audio.

"Yes, it is. How are things out there?"

"Highly unusual," she said. "I really need you to come out here as soon as you can."

"Well, Syd and Ray-Lee are asleep, and nobody knows where Fowler is."

"Have you seen anything about the war that seems to have started in the Middle East?"

"What war?"

"That's my question—or one of them, at any rate. Try to

get a complete wrap-up of what's gone on today, and bring the crowd out here as soon as you can. I'll be up all night, probably.''

"Okay."

"Tim—it'll be safer out here. The worst is yet to come. Excuse me now, I've got to go.''

She rang off before I could ask any more questions, and when I tried to phone her back later, all I got was a busy signal.

II

Fowler showed up around midnight just as we were getting ready to leave.

"I was stuck in the subway," he told us, "and it started running again only about fifteen minutes ago.''

After Fowler had eaten a couple of sandwiches, we piled into Syd's truck and headed off toward Lake Minnetonka. When we turned the corner onto Lake Street, the city's longest no-parking zone, it was clear it was going to take more than an hour to get out there.

City wreckers were just starting to clear away some of the debris from the cars that had destroyed one another during the computer outage.

It was nearly two by the time we pulled up to the Battenberg estate. Oddly enough, the gates were open, so Syd drove in and drove up to the front door.

"Okay everybody," Syd said to Ray-Lee and Fowler, asleep on the backseat. "We're here.''

"What is that?" Fowler asked sleepily.

I looked in the direction he was pointing to see a rank of men standing on the porch, some of them holding what looked like submachine guns in the dim light from the house.

"We're here to see Martha," I shouted out the window.

"Welcome," one of them said rather emotionlessly. "Martha is expecting you.''

For a moment we listened to the crickets.

Then Syd and I looked at each other and said in unison, "They're robots."

"I should have known," Ray-Lee told us. "She's always been a kind of survivalist."

We locked the truck and headed toward the porch. One of the robots—who looked very human indeed—opened the front door for us and said, "Martha will be with you in just a moment. There are some refreshments in the living room. Please help yourselves."

"That's downright creepy," Syd said as we went inside. "I didn't notice them standing there on the porch as I drove in."

"Neither did I," I told him.

"Oh, they're probably some war-surplus special-forces remotes," Ray-Lee added. "Martha always knows where to get bargains."

Fowler launched himself towards the nearest sofa—long enough to fit even him—and went back to sleep. The rest of us stood around fidgeting.

"So what is this place, anyway?" Syd asked, carefully picking his way around the perimeter of the vast array of furniture, studying the knickknacks as he went. "A combination secret army fortress and curio shop?"

"That's a good question," Martha said as she walked into the room. "But let's not answer it until we get downstairs, shall we?"

Maybe it was just the subdued lighting and the night air coming in off the lake, or perhaps it was the khaki safari suit she was wearing, but Martha looked simultaneously older and more energetic than I'd ever seen her. She saw Fowler sleeping on the sofa and murmured, "Oh dear."

"It's awfully late, Martha," Ray-Lee told her. "I think we all should be asleep in bed."

"So do I, child, but it looks as though a new world war is about to start, unless we do something."

After that there wasn't much more anyone could say, so Syd

and I shook Fowler awake and forced him to get up and follow us to the elevator that took us down to Martha's operations center.

III

Martha sat in a plush swivel chair upholstered with a paisley fabric. "All this is just a trial run by the hammerheads," she told us. "They seem to be able to monkey around with the most powerful artificial intelligences with ease. Shutting down city freeway grids is child's play to them."

She clasped her hands together and looked directly at us and asked, "So tell me, what are your attitudes toward drugs?"

I looked around at the others, expecting some sort of arch-conservative, grandmotherly lecture from the twentieth century.

"Depends on the drug," Syd answered.

"You already know my views, Auntie," Ray-Lee said.

"Caffeine," Fowler muttered, rubbing his face with both hands.

I looked around at the bookshelves and the computer equipment that surrounded us, and then at my feet.

"Why do you ask?" I managed to say at last.

"Because I want to have you all help me participate in an experiment to duplicate the way the hammerhead warlords think," she answered. "My generation probably did more experimentation with such things than yours, and I know there are a number of prejudices still lingering out there against us baby boomers." There was something remarkably nervous in her eyes for a moment, then she asked, "What I want to ask you to do requires that I, and any other participant, take some rather remarkable designer drugs."

"I'm always ready," Syd told her, switching his tail.

Martha nodded.

"I think—I'll pass," Fowler said.

"And I think I'd like to know more, Auntie."

"So would I," I added.

"Certainly," Martha said, leaning back in her chair and placing her fingertips together over her lap. "I happen to have a sensory synthesizer that I acquired after the North African Crisis of Twenty-Ought-Nine." She laughed self-consciously. "I guess that *is* before your time, isn't it?" She shook her head and went on. "It's much more effective as a synthesizer of mass thought patterns than the designers intended—if you use some of the modern over-the-counter stimulants and enhancers.

"All that's a long way of saying that I want us to synthesize the warlords' thoughts, and then apply what we find out to what happens after that."

"Just what over-the-counter things are you talking about?" Syd asked in a level tone.

"Oh, mainly phokus and super-rekall. But there's also a rarity from Eastern Europe called perestroika. There's no interaction with those three."

"That's true enough," Syd added. "But how does the synthesizer work using those?"

"It was one of the first nerve-input sets. You know—the thing puts in the maximum amount of information you can absorb, then takes out the maximum amount possible. Most people find it takes the form of an unusual sleep state—often like a bad night's sleep, unfortunately—followed by an extremely detailed, highly memorable dream. The dream state is the important part. That's why we have to record everything, of course. That's the product."

Ray-Lee stood up and stretched. "Maybe I'm just being a spoiler, but isn't Washington already going to be doing this sort of thing?"

"Why, no, child. They went completely to artificial-intelligence simulation years ago. And the problem with that is, it's just not very creative."

"And without trying to repeat myself," Fowler interjected,

"I'm going to bow out. Is there someplace I could lie down and go to sleep?"

After she summoned a robot to take him off to a bedroom, I said, "I'm really worried about burn, Martha."

"There won't be any with these things, child."

I looked over at Ray-Lee.

"What do you think?" I asked her.

"There's nothing to be afraid of, Tim. Johnny used to operate like this all the time."

That wasn't news to me, but I added, "I don't think that's much of a recommendation."

Ray-Lee leaned her head to one side and frowned very slightly. "It wasn't burnout that killed him," she said quietly, in a distant, almost-academic way.

At that I had to turn my head because my tear ducts began to burn, and I had to wipe my eyes. That woman could say things sometimes that could perform microsurgery on my soul.

So I simply nodded in agreement. There wasn't anything more to say.

IV

Martha reminded me of an elementary-school nurse as she handed the three skin patches to me and Ray-Lee. While Ray-Lee and I were applying them to our own necks, Martha was counting out handfuls of the things for Syd, who must have needed at least triple the ordinary dose because of his body mass. When we were finished, Syd looked like some Band-Aid punk from East L.A.—well, at least above the waist.

"All right, dears," Martha said. "I'm going to stay awake through the whole exercise. Normally, each of you should expect to be under for about eight hours. If there's something too frightening—or wrong—or something—you'll wake up, just as you would with a nightmare. Given the subject matter, that is a possibility, and you need to know that.''

She handed Ray-Lee the first of the beige face-masks attached to the synthesizer.

''If you have a nightmare, it's going to be extremely vivid,'' Martha said. ''But just like a bad dream, it will wear off.''

Ray-Lee sat down on a roll-away bed, slid onto it in a wrestler's turn, and put on the mask. Martha bent down and made sure the contacts were solid.

''You've got about twenty minutes before it begins to take effect,'' Martha said as she gestured for me to get into my cot. ''So you might as well get settled,'' she said, helping me put on my mask.

Maybe I'm unusually susceptible to this particular concentration of drugs, but I started to fall asleep as soon as the mask went over my head.

There wasn't much remarkable about the equipment. I've seen masks like them for sale in discount stores intended for people who live in apartments near freeways or train lines. There are even kiddie versions with pictures of cows jumping over the moon on them. They shut out all the light and a lot of the noise, and the more expensive ones usually have some kind of direct nerve-input generators. It's the sort of thing a lot of church groups used to protest against before scope music and the rave-revival started.

Martha's synthesizer must have been pretty special, though. Once the field went on, I seemed to plunge into a full-color dream of being at the beach that I can still recall. The funny thing is, I never have dreams in vivid color like that. Then, almost immediately after it started, I seem to have drifted off to inner sleep under the influence of the generator and stayed there for what felt like a very long time.

Gradually I became aware that I was no longer myself—as you do in dreams. Instead, I was one of the great hammerhead warlords.

I suffered from racking, long-abiding pain.

As did we all.

It was the enemy that had destroyed our soldiers. And as I thought of our lost horde, images appeared in my mind's eye of rank after rank of them marching down the streets of the world's great cities, the broad lobes of their heads gleaming opaline in the sunlight.

And with the destruction of the horde, calamity had descended on our own psychological ecology. We had designed ourselves so that we were all one, perpetually in contact with one another. Now the suffering of the great dying—the destruction of our flesh on the dry land—ricocheted within all of us. Many of the lesser lords had committed suicide by returning to the land.

It was the weakling's escape.

The true course was to die simultaneously with the final destruction of the enemy.

And that was my goal.

I swam to the limit of my depth, and there we gathered—where the pressure of the sea's deeps compensated for its formidable cold.

But after the meeting began, I found I couldn't understand what was being said, though I could see the other greater lords—big as whales—sculling about me.

Gradually, ineluctably, something pulled me back into myself, and I started to wake up.

V

"It was only a dream," Martha told me after I'd finished telling her about what I'd experienced.

"So all right, it was only a dream," I said. "But I can still feel what it was like to be one of the great ones. They're cut off from the land-based hammerheads that were their link to reality. You know, that's what the lobes in their heads are for—it's an organic transceiver. And now they're reeling in pain and madness. Sort of like having a brain tumor or something."

Ray-Lee cried out and lurched up where she slept.

"Another bad one," Martha muttered as she walked over and sat on the bed beside Ray-Lee and helped her remove her mask.

Ray-Lee held her hands over her face, and Martha put an arm around her and rocked her gently.

"Tell me about it, child," Martha said. "It'll all be better after you tell me about it."

Ray-Lee finally withdrew her hands from her eyes and stared at the electronic equipment in the room.

"My God, that was realistic," she said, almost suppressing a small laugh of disbelief.

"It was only a dream," Martha told her, "but we need to hear about it. You can tell us."

Ray-Lee inhaled deeply. "I dreamed they were after me. They're trying to get everyone near to me. It's like some kind of holy war for them." Ray-Lee stared off into space for a moment, and I could see there was something sick inside her when she did that. I'd never seen it before, though I think I might have sensed it at some subconscious level once or twice when she woke me up in the middle of the night.

"But the heart of the matter is that time isn't—wasn't—the same for them as for us," Ray-Lee began once more. "And I dreamed they killed my father. He didn't kill himself, Auntie." She fell silent for a moment, and then she began to cry, leaning heavily into Martha's shoulder. The older woman hugged her as though she were a very small child and rocked her again.

"I was afraid this might happen," Martha said, looking toward the ceiling. "Listen, child," she went on, leaning her cheek against Ray-Lee's head, "I'm sorry you had to go through this. But the important thing to remember is that it helped."

VI

Syd didn't wake up until nearly an hour and a half later.

"Yeah, well, I had some dreams about fish," was all he told us when he got up.

"Oh, dear," Martha said. "Can't you remember anything more than that?"

"Listen—you can ask Tim here—my psychology isn't exactly what it used to be."

"It may never have been," Ray-Lee muttered under her breath; I don't think Syd heard her, though.

"But we need three people at least to get some attitude of centrality for this effort," Martha said.

"That leaves you, Martha," I told her.

"He's right, Auntie. You're going to have to try, too."

"But, damn it, we don't have time."

"Syd, let me fill you in for a moment," I said. "I had this vision of the hammerheads seeking to kill off the human race and to commit suicide at the same time. Ray-Lee had a nightmare of them having changed time and space to get at her, her family, and at Johnny. You had a dream about fish. Can't you remember anything more than that?"

Syd thought for a moment, got up on his four legs, turned to Martha and told her, "Sounds like you're gonna have to take the time out to dream."

"I suppose there's nothing left but that," Martha said. "The problem is that things have gotten much worse in the last eight or ten hours while you've been sleeping. Especially in Eurasia. We seem to have gotten to the point where people are actually killing each other in riots in a number of places; and in a couple of cases, it's not clear who has control of the nuclear codes of several of the smaller states."

"That's bad," Syd remarked as he started peeling the medicinal patches off his torso.

"We're perfectly capable of monitoring things while you sleep, Auntie," Ray-Lee told her.

"I've no doubt you are. But there may come a time when I need to phone a few people. What then?"

"Then we'll have to wake you up," Ray-Lee said.

"I'm so nervous about this," Martha replied, hesitating to look us in the eye. "I'm a notoriously bad subject for this exercise.

"And as for your doing the monitoring, it's all the black propaganda, you see. That's going to be your hardest problem. The hammerheads are geniuses at it. An information-rich, interconnected world like ours is a sucker for the stuff if it's dished out like this. Half the news agencies in the world are putting out completely faked news right now, and the other half are picking it up. That's what you've got to look out for."

"Can you show us how?" I asked her.

"Maybe. It's all a question of time."

CHAPTER 10

Janssen and Allegro-Daumier are standing in front of the control panel of the foundation's research submarine; the transmission is marred by constant static.

"So we've reached our destination, and that's what's causing the breakdowns—is that right?" Janssen asks. He swallows and looks worried.

"Apparently," Allegro-Daumier answers, nodding. She is trying to look calm and collected, but not quite making it. "I don't want to alarm the foundation, but our ship's engineer has turned off the atomic pile and we're running on solar and battery power. We've suffered several serious malfunctions at once. As far as we can tell, all our computing systems have been attacked by the hammerheads, just as they seem to have attacked a number of other computer installations throughout the world.

"But we've survived it."

"We're also broadcasting a distress signal, aren't we?" Janssen says, sounding as though he's under sedation.

"Yes, we are. But more importantly, we're also relaying a constant stream of information on the microwave radiation that the hammerheads are emitting back to—"

"Patricia, you'll have to stop and help me," a man says

from off camera. "We're having trouble with the reactor unit again."

"We'll be back," Janssen intones dully as the transmission ends.

CHAPTER 11

TESTIMONY OF TIMOTHY J. WANDEL

We no sooner got Martha to sleep in the embrace of a mask than Syd announced he needed to go back to sleep, too.

So Ray-Lee and I sat there in Martha's operations center watching the news roll in by ourselves. Ray-Lee was in charge of watching the Western Hemisphere, and I monitored the eastern half of the world. Every major story that indicated war was about to break out we put through a computer program to try to figure out if it were real or not.

The problem was that at this point it was getting very hard—even for the computers—to tell what was really going on.

"Jesus Christ," Ray-Lee said, reaching over to touch my arm. "Take a look at this." She punched a button and the large television monitor in front of us switched from a frosty black to a scene of the flames over the Champs-Élysées.

"The second day of uninterrupted rioting in Paris has left at least twenty thousand dead," a newscaster announced; then Ray-Lee turned off the sound.

"And it's all for real," she said after a while. "We've got direct corroboration of what's going on in Europe out to the Urals, according to this."

"The funny thing is," I told her, "there really isn't much happening in Asia. If it's anything, it's too quiet."

"Try running a direct check with Tokyo."

"I'm not getting anything when I do." And I punched in the codes for direct access to the Tokyo dataspace one more time. At the very least I should have gotten out weather and exchange-rate reports. But I couldn't even get phone numbers out of Japan.

"You're right," Ray-Lee said, getting up and watching me try to reach Tokyo on the system. "Let's try a satellite view."

She dialed up a general-access weather view of the Earth. It was early morning over the eastern Pacific, and there was very little cloud cover.

That was when we saw the explosion.

It grew, spreading out across the Japanese islands and the coast of Korea.

"My God, look at the size of that thing," Ray-Lee said very quietly. "It's got to be a hydrogen bomb."

And then all the electronic gear in the world went out, leaving us in the dark.

CHAPTER **12**

Allegro-Daumier and Flying Eagle, looking as though they both could use a good night's sleep, are standing on the deck of the *Čapek*. Static ripples constantly through both audio and video. Behind them the sea is fairly calm in the morning light; sparse cumulus clouds are visible in the sky.

"Doug Janssen is acting as our cameraman this morning," Allegro-Daumier begins, her voice a little shaky, "because the camera's robotic control mechanism has broken down. Unhappily, because we have had to dismantle the ship's reactor, we are adrift and nearly powerless, more than 290 kilometers from Japan. We are floating atop what appears to be the principal swarm of hammerheads in the world, numbering more than ten thousand."

Flying Eagle leans his sunburned face forward, seeming weary nearly to the point of incoherence, and adds, "We've calculated that figure from separate transmissions, each one of which is the product of a different individual—each with a separate pattern of transmissions."

"The most remarkable discovery we've made, based on sonar imaging, is that there are at least two quite different kinds of hammerheads in this swarm," Allegro-Daumier says. "One group is composed of enormous creatures, some of them perhaps the size of a blue whale, and the other is apparently composed of individuals about the size of a mature dolphin—"

Flying Eagle interjects, "Running from four to five meters up to seven or ten in length."

Allegro-Daumier glances at him, anger flashing, and then looks off-camera.

"What is it, Margaret?" Allegro-Daumier asks.

A heavyset woman with a crewcut leans forward and says quietly, "We're getting some kind of peak load right now from below." Then the heavyset woman gazes out to sea, past the other two.

"Look at that," she says weakly.

The camera turns awkwardly away from the group on the deck and focuses on the grayness of the ocean. A line of darkness has formed some twenty or thirty meters away from the ship. It is a row of hammerheads swimming rapidly in formation toward the submarine. The camera catches one as it breaches the surface of the ocean, and then static engulfs both audio and video and the transmission ends.

CHAPTER **13**

TESTIMONY OF NILS ULLRICH

I

That afternoon I had a meeting set up with my two friends and coproducers, Eddy Corrigan and Joel Terboom. As far as I recall, I sat in the front room of my apartment in Brooklyn typing for several hours and lost track of time. Before I knew it, Corrigan had shown up at my door.

"Have you been listening to the news?" he asked, out of breath from climbing the stairs to my apartment.

"Naw, I've been working on the script."

"Things are going crazy around the world," he said as he entered and went straight to my computer, logged off what I was doing and accessed a news channel.

"Look at this stuff," Corrigan went on. "Three different regional wars seemed to have started today. And the worst of it's in Eurasia. They don't know if the nuclear-weapon codes are safe in some of those countries."

The phone rang. I answered it.

I can't tell you what I heard, because I really don't know what it was. As far as I can recall, there was some sort of noise like a high-speed fax transmission. The next thing I remember, I was sprawled out on the floor, and Corrigan was shouting at me.

"What the hell is going on here?" he hollered as I opened my eyes.

"I don't know," I told him. "But I think you better get me over to Columbia-Presbyterian now." I explained that I was scheduled to go there for tests that evening, and Corrigan called them to tell them what had happened and to get them set up to receive us. Just before we left, Joel Terboom arrived, and I remember trying to explain to him what was going on, although I had trouble keeping my eyes open. Corrigan later told me that I slept most of the way to upper Manhattan on the subway, even though it was only about two or three in the afternoon.

II

There's not much to say about the next several hours. I'm told I slept through most of them; what little time I spent awake I simply don't recall. But while I was unconscious, the staff at Columbia were able to follow the centers of radio reception still operating in my brain at that time, and they discovered that I was receiving extremely low-frequency radio transmissions and, apparently, responding to them.

When I did wake up, it was the middle of the night. All my senses seemed overly acute, especially my sense of smell. There was the musty scent of the antiseptic cleaning fluid they used in the hospital mixed with the smell of the medical staff people; in the distance, there was the sweet, fruity aroma of gasohol that permeates New York all the time, and beyond that, the smell of the Hudson River.

I got out of bed, dressed in my hospital gown, and began walking down the hall. Everything looked like I was seeing it through a star filter. All the lights seem to have a prismatic halo around them, as though there were some kind of fog inside the hospital building. I must confess that I thought I was dreaming at the time.

It never crossed my mind that I should be afraid, or that I was not in possession of my own faculties.

Instead it all seemed perfectly natural. I managed to sneak out of the hospital and found myself on upper Broadway. There was a riot going on, so no one noticed that I was wandering around amid the bodegas and the stalled traffic near the George Washington Bridge wearing hospital pajamas.

It was foggy and misty that night, and I kept near to the walls of the surrounding buildings to keep out of the wet and away from some of the charging crowds storming uptown. I hadn't gone very far when a group of three men walked purposefully toward me out of the darkness and stopped in front of me. All their clothing was ripped—their leader had no shirt on at all—and what was left of their clothes was soaked through. For all I know, they may have swum across the Hudson; I never had the chance to ask.

They stared at me for a moment. Then the man in the lead opened his mouth and emitted a series of sounds rather like those that came out of the phone and knocked me out. After that I joined them, and we walked along Broadway for many blocks.

I'm not clear on what happened to the others. I think they ran off, after we were attacked. Just who attacked us I can't say. I remember waiting, crouching behind a garbage Dumpster. And then I heard the leader's call once more.

What he was saying means in English: "We will kill the ancient gods inside of us." Or something like that, anyway.

I stood up and saw the leader facing a group of armed men. Carrying something in his hand—it might have been a piece of a drain spout—he charged one of the men.

The man aimed his gun and shot, clearly wounding the leader in the chest.

Still the leader marched forward.

Once more the man shot his gun, and then the leader leaped—it must have been three meters at least—and smashed

in the head of the gunman with the pipe. Both figures collapsed against the pavement.

I waited until the armed men dispersed and walked past
the two bodies. Both of them were dead.

Now it seems obvious that the others ran away because a
point-blank shot hadn't stopped the leader. But I couldn't figure that out at the time. All I remember thinking was that it
was strange that the others wouldn't stand and fight. Somehow, that was something I couldn't understand.

For more than half an hour or so I must have wandered
along Broadway. I think I picked up some fruit from a bodega
that had been wrecked and ate it.

But the next thing that I really remember is seeing the
George Washington Bridge rising up into the fog and disap-
pearing there. None of the lights were working on the thing,
so it was like a span leading off into nothingness.

Gangs of kids were trashing the kiosks and fruit stands
along 176th Street as it started to mist once more. I remember
that all the traffic on Broadway had stalled around the entrances to the bridge, and that some of the vehicles were burning. Some time not too long before that there must have been
one of the bigger multiple-vehicle collisions in the history of
New York, because there were trucks burning all along the
street. I'm pretty sure some of the drivers were dead inside
them. At least there were dim shadowy forms coiled over
some of the steering wheels, faintly lit by the flames.

Small groups of police and the national guard were sta-
tioned at the intersections of Broadway and some of the side-
streets there in the 170s. The police watched me cautiously,
their guns partly raised, as I walked past. Only as I got to the
subway station, where there was a large hologram sign announcing "Evacuation Route" glowing in the air, did I have
enough light to see that the side streets were filled with bodies.
They had piled the dead there in their hundreds and thousands until some later time when they could be removed.

Somewhere a few blocks away—that is, downtown, maybe

in the middle 160s—there was the sound of small-arms fire. That seemed to signal something inside me that compelled me to go into the subway.

Although the city's traffic grid system had obviously failed, the subway was still running. There were rush-hour crowds down there, and I remember butting through them. It never occurred to me that people were trying to escape from what was going on downtown, even though I'd seen the evacuation sign. People have told me there were also regular announcements saying which subway lines provided the quickest routes out of Manhattan, but I don't remember any of that.

At the time, I knew only that I had to get inside.

There was just one problem—I didn't have any money or a subway card—let alone a credit card to use.

So I robbed a woman.

She was caught in the crowd immediately ahead of me, her purse slung over her shoulder.

I reached inside and found her wallet and quickly withdrew my hand.

Neither she nor anyone else noticed. I glanced through her billfold, took out all the cash, and dropped it. As the crowd advanced down the steps into the subway station, I quickly lost sight of the wallet.

You cannot imagine the remorse I feel about this incident now, but at the time I felt nothing. It was like breathing—so simple it was nothing you would even remember.

And that was when it began to dawn on me that I was a prisoner in my own body.

Ever since I underwent the transformation and started my way back to humanity, I've tried to behave like a reasonable person. I can't claim to be a very moral one, though, considering the things I did when I was a hammerhead. But stealing was just not something I would ever do now.

Especially in a situation like that.

And then the crush of people forced me and all the others around me down to the gates. I had enough money to pay my fare, and the gates opened for me. For a lot of people the turn-stiles wouldn't open, and they were pushed to one side, some of them screaming and crying, and still the crowd shoved me onward and downward. Finally we reached the platform. There were police holding people back so they wouldn't be pushed onto the tracks.

It so happens there is a vaulted computer center in that particular station on the upper Broadway line. That's not the kind of information that I'm prone to collect, mind you. But somehow that fact reached into my head, and the forces that were controlling me maneuvered me through the crowd of sweating, frightened people toward the back end of the plat-form. There are some old wooden doors there—they made me think of a nineteenth-century schoolroom, for some reason—and I grabbed the doorknob on one and wrenched it with all my might.

An odd sound crackled out of my right hand, and I looked down and saw that I had broken the lock. But I could no lon-ger open or close my fingers, and the doorknob dropped to the tiled floor. In the distant background, as though it were in some mountain valley halfway around the world, the warning chimes sounded and people started pushing toward an arriv-ing train.

That's when I stumbled into the computer vault. I shut the door behind me, and my eyes quickly adjusted to the dim greenish light from the telltales and readouts.

Gradually the pain from my broken hand began to spread up through my arm, but I was nevertheless forced forward to the control panel. With my left hand I started typing com-mands into the computer. Although I know a few things about computer programming, I had no idea what I was doing.

But of course the great ones did.

It's a sign of how far gone I was that it didn't occur to me that I was being controlled by the great ones until that mo-ment. As I started running a series of subroutines on the com-puter—none of which I had ever dealt with before in my

life—I began to realize that the great ones had prepro-
grammed me for this very instant.

They had a million people like me doing their bidding that
night, lots of them in even nastier situations.

Then the central screen began blinking, in red, "Access denied." My fingers flashed across the keyboard again for several
minutes, and then the "access denied" screen started blinking
again, only to be replaced by a "terminal closed to all access"
screen.

At that I frenzied.

I burst backwards out of the computer vault and stumbled
into the crowd. Like a berserker, I charged at the people standing between me and an incoming train. There were two
teenaged boys, a middle-aged businessman, several jones old
people, and one little girl standing in front of me. I was being
commanded forward to push them onto the tracks and to
throw myself after them.

There is a killing lust in people, but this was more than
that. It was ecstasy, and at the same time it was like trying to
perform an appendectomy on yourself. Without anesthesia.

I didn't seem to have any control over myself anymore. And
as I started to rush forward into a charge, I sought to grab onto
the people nearest me with my good hand. If I could stop myself for a moment, I thought, maybe I could stop the great ones
from telling me what to do.

I'm not sure if I actually managed to force one of my feet to
stop or if I simply tripped over something on the floor; but
right then, down I went. My head bounced against someone;
otherwise I would have landed on my face.

There is an alternate explanation for why I fell down just as
I was being compelled to murder those people in front of me
on the subway platform.

It may have been the precise moment when the great ones
committed suicide. I can't be sure, of course, but the fake nuclear explosion that signaled their end occurred about then.

At any rate, after dozens of people filed past me, two policemen helped me up and put me on board the train. The next thing I knew, we were being let out at a station in the Bronx.

III

My head was clearer again when I got out of the train; but the guilt that welled up inside me, accompanied by the pain from my right hand, made me so weak I could hardly stand up.

"What happened to you, buddy?" a policeman asked me as I walked out onto the street.

"I don't know," I told him.

"Was it an incident or an accident?" he went on.

"What d'you mean?"

"Well, there's different insurance for 'em. Go over to that van if it was an incident, or over to that one down on the corner if it was an accident."

I shuffled down to the van for accident victims. By this time the blood from my hand had spread over most of my pajama front, so people made way for me.

"My God, man," said the woman seated inside the van who was filling out forms for the city. "Have you been shot?"

"No. It's my hand. I think it's broken."

"Yo, Floyd," the woman shouted. "Come help this guy down to the first-aid station, okay?"

Floyd strolled up—he was three times my size—and asked me if I could make it down the block to the laundromat, where they'd set up a small field hospital. I nodded, but I'm sure he would have carried me if I'd asked.

They bound my hand in gauze at the first-aid station, and that's where they noticed that I had a hospital ID tag around my wrist.

"What happened to you?" the man who bound up my hand asked.

I lied and told him I guessed the hospital security system had gone down and that gangs must have attacked the building.

They let me sit in a plastic chair and try to sleep. A radio was playing in there, and that's where I first heard about the fake nuke and the end of the great ones. Somehow it seemed natural to me that they would do that; but by that time I'd started to realize that I had been part of their armed memory—that they'd used me and millions of other people to try to take down New York and London and Paris and Tokyo and Rio and all the others.

It's very hard for me to say this. . . .

But as I sat there, where we could smell the smoke from the burning cars and the dead bodies mixed in with the gasohol scent of New York, I started crying. You see, even though the great ones had intended to kill themselves all along, they intended to take us all with them. What they taught us was that they were the ancient gods who had to perform the cleansing ritual upon the Earth.

And I thought they had succeeded, and that I had helped them. And I sat there in that plastic chair and cried as silently as I could.

CHAPTER 14

EXECUTIVE SUMMARY OF THE REPORT OF THE SENATE SELECT COMMITTEE ON THE MICRODE CITY INCIDENT AND ITS AFTERMATH

I n less than twenty-four hours, the rioting and programmed attacks caused by the hammerheads led to:

—The death of more than 150 million people throughout the world;

—Property damage in excess of $400 billion dollars (in current dollar terms);

—Destabilization of the world banking system, followed by economic crises that have taken nearly ten years to resolve;

—And, among others, the loss of the research vessel *Čapek,* and with it, some of the foremost scientific authorities on the hammerhead threat.

CHAPTER **15**

TESTIMONY OF TIMOTHY J. WANDEL

I

After a few seconds, the emergency lights flickered on.

"We'll have to wake Martha up," I said. Ray-Lee nodded, went over to Martha's cot and started the downloading procedure for the dream generator. I kept tweaking the TV equipment to see if I could pick up any transmissions from anywhere on the planet.

Ray-Lee must have jostled Syd because I heard his hooves clamoring as he got up and walked toward me.

"Why are the lights flickering?" he asked.

"We're on emergency energy," Ray-Lee told him as he walked past her and Martha.

"It looks like a nuke's gone off," I told him, "and there's been an electromagnetic pulse that shut down just about everything around the world."

He whistled.

"What happened?" Martha said loudly. I looked over and saw that she was sitting up in bed, patting her hair.

"There's been a nuclear detonation over Japan," Ray-Lee answered, "and the EMP seems to have shut down everything."

"Jesus," Martha said, once more too loudly. "Do the phones work?"

I patched in a phone and we got a dial tone.

"At least the local net is up," I told her.

She nodded and walked unsteadily toward the console and sat down across from me. It took her a moment to focus; she was still numbed by the dream generator, but at last she managed to dial a long-distance number.

A voice announced from the speaker, "United Nations Control Center, Ledbetter speaking."

"This is Martha Battenberg," she said into the microphone. "May I please speak to André Chastaine."

"Certainly."

After a moment a very husky-sounding man's voice answered from the speaker. "Martha, what on Earth are you calling for?"

"I've been monitoring what's going on here at home, André," she responded. "There's been some sort of nuclear explosion over Japan that seems to have shut down everything but the phone net."

The man laughed briefly. "It wasn't a real nuke, Martha. The people in Japan we talked to a few minutes ago are just fine."

"Then what was it, André?"

"An illusion."

Martha raised her eyebrows and looked up at me briefly, then lowered her gaze again.

"If it's an illusion, it seems to have fooled most of the world's telecommunications net."

"Yes. Well. Most of the world's artificial intelligences were so fooled by it that they shut themselves off. And at the same time, it seems to have killed off most of the hammerhead group swarming in the Pacific near the Japanese islands."

"So you're saying the hammerheads generated this somehow?"

"At this point, Martha, I'm not saying anything. You'll have to excuse me now. Things are pretty bad here in New York. There's a combination gang war and riot going on throughout most of midtown Manhattan, and we may have to evacuate. So bye-bye."

"I'll call you later, André. Good-bye."

There was the sign-off tone and the line was broken.

"I guess it's a good thing I called the United Nations first," Martha said. "Washington wouldn't have told us that much in five hours."

She pulled a flat-screen monitor toward her and started scanning through the incoming news stories.

"Oh, this is awful," she said at last.

"So what do we do now?" I asked.

"Pitch in any way we can," she told me, nodding her head to one side. "With this sort of destruction, it'll take years to repair the damage here alone, let alone in the places where the real destruction occurred."

II

"I say it was suicide," I told them as we drank our coffee and watched the sun coming up over Lake Minnetonka.

"That may very well be," Martha told me, "but the important thing is that it was a simulation that was so real that most of the world's electronics net behaved as though the electromagnetic pulse were real. And that suggests the hammerheads intended it as a weapon."

"But Martha, it's just like I dreamed it," I said. "They wanted to die and take everything else with them. So it's a case of suicide. They were just crazy enough to think they were taking the rest of the world with them at the same time." I thought about the first pictures broadcast when the world net came back up—the floating bodies of the dead hammerheads, bobbing in the Pacific off Japan.

"To me it suggests a quality of intelligence quite different from our own." Martha folded her hands behind her neck. "Maybe they were already spinning into some kind of fantasy realm we lack the brains to understand. With the elimination of their foot soldiers—through which they remained in radio contact with land-based life—they clearly lost touch with reality in some essential way. But how they compensated for it!''

Fowler interjected, ''If I may say so, that's not going to help the people who died in the riots last night all around the world.''

No one said anything for a while after that. Fowler had a way of stopping any conversation dead in its tracks.

Ray-Lee finished her coffee and told Martha wearily, ''Auntie, I'm grateful for everything you've done. But I'm afraid we should be going.''

''Oh, I suppose so, child.''

''Uh, I'll go start the truck,'' Syd added, and he got up and cantered off toward the front of the house. Fowler smiled and said, '' 'Bye,'' and followed Syd.

''It was good meeting you,'' Martha called out to them. Syd turned and waved, but Fowler acted as though he hadn't heard her.

''And it's been good meeting you,'' I told Martha. She leaned across the table and clasped my right hand in hers.

''I wish I'd been able to finish my own dream, so that I'd have something as worthwhile talking about as you have with yours,'' she said.

I nodded.

''Tim, would you excuse us for a moment?'' Ray-Lee got up from her seat.

''Sure.'' I got up and walked away toward the front of the house. The robot guards were gone from the veranda, and Syd was sitting in his truck, waiting. Fowler was leaning out one window.

The two women followed after a few minutes. Martha muttered something to Ray-Lee, kissed her on the cheek and, to my surprise, came over and kissed my cheek as well.

''Do stay in touch,'' Martha said with a small wave of her hand, and then we got in the truck and drove away. I looked back once near the bottom of the hill and saw that she was still waving to us, standing small and fragile against the stonework of the mansion outlined against the morning sky.

III

Syd offered Fowler a place to sleep at his apartment, and after they dropped us off, Ray-Lee and I slept through the rest of the day. I woke in the early evening.

Ray-Lee was already up and packing her clothes.

"I'm sorry," she said, looking up from her suitcase. She was wearing a green dress that made her look very pale. "I didn't mean to wake you."

"No, it's better that you did."

She bit her lip and gazed at me. Outside, birds were singing, and a breeze came through the screen, blowing the curtains behind her.

"I'm going to go, Tim."

"Yeah. I see that."

She shut her suitcase and locked it.

"Would you like something to eat before you go?" I asked.

"No." She didn't sound very sure. "No, thanks." She walked over and sat on the edge of the bed and put a hand on my shoulder. "Tim, don't be mad or hurt by anything I'm going to say. You've done a lot of things to help me." She stopped speaking, turned her head away from me briefly, and then she looked back. "If I stayed, I'd be using you as a substitute for Johnny. I've already been guilty of doing that. It's been stupid, and it's hurting me already."

"Ray-Lee, you always say these enormous things to me when I'm half-awake and I never have any idea of what to say—" I exhaled and looked out the window at the tree branch between my building and the one next door.

"But the big thing you've done for me is to make me realize that I don't owe Johnny anything anymore. I went to jail for him. I've paid off my debt."

After a while, I asked, "Where are you going to go, Ray-Lee?"

"I don't know. But it's time now." She leaned over and kissed my cheek. I tried to hug her, but she pushed away, got up and grabbed her suitcase.

"Would you show me to the door?"

"Sure." So I got up, dressed only in my gym shorts, and followed her out to the elevator lobby.

She pressed the call button and we waited in silence. When the elevator doors opened, she turned back and said, "I'll miss you, Tim."

"Whatever, Ray-Lee." I guess I closed my eyes when I told her, "I love you, you know."

"You probably do," she answered, frowning. She gazed at the floor, her back hunched. "But this whole thing has been wrong from the very start, and it's my fault."

"No it wasn't, Ray-Lee. I'm just not anything like Johnny, and I never will be."

The elevator chimed behind her but she ignored it. "Tim, you've been sliding through life for as long as I've known you. If I stayed around, you'd still be doing it ten years from now. And then maybe I'd be doing it, too."

"Ray-Lee, please don't go."

At that point, one of my neighbors pounded on the inside of her apartment door. "If you're gonna have an argument, have it somewhere else!" the woman shouted from inside her cubicle, never opening the door to face us.

Ray-Lee shook her head and said gently, "Go find yourself, Tim." After a moment, she added, "Good-bye."

I said, "Good-bye," too.

She nodded and almost smiled, and then walked into the elevator.

The doors closed. It was the last time I ever saw her.

IV

Martha Battenberg called me about two weeks later, after Syd had made the big discovery about the retrovirus Johnny had designed.

"I'm afraid I've got some bad news, Tim," she told me. "I just got off the phone with people in Washington. I thought I'd allow some time for things to cool off and then call and ask about the pardons. You know, the ones you requested for the people who were busted for working for your cousin."

"So what happened?" I asked.

"They told me the president's dead set against it. Apparently, political ecology is too hot a subject for her to deal with right now."

"That is too bad." I thought about it for a few moments and added, "So what do you think—is there any chance we could try again after a few months?"

"Maybe. But I doubt if this administration will ever seriously consider the idea."

"Well, thanks for trying, Martha."

"You're welcome. And on an entirely different subject, have you heard anything from Ray-Lee?"

"No."

"I don't think you're likely to for a long, long time. She's strange that way. And then suddenly she'll pop up again as though no time has intervened since the last time you saw her."

"Somehow I don't think she'll be in touch with me again."

"Well, perhaps not. At any rate, I wanted you to know that about her. The popping-up part, I mean."

"Well, thanks, Martha."

"Remember what I said the other night, Tim. Pitch in any way you can."

"Okay."

We rang off.

I was stunned when, a few days later, my computer alerted

me to Martha's obituary. I wouldn't have known she had died if my network didn't have an alerting programming for people I've had contact with.

It seems outrageous that in this day and age someone could die from a cerebral hemorrhage. But that's what happened to Martha.

My life was that much emptier because of her passing.

V

Sometimes there seem to be knots in time where gigantic events and peoples' lives get all snarled up; and when the knots are finally undone, nothing's ever the way it was before. That's the way the world has been for me since the hammerheads committed suicide.

It's what Jung called synchronicity, I guess. Everything happens at once, and then we spend years trying to explain what went on as fate or luck or chance. It's what the Russians have been trying to control with smart drugs like udacha.

But to me it just seems like a bunch of knots unraveling.

Syd showed me the first hitch of the knot when we stopped in the country and he told me he didn't have any desire for human women any longer. That was when I started realizing how different people could become—psychologically—because of microding.

At least Syd's taken charge of his life; he joined a centaur commune in New Mexico.

I've been trying to take charge of my own life, you see, but what I've been fighting all along is comparing myself to my cousin Johnny. There's no way I could ever be that sort of person.

And what's helped me the most is to remember that Johnny trusted me the way he did. When he thought there was a chance he might be killed, he made plans for me to carry on. I keep reminding myself of that when I feel like the problems are just too big to handle.

That's what I wound up telling his mother when I finally reached her, weeks after the fake nuke went off. But I never told her what Johnny thought about reincarnation, or Jim Morrison, or the world serpent. She never would have understood.

I'm not so sure I do, myself.

What worries me most is that somehow, someway, somebody is going to come along and say that the money from the lottery isn't really mine. One court in Switzerland has already ruled that the kind of system Johnny appears to have programmed his computer to use—a random-process selector that picked out a lot of lottery tickets in my name—is perfectly legal. That gives me some comfort. But nevertheless, I've only been using the interest on the money that's left, just in case they ask me for the money back some day.

Then again, although maybe everything I've been doing is really just a way of trying to measure up to Johnny, it at least makes me feel like I'm doing something worthwhile. Because what I've done is to set up a nonprofit institution to deal with the aftermath of it all. One part of the foundation works on cleaning up the Pacific. The bloom the hammerheads left is a vicious superalgae, and it'll be years before we get things back on an even keel there.

The other part of the foundation is set up to help the transformees—the people who were turned into hammerheads and then retroed when Johnny released the virus. A lot of them are mentally incompetent, and somebody's got to take care of them.

But not all of them. It's the ones who recovered who should be able to tell me how the hammerheads simulated a nuclear blast so effectively that the great ones blew out their own brains with it.

It's the answer I really owe myself, and everyone else as well.

Besides, it's the only way I can take hold of my life, just like Ray-Lee wanted me to.

CHAPTER 16

EXCERPTS FROM THE TESTIMONY OF EDWARD CORRIGAN BEFORE THE SENATE INTELLIGENCE COMMITTEE

U nlike the others who have testified before this committee, I have not come here prepared to tell you about my own experiences during the series of events you are investigating here.

My role in these developments was occasionally near the center, even though I was not conscious of it at the time. However, my subconscious must have had some grasp of my own nearness to the locus of events, because I went through a prolonged period of several months' duration during which I felt that some enormous change was occurring in the world.

Yet I was unable to understand what the change was all about until much later.

Perhaps that's natural. I was in the midst of a disintegrating relationship, and that was the most important thing in my life then. Certainly the relationship I had with my fiancée seemed more important than my work at the time; and when I spent too much time mourning the end of that relationship, I neglected my job and lost a steady means of support for several months.

Oddly enough, that was fortuitous. I needed time to think, and I didn't have that before then, when I was effectively working several jobs at the same time. And during those days, after the great retro but before the disaster struck, I resolved a number of questions in my own mind that I put into the article I wrote and published about what the new era of mutability meant to our poor attempt at creating a civilization.

It seems like another era to us now, of course. But when Johnny Stevens set up his company nearly ten years ago, almost everything he did was based on twentieth-century icons. His first microdings were renditions of superheroes that, at the time, were almost one hundred years old. Punk parodies of his original icons quickly followed—most notably the wolfman cult that developed within the demimonde. But by the time of his last collection of designs, shown publicly just hours before his death, Stevens had moved beyond the realm of the icons. He'd entered the realm of the new mutability.

All of his last designs contained some element of the chameleon in them, and that ability to transform oneself rapidly was intended as a metaphor for the new capability he made available to the world with the perfection of the Salvatore process. It is doubly unfortunate that Dr. Salvatore, one of the most brilliant biochemists of the century, died in the attack on the Microde City laboratory near Branchville, Connecticut along with Stevens and a number of others. If she had lived, unraveling some of the work of the hammerhead keiretsu would have been made that much easier.

In short, Stevens is responsible for moving us beyond the era in which culture became nothing but the regurgitation of icons—the phrase "pop will eat itself" comes to mind to describe the condition—that set in during the seventies of the last century.

And when you consider what Stevens has done to us all, then you must argue that no other single person has ever so affected the entire human race.

CHAPTER **17**

I

In the morning, a city van drove me back to upper Manhattan. A number of buildings were burned out, smoldering hulks in the light of a gray, cloud-covered morning. But the robots were already out there, cleaning things up.

I stayed in the hospital for the next week. At first the doctors didn't want to tell me much about what had happened to me, and it took that long for me to recover from the experience in order to be able to talk about it.

And then the information from the archives of Microde City popped up on the computer networks.

One of the researchers who had been studying me, a young man named Cassell, came in one day to tell me that they had discovered that the retrovirus that had turned me back into a human being was also designed to change some essential parts of my brain.

"There are brain-chemisty centers that help to produce some general attitudes in people," Cassell told me. "One of the things the hammerhead microding was intended to do was to make you more like a predator in a number of ways. By contrast, some of what the Stevens microding was intended to do was to make you more altruistic. That's as much as we've figured out so far."

"So when will I get back to being just me?"

"In some ways you're never again going to be the person you were. It's as simple as that."

I nodded and said, "It's just as well. I wasn't such a great guy, anyway."

After Cassell left, I found myself crying. I was simultaneously incredibly happy about surviving, and assaulted by what the hammerheads had tried to force me to do.

There was no doubt they had tried to get me to kill thousands of people. If they had succeeded in reprogramming the subway computer through me, people would not have been able to escape from the rioting in central Manhattan. That alone would have made things much worse.

But, worst of all, they had tried to compel me to push innocent bystanders onto the rails in front of an oncoming train.

They'd planted a series of programmed moves inside me, and with one telephone call and a few low-frequency radio transmissions, they'd armed the memory, and off I'd gone to wreak destruction for them.

Up until that time, I'd thought I was free of the hammerheads. My body was nearly back to normal, and I could stand to look at my face in the mirror in the morning without throwing up.

Okay—maybe I'd asked for what happened to me. Even at the time I started making the film about the 'heads, it was generally known that they had begun kidnapping people who reported on them. I should have taken that as a warning, I guess.

But you see, one of the things they managed to implant in their victims' brains—it was certainly in my brain—was the need to be part of the pack. When the great retro took place, that was the first part of their programming that dried up inside me. So I figured I was that much nearer to being completely free.

Nevertheless, I've got to admit it left me needing something more in life. If I were a religious person—after that—

maybe I would have become intensely involved in church work. I'm not, so I don't know what would have happened.

But more importantly, I'd taken some steps to assert my independence, too. I've already mentioned that I stopped using the nickname I'd used since I was a kid. When my head starting looking human again, I went back to being plain old Nils.

And the second thing I decided to do was to make a film about how the government had put together a program to help those of us who were transformed. Doing the writing and starting the production of the film were the first things in my life that I felt good about for a long time.

And then the great ones grabbed me again.

From inside my head.

That was the hard part.

At least I wasn't alone. The night of the fake nuke, nearly all of the transformees throughout the world went on rampages of one kind or another. We'd all been programmed to do that, of course. New York suffered immensely as a result because of the frenzies that erupted from the federal treatment facilities in Brooklyn and New Jersey.

And then, at last, about four o'clock that morning, we were all freed.

II

The great ones killed themselves by simulating a nuclear explosion so well that most of the world's computers shut down to prevent themselves from being fried by the electromagnetic pulse of the bomb. That's testimony to the kind of power they had at their disposal.

Now, as far as we've been able to find out, none of the bodies of the great ones we've recovered show any effects of actual EMP damage to the radio-reception organs located in the lobes of their heads. So the way I figure it, they must have believed so strongly that the pulse would kill them that it did.

Some people say that kind of belief is impossible. I usually tell them about some of the famous mass hallucinations of the last couple of hundred years—the angels of Mons in the First World War and the power riots are the ones I usually talk about. That seems to remind everybody that even fairly normal people have had truly bizarre experiences as a result of shared, but abnormal, psychological states.

Of course, when you start thinking about the great ones, you're dealing with people who had transformed both their bodies and their minds far beyond anything like what's ever been attempted before.

And besides, they were all preselected for criminal behavior. Beyond that, you have to bear in mind that the hammerhead keiretsu was working on brain reconstruction for years before they kidnapped the scientist who developed the microding formulas for Johnny Stevens. We've found the records of that research in two different hammerhead front corporations set up to hide what was going on.

Alongside that kind of research they were drawing on a one-thousand-year-old tradition of rigidly enforced criminal discipline to maintain a secret organization and to use it to undermine the competition—in this case, all land-based life.

As far as I understand it, there was a kind of Buddhistic quality in that effort. They never talked about sin but about "wrong turning," which was something much more serious, really. They believed that the rise of land-based life constituted such a "wrong turning," and that it could only be corrected by eliminating it.

And there was a Marxist-Leninist aspect of their belief, too, insofar as they disparaged all society as, well, jones—that is, bourgeois. What they intended to replace it with was supposed to be a society without any economy at all: just a collection of highly intelligent creatures who would hunt up their own food for themselves in the seas.

I'm not really sure where it came from, but there was also a mystical tradition that they drew upon—though I confess I don't know much about it, and no one's been able to help me learn much more. I guess it stems back to their medieval tradition. What it amounts to is that they thought the structure of the human brain was the physical manifestation of the ancient gods that forced life into the wrong turning, or onto the land.

That's also where their worship of the shark came from, I suppose. At any rate, the shark is a symbol of power in many religions around the world, so their use of that symbol isn't all that surprising.

One of the things I ask myself is what would have happened if the hammerheads had succeeded in eliminating all land-based life. You see, all of us who were transformed were promised that we would undergo a final change when we won, so that we, too, could go back to the sea. Eventually we were all supposed to become one with the ocean, and we were supposed to create a society without any need for a technology, or an economy, or any kind of political system.

Because the great ones had incredibly sophisticated computer and communication abilities built into their heads, however, there would have been two tiers to that society. But that division would have been maintained by the religion they created because the great ones taught that they were the physical manifestation of the gods who had opposed the wrong turning onto the land all those billions of years ago.

What that means is that the "new turning" would have created a society in which the hunter-killer behavior pattern would have been restored as the basis of society. Besides eliminating social structures like political and economic systems, they would have eliminated the family as we know it. But I guess there would have been some kind of culture under that system. Science probably would have continued to exist under them, though it would probably have been something more like science in ancient civilizations than what we're used to.

You see, the gods themselves would have been the scientists.

So what it comes down to is that the hammerheads had developed the kind of belief system that made them think they could control the universe directly through their brains. They thought they were beyond the bounds of plain old everyday humanity. And when they suffered overwhelming defeat—and that's what the great retro was for them, don't doubt that for a second—then they were determined to commit ritual suicide. For all I know, that may have been their intention all along. For some time now, I've been thinking that's what their chant about "killing the ancient gods within us" really means.

You see, no matter how radically they changed themselves, they knew that somewhere, deep inside their brains, they remained human—or at least partly human.

And they also thought they were taking the rest of the world with them.

None of that analysis occurred to me until I survived my night in the subway station in upper Manhattan.

In fact, it wasn't until I met Tim Wandel for the first time that I started putting together a lot of what I knew into this kind of coherent picture.

My friend Eddy Corrigan introduced us. It turns out that Wandel had read an article that Eddy had written about how pop culture had been affected by the hammerhead era and had contacted him about it. Several weeks after the night the fake nuke went off, Wandel visited New York, and that's when I met him for the first time. Corrigan brought him over to my apartment one afternoon. I didn't have very much money, but I did have a couple of sodas and some pretzels that I served them.

I remember telling Wandel that I felt this uncomfortable mix of anger and guilt when Corrigan introduced us.

Wandel shook his head and asked me why I felt that way.

"It's hard to explain," I told him. "I guess I've got several layers of guilt going through me. Most of it's about what I did as a 'head. I remember everybody they had us kill, you know."

"Okay," Wandel replied. "I get that. But what are you angry about?"

That's what made me most uncomfortable, of course, but I had to get it off my chest.

"It's because I blame your cousin for what happened to me," I said.

Corrigan shook his head, nearly spilling his can of soda.

"He doesn't mean what he's saying," Corrigan tried to tell Wandel.

"I sure do," I said.

"But listen, Johnny didn't have anything to do with creating the hammerheads," Wandel answered. "You've got no reason to feel that way."

"Maybe he didn't create the 'heads," I said, "but he created the preconditions for them."

"Oh, God!" Corrigan moaned, putting one hand to his forehead. "I write one lousy article and everybody who reads it thinks he's an expert."

"Can it, Eddy." I was starting to feel as close to really angry—the way I used to feel all the time—as at any moment since the great retro.

"Seriously," Wandel said, "you shouldn't feel that way about Johnny. There were lots of other people who were about to do what he did at just about the same time, eight or nine years ago. He was there just barely ahead of a lot of others—that's all."

"Well, it's the way I feel," I told him. "And what's more, I'm not grateful that I survived the retro. All it did for me was let me realize how horrible things were when I was running with the 'heads."

Wandel thought about that for a while before he replied. "Listen, Ullrich, you've got to realize one thing, if nothing else. When my cousin released that virus, it did a lot more than just change you back into a human being. It infected everybody. Maybe the effects don't show yet, but they will.

"Because that virus was designed to do two things. First, transform the hammerheads." Wandel said, holding up his forefinger. "And second, to make everybody smarter and kinder and more loving." He shook two fingers at me. "Now go figure that."

"Who gave him the right?" Corrigan asked kind of quietly.

"Damned if I know. But that's what he did."

We all sipped at our drinks.

"You know," I said after some time, "that jibes with what they told me at the hospital. They said my brain chemistry was being transformed to make me more altruistic."

"I have to hand it to my cousin," Wandel told us. "He was really amazing when it came to design. He put together this dual-purpose virus and modified it so it would infect the whole planet and then die out. A guy who's been doing some re-search for me figured out that about ninety-nine percent of the human race was actually infected by it."

"So what does that mean is going to happen to us?" Corri-gan asked.

"Maybe everything will improve," Wandel answered. "I hope so, anyway. But it could also mean we might just become that much better at getting lost in our own fantasies."

"You mean like the great ones," I said.

"Yeah—that, too." Wandel nodded, smiling. "But I was re-ally thinking more about Johnny. He got to the point where he seemed to have realized every dream he ever had. He wanted to be the lizard king. So that's what he became.

"And then he grew tired of it. Just before he died, he told me he was transforming himself back to something very much like his jones self."

"That's funny," I said. "Because all the pictures always showed him as total jones."

"He only let people photograph his remotes. And I never saw him go out in public unless he was using one."

We went on talking for a long time and finally decided to go out for dinner. While we were eating at a Chinese restau-rant, Wandel asked me and Corrigan to work for this founda-tion he was setting up to aid the transformed.

Both of us said yes without hesitating.

III

And that's how I joined the Transformation Foundation and got into the business of trying to help people.

As I said earlier, that's not exactly something I've ever done before in my life.

So now, when I have flashbacks of guilt about what I did when I was running with the 'heads—and I still have them—I have something to balance them with.

I admit it—I went looking for trouble. That's the way I was, and I loved it at the time. In fact, I wanted to scare people for a living, and it was that much more awesome because the mental-health laws made it illegal. So I grabbed onto the hammerheads. They were news; they were real; they weren't something the censorship board could say I made up to scare people with.

The 'heads got me for doing that, of course.

And then this guy named Johnny Stevens came along, a guy I never met, and saved my life. He saved a lot of other peoples' lives, too. That's something that all the lawsuits against his company and against the people who worked for him have tended to obscure.

Now, there is no way that I'm ever going to be able to do as much good for as many people as Stevens did. But for every little bit I do, I make up that much for what I did when I was down with the 'heads.

Without trying to sound like I'm exaggerating, there's more to it than that. In a way, an organization like the Transformation Foundation is intended to help evolution get us beyond the point we're stuck in. Maybe it doesn't seem that way to you, but to me at least it seems like we're in a gigantic rut. We may have found a few ways to feed people with less energy input, and maybe we've discovered how to grow plants that produce oil instead of using fossil fuels; but has government gotten any better? Have people gotten any better?

I don't think so.

So what we need to do is to evolve.

It wasn't until after the night the great ones destroyed themselves that I figured that out; you see, thinking about how a simulation killed them made me realize how far they had gone in developing the science of programming the human brain. Since then, of course, everybody realizes we've all been made into mutants. Johnny Stevens's retrovirus has worked on all of us.

Now, nobody asked Stevens to do what he did, but for better or for worse, he's made us all guinea pigs in an enormous experiment. As far as I've been able to figure out from talking with people who knew him, Stevens probably thought of it as an effort to liberate us from the tyranny imposed on us by evolution.

Here's his argument, at least as far as I'm able to understand it: psychologists say that about 60 percent of human intelligence is innate—that means it's what's hard-wired in us. And part of that 60 percent contains a lot of encoding for hunting, for fighting, and for killing.

It's the part that's responsible for anger, for murder, for wars—you name it. That's the dangerous part inside of each one of us that Stevens was trying to change.

Okay—granted, there are enormous risks in doing what he did. Things like intellectual curiosity and self-preservation are probably tied up in the complex of brain structures that he tampered with. And that means that maybe the worst outcome would be if we became so docile that we lose our ability to cope with life. It's possible. We just don't know yet.

And here's the scary parallel between Stevens and the 'heads: in his own way, Johnny was trying to kill those ancient gods within us, too.

IV

Every morning I look at myself in the bathroom mirror and I remember that night in the subway. Without wanting to, I think about the danger that somebody could try to reprogram me or anybody else all over again. Nowadays it isn't too difficult to imagine somebody trying that.

And then I go to work and try to do something about it at the Transformation Foundation. We're trying to monitor the transition and to report about it as clearly as we can to the public. Part of our work includes taking samples of airborne viruses every day of the year at twelve different sites around the world. We're also supporting research laboratories in three countries that measure what's happening to people's brains as a result of Stevens's microding.

Maybe what I'm going to say will come as a shock to you, but I've never paid much attention to what goes on in Washington. In fact, I've never even visited the city before. Last night I saw the Jefferson Memorial for the first time. Inside the dome of the monument there's a quote from Jefferson about how he swore vigilance against tyrannies over the mind of man. It stunned me. Here was a man who died more than two hundred years ago, and he was talking right to me, right now.

Without realizing it, at some point I guess I came to the same conclusion Jefferson did. Sometime during the week after the riots, while we were burying the dead and trying to rebuild New York, I decided the only way to help was to tell people my story and go on from there to try to keep the worst from happening.

It's going to be a long vigil.